MAXIME

ALSO BY DANIE BOTHA

Be Silent
Be Good

MAXIME

Danie Botha

For Isabella

Author's Note:

1

Maxime Discovers A Lump

Maxime was worried.

He had a doctor's appointment. That was not why he was worried: he might be late. Maxime was never late. Anybody who knew anything about punctuality and who knew Maxime knew that being late could never be a bloody option.

Maxime was a private man. His life was structured and lived by a set of rules—two full pages if he wrote it down, double-spaced. He did so once. These were not *actual* rules, Maxime believed, only life beacons. Since his earliest memories, it had been this way. It started with his father. Not that he resented the man—he was a good person, a devoted father, and Maxime was comfortable with this life guided by rules. He was certain that Donna suspected as much—the rules thing—but was too sensible a woman to make a scene about it.

Maxime was a man who doesn't speak out of turn or put his nose into other people's business where it didn't belong. He had learned these rules from a young age, and they served him well, helped keep his nose clean and relatively straight, not crooked like some second-class boxer's.

He leaned closer to the mirror, taking care not to skip a spot on his cheek. He couldn't stand electric shavers and preferred the sleek contour type, the manual ones. The only problem with his preference was the exorbitant cost of the disposable blades—why the government didn't do something about the exploitation of the poor consumer was beyond his comprehension. *Bloody capitalists.* And then they expected him to vote for them.

Perhaps it was time to print out the letter he had written years earlier in this regard, and mail it to the Minister of Natural Resources—he would just have to change the date. The thing that held him back was the second rule on page two: *Don't stir things up.*

He leaned closer and concentrated. The tricky part: the three-quarters of an inch between his almost straight nose and his upper lip—these triple blades were sharp. Maxime couldn't stand facial hair. Never could. He turned his head. He had missed a spot: a small patch of hair in front of his ear. He jutted his chin sideways, leaning even closer.

"Damn it!" He had drawn blood.

Maxime hunched over the sink and dabbed cold water from the tap onto his cheeks. The cut stung. There was blood on his hand and in the water.

Donna. Where is Donna when I need her? Kleenex. He pressed a wad of tissue paper on his cut and dried the remainder of his face with his black towel. He made certain he didn't touch Donna's white one on the rail next to his. One glance at the clock on the bathroom wall made him realize he'd better hurry. His appointment with Dr. Moller was in less than half an hour. It was past nine already. Two weeks earlier he had arranged with his boss to take the day off—medical urgency, he had claimed. His boss hadn't hesitated. Maxime never took any sick days. He was never late. He never complained. His work was always beyond reproach—in one word: outstanding. However, what Donna and his boss didn't know was that he wasn't planning on returning to work later that day, in spite of the guilt that sat as an accuser on his shoulder.

Maxime tore off a small piece of Kleenex, folded it into a tiny square and stuck it on the cut. *Bloody spring-mounted blades with their pivoting heads—I could have severed an artery.*

He grabbed his ironed white shirt and slipped it on. He already had on his suit pants, and his yellow socks with the gray stripes. Maxime always wore a lambswool suit to work and when he visited his doctor once a year. Today was an exception: it was his second visit to the doctor this year. But he still had to wear a suit—and a tie. Anyone who knew anything about suits knew that a tie was non-negotiable. Maxime had little time for those amateurs who wore bloody T-shirts to work.

He was not a little proud of his knots. He had taught himself. He folded the collar down and tightened the knot. Perfect.

Maxime glanced at the wall. Ten past nine. He leaned closer to the mirror for a final inspection: his hair was gelled and parted on the left, perfectly straight, as if he had used a measuring stick. A red blotch on the collar stared back at him. The cut.

"*Scheisse!*"

The tie went flying, then the shirt. What did Donna always say? *Use cold water for removing bloodstains, Max.* He scrubbed the collar with a nailbrush. There was another ironed shirt in the closet, but that was for work, for tomorrow—it was out of bounds for today.

Donna, where's your blow dryer? Maxime found the dryer but abandoned it after thirty seconds. *The iron will be faster.* He pinched his fingers in the process of opening the ironing board. The collar was easy enough to dry, and he slid the iron down to the shoulder, which was still soaking wet. Anyone who knew anything about sheep knew that one didn't wear wet shirts under one hundred percent wool suits, not if one didn't want to smell like a sheep shearer from Down Under.

Nine seventeen.

Maxime turned the temperature higher and held the iron steady. That should get the shirt dry in no time. *I'd better move my ass.* A cloud of dense steam engulfed the iron, and he jerked it away. *That's not steam, Maxime Baumann.*

There was no time for a plan C. Maxime put on the now dry shirt with an ebony iron mark on the shoulder, knotted his tie and grabbed his suit jacket. He ran through the house, unhooked the keys in the mudroom and barged into the garage.

He was confident that he would require time for reflection after his visit to his family doctor. He knew himself.

It was serious business: first the lump, and now the bloody shirt. Donna was going to have a fainting spell when she saw the shirt.

He had noticed the soft swelling, the lump, three months earlier. It had slowly, inconspicuously, grown bigger. It was still small, so small that Donna didn't notice it, not even when they were intimate. He would not be able to hide it from her much longer—that's why he had phoned the doctor's office.

When he had informed her, only yesterday, about his doctor's visit, she had been alarmed. So great was her concern that he had brushed it off with "Oh, it's nothing, darling. Just a routine examination."

He had refrained from telling her that he wasn't going back to work for the remainder of the day. That wasn't lying—he didn't want to burden her with the extra knowledge. Maxime loved his wife of thirty-seven years. Still, he knew that she would not back off if she suspected him of withholding crucial information.

He knew of a little coffee shop where she wouldn't find him. He would read the paper and take a book along too. Maxime was a wise enough man—he'd go home at the usual time, three thirty.

Dr. Moller's offices were in a big strip mall not far from the highway. It was a six-person group practice—two of them were lady doctors, all lovely and helpful, but he still preferred Dr. Moller. The doctor also knew a few German words, which always helped Maxime relax. When he went for his annual visit, they stuck to English, Maxime's third language. It wasn't a problem since it was the language he spoke with Donna and the boys.

It never ceased to amaze him when people declared that he had a distinct accent—as if *they* did not. Incredible, he thought, the sheer ignorance of some. He made a mental note to work harder on the elocution thing. Perhaps it was time he learned a fourth language, just to trouble those individuals more.

Maxime had trouble with wasting time—life was too short for that. And with doctors, the accepted norm was to let patients sit and wait for goodness knew how long, wasting their lives away in spite of having been given an exact time to show up. Why did they bother with a time when they could have given only the date?

Dr. Moller's first name was Manie, but Maxime would never call him by that, although the young doctor was barely a year older than Maxime's youngest. Maxime's father (God rest his soul) had brought him up with the notion that you showed respect for other people's professions.

It took Maxime a full five minutes to find a satisfactory parking spot: it had to be a double vacant space in the corner of the lot. He could then park at an angle, and prevent an asshole from squeezing his vehicle into these too tight spots, making it impossible for anyone to get in or out without requiring a new paint job on the door. He was sure that those idiots who parked three inches from you slipped out of their cars through their sunroofs, or even crawled out through their trunks. Imbeciles.

Maxime reported to the front desk, mortified: he was two minutes late. He smiled at the young ladies behind the counter, then shook his head in disbelief and looked again. One of them—a brunette—had to be a new addition to the family practice team.

She did it, just being her gorgeous self, on purpose, as a punishment of men in general. It was impossible to look and not be enraptured—compelled to look again, drawn to follow the sleek contours of her facial features, down, down into cleavage that beckoned with glorious abandon. He sucked his breath and commandeered every morsel of testosterone to ignore the phenomenon, the vision. His Donna was attractive, even at fifty-eight—she took great care of herself—but this was tough.

Maxime swallowed and forced a smile.

"Yes, sir?" the Vision purred.

"I'm here for Dr. Moller," he spluttered.

"Do you have an appointment?"

Why else would I be standing here? "Yes … I *do*."

"Your name, sir?" She was purring again. Maxime relaxed.

"Maxime. Maxime Baumann."

"MacSeem?" He was certain she was unaware of how her breasts jutted forward. He averted his eyes.

"*Nein*. It's Maxime. M-A-X-I-M-E. Maxime, with an *m*. Baumann—two *n*'s."

"Thank you, Mr. Bowman. I have it. Date of birth?"

"1951."

"There we are. I have your file." She clicked the mouse several times and smiled up at him. The cleavage beckoned again. *Oh, Lord.* "Please have a seat."

He sat down—just in time, as his knees gave way. In his haste, he discovered now; he had forgotten to bring his book. He always carried a book. At least these younger doctors had the common sense and decency to stock fresh-off-the-press magazines, not only ancient issues of *Chatelaine* and *Reader's Digest*. Not that there was anything the matter with those, it was just that he preferred to stimulate his mind, such as by reading *The Economist*. He leaned back and prepared for the long haul of the wait. He turned to the first page: *The gutsy Greek government and their lack of respect for the euro.*

Dear Lord, he prayed, *perhaps Mr. Papadopoulos can help me apply the same brazenness to my dealings with this unwelcome fiend in my bosom, or rather, in my nether regions.*

2

The Doctor Makes A Diagnosis

The Vision reappeared.

"Mr. Bowman?"

Maxime rose as if hypnotized and followed the young lady down the endless hallway toward a small room at the back. Shafts of morning light burst in through a side window, enveloping them in gold and accentuating the female form that floated ahead of him—the black leggings hugged her perfect bottom, firm thighs, and toned legs. *Dear Lord, this hallway had better come to an end.*

He immediately recited the fifth rule on the first page: *Don't take what does not belong to you.*

Maxime, don't be an asshole.

Dr. Moller was going to be so upset with him, thinking he had been neglecting his blood pressure, while it was all due to this enchantress, this Siren. He should tell Dr. Moller to make his staff wear shapeless scrubs, with long lab coats buttoned closed at the neck, that covered everything. Anybody who knew anything about white lab coats and body contours and testosterone would bloody well know this was the smart thing to do.

"The doctor will be with you shortly, Mr. Bowman," the Vision murmured.

"*Danke*," Maxime whispered as he dropped into the chair in the small examination room, grateful for time to compose himself. He closed his eyes and focused on his breathing.

He could feel his heart rate settle down.

Maxime loosened his tie. He felt warm and slipped out of his jacket. The room was too small. Dr. Moller wouldn't mind—he had the impression that the doctor was always overheating, hence his customary wearing of short-sleeved Hawaiian shirts. Maxime remembered the burn on his shirt, sighed and slipped his jacket back on.

Maxime owned five suits and ten collared shirts. There was one suit for each workday in a week. Today he had on his newest suit, the gray one with the thin stripes, the one he had bought in January. Maxime always wore white shirts to work or when he went to see his doctor. It was the right thing to do. Maxime believed he knew a thing or two about fashion; scheduled today: tan shoes and a tan belt. Shoes had to match the belt, and ties always matched socks. Anybody who knew anything about fashion and dressing smart, even if they were sixty-four-and-a-half, bloody well knew that.

Maxime Baumann was a modest man, insofar as he could speak for himself. Didn't he painstakingly follow rule eleven on page two, which stated: *Don't ever think of yourself as a smart aleck*? He could never understand the gentle smirks he received from Donna and the boys when he claimed just that, especially when they noticed his socks. For the past ten years, but more so the past five, the one thing Maxime had spoiled himself with was colorful socks.

Today was his yellow-socks-with-gray-stripes day.

Maxime thought about Mr. J. Johnson, his boss. He had his reservations about whether one should call him his "boss," since he was only the senior partner, in charge of Johnson, Johnson & McBride, attorneys at law. Maxime snorted. They were nothing more than glorified underwriters of properties (business and residential), mere pencil-pushers. They were real estate lawyers. Maxime stuck to what he loved: residential property. He always prayed that his clients would be honest and not succumb to fraud, and it served him well. He couldn't remember when he had last seen the inside of a courtroom. He was okay with that. He was a senior partner now. *Haha,* he snorted again. *Senior partner*—the *only* other partner.

He, Maxime Baumann, had been hoping he could retire in six months' time, at sixty-five. But no. Mr. C. Johnson, the brother of Mr. J. Johnson, had to go and have a massive heart attack. Died on the spot. Just like that, without even consulting Maxime. Inconsiderate man. That had been over a month ago.

Mr. J. Johnson had called Maxime into his office soon after the funeral and made it clear that since the whole team now consisted of Mr. J. Johnson, Maxime, and two junior colleagues, early retirement would be discouraged, if not entirely impossible, if Maxime understood what he meant. Understood? Impossible?

Mr. McBride had passed on more than ten years ago, but Mr. J. Johnson had never felt the need to change the firm's name. Too much paperwork, he had said back then.

But the idea that Maxime should wait until the two junior lawyers could manage without training wheels was preposterous. They would need to be babysat for at least another five years. That would make him sixty-nine-and-a-half, and chances were high that, given Maxime's boss's family history, Mr. J. Johnson might by then have followed in his brother's footsteps, adding at least another five years before retirement for Maxime. Then he, Maxime Bastien Baumann, would be seventy-four-and-a-half. Outrageous.

The door swung open, and Dr. Manie Moller rolled in. "*Guten Tag, Guten Tag, Herr Baumann!*" he roared as he shook Maxime's hand, clasping it with both of his, each the size of a bunch of bananas. He was a burly man, strong as a bear, and sported a free-hanging short-sleeved shirt printed with palm trees.

"*Guten Tag, Herr Doktor,*" Maxime said, immediately relaxing. It is what he loved about the man: genuine, going out of his way to being helpful—there was no bullshit.

Dr. Moller plopped down with the folder. His ample girth strained against the desk. He activated his computer screen and looked up at his patient, the warm smile never leaving his face. "What brought you to us today, Mr. Baumann? Your annual was five months ago, and everything seemed fine then."

Maxime cleared his throat twice—his protocol when he had something important or embarrassing to discuss.

The doctor raised his eyebrows. "*Was ist loss?*"

Maxime found his voice. "I have a swelling ... in my groin, doctor." He gestured down toward his right side.

Dr. Moller asked many more questions and listened with intent, then asked Maxime to take his shirt and shoes off and sit on the examination table. They would start with his blood pressure. Maxime undid his yellow tie and slipped with a convoluted maneuver out of the white shirt and jacket at the same time. What would Dr. Moller think of him if he saw the burn on the shirt? Certainly, that he, Maxime Bastien Baumann, was an everyday cheapskate. He would then die of shame.

Dr. Moller didn't favor those new automatic machines that some of his colleagues loved, the ones that squeezed your arm until the blood supply was cut off and your hand turned blue, deflating only moments before gangrene started.

One thing to be grateful for.

"Pressure is good, Maxime."

Maxime laughed, relieved and relaxed, as his doctor's expert hands traveled over his body, probing, palpating and checking. Dr. Moller had him pull his pants down, and then, after covering him with a thin sheet, his underpants.

Next, he made Maxime stand, told him to cough and compared the two sides of his inguinal canals and both scrotums. Then it was on his side; a rectal examination followed, and then onto his back again.

"Open those legs wider, please, Mr. Baumann. That's it. Thank you."

Dr. Moller palpated Maxime's abdomen a second time and finally zoomed in on the swelling in his right scrotum, squeezing it ever so gently.

"Does that hurt?"

Maxime shook his head, but the heat rose to his face.

The doctor stepped back, washed his hands, instructed Maxime to get dressed and tapped away at his keyboard.

Maxime barely waited until he had tucked in his shirt and fastened his belt before he blurted, "It's not something serious, is it?" He slipped his shoes on and sat down, on the edge of the chair. "It's not cancer, *Herr Doktor?*"

Dr. Moller paused his mouse-clicking and made eye contact. He smiled, then put a hand on Maxime's arm. "No, Maxime. The chance of that is almost zero. You have a hydrocele. It's benign."

Maxime coughed. "Hidro-seal?"

"Hydrocele, Mr. Baumann. It's a fluid collection around the testis, inside the scrotal sac. A simple operation will solve the problem."

Maxime wanted to break out in a dance. It wasn't cancer. But he immediately stopped dancing in his head. He was in need of an operation, would have to be cut open.

Maxime had never had surgery in his life—no tonsillectomy, no appendectomy. Not even a mole excision or circumcision, thank you very much. And he would have liked to keep it that way. *Simple operation.* Anybody who knew anything about operations and surgeons knew that there was no such thing as a *simple* operation—small, perhaps, but never unimportant. That much was bloody obvious.

Maxime's blood pressure shot sky high. He stiffened up like a broom in Donna's kitchen closet. "Operation?" he said. "Do *you* perform the operation, Doctor?"

Manie Moller laughed. "No, no, Maxime. I'll refer you to one of our urologists. He'll see you and then discuss the options."

So there was hope—a way out.

"Options, Doctor?"

"Well, Maxime, he has to examine you, confirm my diagnosis and then discuss all the pros and cons—the options."

"So there *are* options?"

Halleluja.

"Not really. The hydrocele will only become bigger and cause more discomfort." Dr. Moller paused. "Do you have any preferences for a particular urologist, Mr. Baumann?"

The doctor's question embarrassed Maxime. It was a miracle that he had made it through law school, with him not being exceptionally gifted with technical terminology. But then again, perhaps it was only the English-language thing. *Urologist?* He'd made peace with that long ago, the not-so-gifted thing. He had to work twice as hard as the other students. He could take nothing for granted.

He wasn't stupid, far from it—only different. He always thought he had a flair for languages. Perhaps not. Mother had called him "quintessential." Gunther had called him "my special brother" but always made him feel strange about it. He used to know what a urologist was. *Damn.* A faint light went on: something to do with water. Ah, a human plumber.

He recovered with lightning speed. "But there's nothing the matter with my waterworks, *Herr Doktor.*"

Manie Moller chuckled, louder this time. "You're right, and they're fine for the most part. I'm referring you to Dr. John Williams."

"Dr. Williams?"

"Yes. A good chap. Studied in Britain, came to Saskatchewan years ago and did the Canadian exams—nice guy. *Jolly good* fellow. You'll like him."

Maxime jumped to his feet. It was all nice and dandy if this Brit was a pleasant person, but was he any good?

Dr. Moller raised his hand. "Sorry, Maxime—one more thing. Your medications: you still take only the daily multivitamins and the little blue pill when needed?"

Maxime sat back down. He nodded.

"Have you noticed any difference in your ability to maintain an erection during intercourse since the swelling started?" On Dr. Moller's face was only an expression of genuine interest and vast intellect. He meant no malice, Maxime decided.

Maxime Baumann was a private man. He could feel the crimson creep up his face. "*Nein, Herr Doktor,*" he whispered.

This time Dr. Moller got to his feet and took hold of Maxime's hand, again shaking it with both hands. He even patted him on the back as they turned to the door. "Please don't worry, Mr. Baumann. I'll set up an appointment with the urologist—he'll see you and set up a date for the operation. Don't lose sleep over this."

Might I lose sleep too? The color drained from Maxime's face.

Dr. Moller quickly added, "Remember: it's not cancer. You'll do just fine. My receptionist will get in touch with you and give you the particulars of when and where."

They were soon in the long hallway, bathed in light.

"*Auf Wiedersehen, Herr Baumann.*"

"*Wiedersehen, Herr Doktor.*"

As Maxime passed the front desk, the Vision looked up and beamed at him in all her innocent sincerity, still all cleavage and straining bosom. "Goodbye, Mr. Bowman. Nice tie." Both the Vision and her colleague grinned and waved goodbye.

Maxime smiled as he dashed for the exit, his face flush with heat. Anybody who knew anything about cleavage and spiking blood pressure knew that seemly attire covered *all* exposed skin. Buttoned-up white lab coats with modest scrubs.

3

Maxime Considers Sharing The News

The last rule on the first page stated: *Listen to your heart.*

Over the years Maxime had learned to do that. It had saved him from certain annihilation on several occasions. Now would be one such occasion. He would not go back to the office, or even home, for that matter. He had to regroup. Rethink his life—his options—his future.

That is why, thirty minutes after leaving Dr. Moller's office, Maxime sat down in a semi-dark coffee shop. He had ordered his first tall skinny vanilla latte for the day. He had ordered only coffee. He wasn't hungry. He had made certain the barista got the recipe one hundred percent correct—the way he liked it—and extra hot. He had put the plastic lid on as well, keeping the drink scathingly hot. He was confident that the environment would survive his humble contribution of the waxed paper cup and lid. He needed this. It was a matter of life and death as far as he was concerned, this caffeine-laden therapy session.

Maxime draped his gray jacket with the thin stripes over the chair back—nothing should touch the floor—then loosened his yellow tie. He pushed the cup to the very edge of the little table to make more room for the newspaper. He always started with the business news. When would they ever stop yapping about the oil sands? It was just oil sands, oil sands, oil sands. He was sick of it. Imagine: *fracking*. What were they thinking, luring every second person in the country to load their U-haul trailers and pitch their tents in Alberta? And then, *kaboom!* The oil price plummets through the blooming basement and every second person in the oil business is unemployed.

He was so glad that he had refrained from investing in oil stocks—the few thousand dollars he had set aside over the years. They were *fracking,* fracking wrecking the environment. The oil people were—not him, with his plastic coffee cup ending up in the landfill. Anybody who knew anything about oil and pipelines and fracking knew it was impossible not to screw up the lakes and groundwater, that all the PR was only talking and making a good impression. The goal of the oil business was simple—make a vault full of dollars.

Settle down, Maxime. Settle down. Your blood pressure, remember? He felt a jab in his groin where the swelling was. *Mein Gott. I'm dying. Never mind my blood pressure—it's this swelling, this thing that's growing in my body.* That young Dr. Moller must have been wrong. This hydrocele was more serious than he wanted to let on. Maxime wiggled on the chair to find a comfortable position. *As soon as I get home, I'll Google it—do my research.*

He resumed reading but turned to the sports pages. He sighed. Football and hockey. Bloody football and hockey—on every single page. Oh, and then right on the last page, page eight, just before they ran out of space, the smart aleck editor had printed the results of the soccer and tennis and baseball and judo, taekwondo and darts and bingo and what not. Squeezed it all in, as if offered in apology.

Soccer. Now that's a game for men. That's what Maxime had grown up with—and speed skating in the winter on the frozen lake and river. Gunther had beaten his ass in the speed events, but only while they were teens. Once Maxime turned eighteen, he frequently made his older brother watch his backside down the ski trails.

These football hooligans with their padded clothing, weird helmets like they were Hell's Angels, and spandex pants like male ballet dancers, showing off their jewels to the whole wide world, constantly hugging their crotches. No, thank you. Oh, they were fit and powerful, but still. And the hockey players—who were they fooling with their skimpy plastic helmets? Useless rubbish. It was like in Roman times: the crowds demanding blood—all the fighting that was allowed, even encouraged, on the ice. A bunch of ruffians, assaulting one another, concussion after blooming concussion. The only punishment for breaking someone's skull was five minutes in the box. *Imagine.*

No, give him soccer. It was fast. Those men and women were fit; there was no intermittent resting, no fighting, no bullshit. If you played foul, you got a yellow card. If you did it again, you got a second yellow, or a straight red—and you were gone. Not for five minutes, either—suspension was automatic for the next game. Or, if you messed up badly, you were banned for longer. Pure, clean and swift.

One, two, three, pass—and goal!

Maxime sipped a mouthful and put the paper down.

You'll have to tell her, Maxime—Donna. And Sandro and Simon. And Mr. J. Johnson. Perhaps even Gunther.

Donna—his Donatella—wouldn't be a problem. The boys were responsible adults. They would have little issue with their father's altered health.

But Maxime cringed at the thought of Mr. J. Johnson's response.

Do you want another doctor's appointment, Maxie? You just had one. You want a second opinion, is that it, Maxie?

He hated it, called Maxie, but the older Mr. J. Johnson had refused to call him anything else from the day Maxime had started working there more than thirty years ago. Mr. J. Johnson was probably close to eighty now and had even said in so many words that he wasn't planning on retiring. Ever.

An operation too, Maxie? How long will you be off, then? Is this serious? Should I be worried about you? You're falling apart, Maxie. Do you think we should interview for a third position to help us? Perhaps acquire the services of a paralegal?

Over the course of the next four hours, Maxime had two more lattes and a toasted multigrain bagel with plain cream cheese. He finished the paper and five chapters of his book. He didn't read fast—he always read with a pen and made notes, even with fiction. Rule number four on page two: *Remember the worthwhile things. Write them down.* When he finished a book, he would transfer his brief notes in the back to a bigger notebook he kept in his home office.

He had to go to the washroom twice—those waxed cups were tall and wide. The caffeine must have squeezed his kidneys.

At exactly three forty-five, Maxime Baumann turned into his driveway. He would not be going to the gym today as he did every weekday, Monday through Friday. His gym bag was in the trunk—packed and ready—but he had decided against it as soon as he had left Dr. Moller's office. The gravity of the whole situation pressed too heavily on him.

There was a movement in the living-room window, next to the front door. It was Columbus, Donna's Devon Rex cat. That the cat always, without fail, managed to appear in the window at the exact instant Maxime turned up the driveway was unsettling. The cat just seemed to know. When Donna was at home, he treated Maxime with guarded contempt, but his innate curiosity made it impossible not to be the one to inform his mistress that the old guy with the suit and the funny tie and matching socks was home.

The automatic garage door stuttered open like something that had suffered a stroke. Maxime fumed as he pulled into the attached garage. He had to remember to give the overhead door guy a call—tell him to fix his screw-up.

People don't take pride in their craft these days. Shameful.

Fortunately, the motor was still under warranty. He had told the man to install the three-quarter-horsepower model. But no, the man was too smart, insisting, *the half-horsepower will suffice, Mr. Bowman. It's the norm for residential use.* For crying out loud.

"The norm. Residential use," my ass. The poor idiot. How could half a horse do anything? Anybody who knew anything about overhead garage doors and horses could tell you that half a horse would only be good for a half-assed job. Bloody amateurs.

Donna and Columbus were waiting in the kitchen. There was no escape. Donna worked five half-days, mornings only, in a chiropractor's office, or "chiropractic," as they called themselves. This arrangement—her working at the tug-and-pull doctor's— was much against Maxime's wishes. She was squandering her talents. Donna, working as a receptionist when she had a master's degree in English and used to teach grades ten through twelve. One day, three years ago, she had simply had enough of the students and told him she resigned—or, rather, took early retirement, with a pension, at fifty-five. She had immediately accepted a job at the "Realignment Center," as Maxime preferred to call her present place of employment.

He had problems with the philosophy that some part of the human body could be skewed, out of alignment, and therefore responsible for all its ailments and misery—and could be fixed by simple manipulation. *The only thing that was misaligned was people's heads—their brains.*

He was not a little proud of his darling, though, having had the guts to make the switch back then. She loved her present job. She missed the students, but not all their emotional baggage, which she would come home with, burdened like John Bunyan's Pilgrim. And then, somewhere over the course of the weekend, would unload it on him, seeking his advice, making him the second pilgrim, the one carrying the pack.

Donna smiled up at him now and hugged him tightly. She showed no cleavage but had beautiful full breasts, which he adored, and he hugged her extra long. Donna melted into his embrace. She was much shorter than Maxime, which made it easy for him to kiss the top of her head. He took a deep breath and closed his eyes. He inhaled her warm body and apple blossom aroma.

Columbus, however, was of the opinion that the smooching had lasted beyond what was appropriate for people the age of his owners, and he gave a protesting meow, pressing his arched back against Maxime's legs. Maxime shooed him away and kissed Donna on the lips before slipping into a seat across from her at the little kitchen table. She had two coffees ready—she must have waited for him and poured it as he turned into the driveway.

Donna was silent, only smiled at him as she sipped her coffee. She waited. He would tell her when he was ready. Columbus dropped down at their feet, contented: the guy with the yellow tie who still made his mistress's heart race was home. He purred like a miniature tree-shredder.

That's why Maxime loved his Donna so much. She was the smart one—much smarter than him. She knew him so much better than he could ever dream to comprehend *her*. He sighed. Rule one on page two stated: *Accept what you cannot change.* Him not fully understanding her was one such thing—unfathomable and unchangeable in his universe. Not that he wanted to change her.

He was almost ready to tell. He sighed again. *Lieber Gott, ich liebe diese Frau.*

Maxime looked Donatella in the eyes and began. "Sweetheart … I have a swelling in my right scrotum—Dr. Moller calls it a hydrocele—not something deadly, he says, and he's referring me to a specialist, a urologist, for an operation."

He managed it all without taking a single breath.

She grabbed his hands. "How long has it been there, Max? And is it big?"

Maxime shrugged his broad shoulders. "A month. Maybe two." He remembered rule three on page one: *Don't ever tell a lie.* "Perhaps three. No, it's relatively small."

"And you need an *operation?*" She knew what Maxime thought about surgery. She could recall as if it was this morning when she needed the Caesarean sections for the boys—how he had almost passed out. Her big strong man, this sturdy Swiss fellow from the Davos Valley. He was all right with blood, but the mere thought of being cut open was problematic.

Maxime nodded. "Although Dr. Moller said the urologist, Dr. Williams, will discuss the options with me."

"So he won't necessarily operate, *mein Schatz?* There are options?"

Maxime was exhausted. "He used the word 'options,' but I think they will have to operate. The thing will only get bigger."

"When?"

"That depends on Dr. Williams."

Donna and Maxime finished their coffee in comfortable silence. She put one load of laundry in the washer and then it was cool enough for them to go for a walk. They loved walking—when it was cool—down to the river. Columbus stayed behind: he was a house cat.

Donna was contented. They would talk more during the walk, much more. Tonight he would make love to her—passionately, as he usually did. It would be lovely with or without the help of the little blue pill. He was a determined man, and she was a patient woman.

4

The Services Of A Specialist Are Required

Two days later, Maxime sat at his tidy office desk watching the second hand complete its circular journey. It was only minutes after eight when Mrs. Long, the receptionist of Johnson, Johnson & McBride, put the call through.

He might have forgotten the other day what the English word for a bladder specialist was, but he never failed to remember a voice. It was that foxy lady from his family doctor's office.

"Mr. Bowman?"

"Speaking."

"Samantha here, from Dr. Moller's office."

So the Vision had a name. Maxime sighed. "Yes ... Samantha?"

"Your appointment with Dr. J. Williams is at exactly 1:45 p.m. on Tuesday, September fifteenth, three weeks from today."

"*Danke*. Thank you, Samantha, from Dr. Moller's office."

Her laughter bubbled over the line—uninhibited, like champagne fizzing over. Then she gave him the address and phone number.

Maxime wrote it down. "You say it's at *exactly* 1:45 p.m.?"

"That's correct, Mr. Bowman. Goodbye then, sir." Again the bubbling champagne chuckle.

Maxime sat in a semi-stupor for a full five minutes. He barely breathed. Then he jumped to his feet, took his ironed white handkerchief from his trouser pocket and wiped his glistening forehead. He questioned the wisdom of picking the black suit. The day had barely started, and already he was perspiring like a hog.

Lieber Gott, das Mädchen.

Maxime Baumann, you're an absolute idiot—an asshole of the first degree. Donna does not deserve this. He felt ashamed as he wiped his forehead a second time.

Maxime did not think of himself as being anally retentive. The fact that he possessed only white handkerchiefs had nothing to do with anything. And they had to be ironed—which he did himself. Anybody who knew anything about men's pure cotton handkerchiefs could tell you that this was a sure sign of sophistication. Bloody uncivilized brutes who wandered around the globe, without an ironed handkerchief, or worse—no handkerchief at all. What was becoming of the world? What if your forehead broke out in a sweat, or a woman standing next to you started weeping?

His first client was not due until nine. Thank God. He was in no state to face anybody. Not yet. He chastised himself for another five minutes before making a decision.

He opened the top drawer of his desk and took out the new paper folder labeled MY SURGERY. Inside were the print-outs from his online search for "HIDRO-SEALS," which had turned up nothing. He had typed the word over and over before accepting the only option given him: *Did you mean: hydro-seal or hydrocele?*

He had picked *hydrocele*.

He reread the Wikipedia article: "It is often caused by fluid secreted from a remnant piece of peritoneum wrapped around the testicle, called the *tunica vaginalis*."

Why didn't he notice this last night when he printed it? *"Tunica vaginalis." Mein Gott. So I have some part of a female inside me? No wonder Gunther insisted I was special.* Maxime scribbled down several notes, which he would request Dr. Williams answer to his satisfaction.

His eyes caught a phrase further down the page: "develops in the elderly." He bolted upright, ripped his reading glasses off and mumbled, "Elderly, my *ass*. I'll tell them who's elderly: centenarians. The blooming word for me is *senior* or *mature*."

Maxime continued reading until his phone buzzed. It was the inside line—Mrs. Long. His first client would be fifteen minutes late. Just as well, he had more to read. He had even printed out two articles he had found on PubMed but hadn't read. He made additional notes. Signs. Symptoms. Diagnosis. Treatment Options.

Maxime snapped upright. *See. Treatment options. PLURAL.* He had to have a man-to-man talk with that Dr. Moller. Not that he, Maxime Bastien Baumann, was a smart aleck of any kind. First, Dr. Moller did not shine a light through the swelling, as this article recommended. Second, he did not tell Maxime two more options were possible. These being (a) doing nothing since a large percentage resolved spontaneously or (b) aspirate it with a sterile needle, which would also make it disappear.

Maxime beamed, much relieved. He closed the folder, returned it to the top drawer and created order again on his desk. He was ready for the first client.

———

Maxime arrived ten minutes early, at 1:35 p.m., at Dr. John Williams's office. He had had less difficulty than anticipated finding two adjacent empty parking spots in the corner of the lot.

Thank you very much. This time I've snuffed you, bloody parking-site assholes.

As he took his seat in the waiting room, Maxime reflected on the differences between the two offices. Oh, the staff here were all quite professional and courteous, but Dr. Williams preferred personnel with more years of experience—decades more, by the looks of it. Perhaps that was a good thing, experience. Maxime had always been of the opinion that book knowledge could never be a substitute for savoir-faire. One just couldn't buy know-how. He scanned the reading material—only yellowed copies of *Chatelaine* and *Reader's Digest*. He would have to deduct one star in his rating of the waiting room. He opened his MY SURGERY folder and reread the questions he had written down on a separate page.

By two thirty, Maxime had realized the wisdom of having informed his partner/boss, Mr. J. Johnson, that he would not be returning to the office in the afternoon. His sixth sense had forewarned him, or perhaps it was only his cynicism about the health care system that helped him make the decision. He reread the two journal articles. By three, Maxime had read all his notes, questions and printouts a third time. He was having his doubts about several of his questions: the swelling had enlarged significantly during the past two weeks. It was now the size of an orange.

"Mr. Bowman?"

It was 3:06 p.m. Maxime yanked himself to his feet, eager to get this over. He had long since made peace with the fact that people could not pronounce his surname correctly. The kind lady waited for him. He followed her down the dimly lit short hallway, her plump features wiggling ahead of him.

Dr. Williams didn't make him wait long. The door swung open seconds later and a gangly man towered above Maxime. "Mr. Baumann. A jolly good day to you, sir."

They shook hands. Dr. Williams must be in his mid-forties, Maxime thought, looking up at him—not even gray at the temples, only those willful red-blond curls.

"Dr. Williams."

"Sit down, sit down, please, Mr. Baumann. I have Dr. Moller's notes here. He states everything is fine, except for the scrotal swelling. Is that correct?"

"*Genau.* Oh—yes, *Herr Doktor.*"

"What was that?" Dr. Williams laughed. "Sorry, old chap, never got further than one year of German. My Spanish is much better. I lived in Spain for almost a year. So, the hydrocele—tell me about it, please."

Maxime relayed the history of the past four months, especially how the swelling had tripled in size during the previous two weeks. Dr. Williams examined him and, much to Maxime's relief used a light to illuminate the cystic swelling.

"See, Mr. Baumann? No doubt about our diagnosis."

They discussed treatment options, and, much to Maxime's satisfaction, Dr. Williams used the plural form of the English word: *options.*

That evening, Maxime consulted his *Webster's* dictionary. It confirmed his hopes. *Option(s): to wish, to desire, to choose, prefer. 1. The act of choosing 2. The power, right, or liberty of choosing. 3. Something that is or can be chosen.* He was immensely relieved—he was planning on option number 3.

Dr. Williams informed him he was going to treat the hydrocele conservatively and initially would only aspirate the fluid. Chances were, it would resolve; if it didn't, or if it became enormous, *then* they could consider surgery. And only then would they remove the *tunica vaginalis.* Dr. Williams explained the embryological development of the fetus and the weird Latin words which were used to describe every part in the body.

Maxime sighed—so he *was* still all male. He found great solace in his sixth rule on the first page: *Consider all your options. Always.* He did just that.

MAXIME

By the time Maxime Baumann reached his car half an hour later, he was the proud owner, once again, of a normal-sized right scrotum. Anybody who knew anything about the male species and body awareness knew that even the smallest collection of fluid inside the *tunica vaginalis* could have a disastrous effect on the male psyche; it could be bloody catastrophic.

5

Fluid Collections Inside The Tunica Vaginalis

Maxime's life returned to normal.

He showed up for work every day, punctually as always, dressed in a different suit. Each suit was dry-cleaned every fifth week because this was the right thing to do. Five days of wear— that was it. Each day's suit was aired at night and put back in the closet the next morning. He ironed his shirts because he could not see why he should pay the dry cleaners three dollars per shirt. This rule he had borrowed from his father: *Don't waste money— not a single mark, or even a bloody franc.*

Mr. J. Johnson showed no sign of any plan to follow his younger brother into the next life and wholeheartedly believed that "Maxie's delicate personal problem" was a thing of the past.

Plans to hire a paralegal were put on hold.

Maxime returned to his schedule of going to the gym five days a week, for an hour of cardio, stretching and resistance exercises. This was followed by a refreshing shower, before dressing in his suit again and heading home for supper at six-thirty with his beloved Donna. And in the living-room window, facing the street, Columbus would sit, watching the master of the house drive up the driveway and wait for the stuttering garage door to finish rolling open.

Even after all these years, Maxime had not gotten used to the Canadian practice of having supper at exactly six p.m. He was certain the proximity to the polar cap had something to do with it. It just made no sense to him. Inconceivable. How had it ever become a national institution? Anybody who knew anything about spacing your meals and eating when you were ready and hungry could tell you that it was a mistake. Bloody ritualistic habitual eaters. His Donatella had no problem if they had supper at seven, after their walk, before the damn mosquitos came swarming.

Maxime put on hold his plan to inform the boys that they had to "come home" because their father was ill. He had bounced back into the second prime of life. He resumed sexual relations with his Donna without the slightest discomfort. He even managed without the aid of the little blue pill.

He mowed the lawn again with gusto, and used the edge cutter with fervor (usually a thorn in his side, what with the winding in the correct direction of the ridiculous orange and sometimes light blue cutting cord), without so much as once resorting to spicy German utterances. He even mowed the lawn across the street, owned by little old Mrs. Nightly, who used a walker.

Mrs. Nightly refused to tell them her age, but Maxime placed his money on the mid-nineties. She was scrawny and sinewy, her skin transparent, but she brimmed with fire. Maxime's particular concern was that she still drove a motor vehicle—a 1988 Jetta, a faded metallic silver sedan. Maxime would pause whenever he noticed her getting into her car. It was a fascinating ritual.

Some people have rules; other have habits.

Mrs. Nightly's single-car garage was attached to the house, but she refused to use the inside door. She would scamper along the path from her front door with her walker, her purse swaying on one arm and the always present transparent pink water bottle swinging merrily on the opposite side, clipped to the frame. If she saw Maxime, she would pause and call out, "Greetings, Neighbor Maxime!" before continuing down the path. Outside the garage door, she would park the walker, press the remote and wait for the door to open—she was in no hurry. Then she collapsed the walker and stuffed it into the trunk, water bottle and all. It took her a full five minutes to back the car out of the garage. Maxime had timed her: fifteen minutes usually passed from the moment she emerged from her front door until the Jetta chugged down the street.

She followed the same ritual in winter. Maxime always shoveled her path and driveway. He often pondered whether he could place winter rubbers on her walker, to give her more grip. She had one daughter, who lived in Texas. They did not see an awful lot of each other because Mrs. Nightly refused to leave the city. Every day, either Maxime or Donna would go by the house to make sure she was okay.

Life was good to Maxime. He resumed his habit of enjoying a glass of sherry before supper. The beer he drank when the boys visited and barbequed—he never could develop a taste for the bitter stuff.

He and Donna even finalized their plans for the December holidays. The tradition at Johnson, Johnson & McBride was that the period from the week before Christmas until the weekend after New Year's Day was vacation time for the entire firm. Compliance was the accepted norm. Maxime had no plans to break the tradition. It would be sacrilegious. When he found himself questioning the wisdom of this enforced practice, his eighth rule on page one helped: *Show respect for other people.*

When Maxime Baumann woke up on Saturday, October third at six a.m., as he always did (except for Sundays, when he got up at seven), he realized that something was the matter. He lay dead still and listened. There was no out-of-place sound. Donna breathed regularly next to him. Relieved, he turned on his side—and felt a jab, a knife driving into his groin. He rolled back. The pain in his groin had woken him.

He snapped upright, making Donna murmur in her sleep. *Lieber Gott, the hydrocele has returned.*

He wormed out of bed, gentle, so as not to wake Donna or Columbus, who always snuck into their room sometime during the night, and limped into the bathroom. An inspection was due. He pulled Donna's hand mirror from the drawer and scrutinized the swelling with the aid of the bright vanity lights. He thought himself a reasonable expert by now at assessing scrotal swellings and irregularities.

Unmistakable: the enemy had returned. It was already the size of a large lemon, and more tender than before. He went to the front door to get the paper and sat down at the table in the kitchen. Columbus tagged along. Maxime would wake Donna at seven with coffee. He wouldn't tell her a thing—well, not initially.

He would try Dr. Williams's office at ten. He could also go to Emergency, embarrass himself in front of the triage nurse and wait eight to ten hours, if he was lucky, to see the doctor. The medical officer, who would by then be pissed off to be bothered at six p.m. (on a Saturday *evening*) by an old geezer with a recurrence of a small hydrocele, would make Maxime lose his decorum. The doctor would then definitely ask him, "Exactly why couldn't you have waited until Monday and gone to your GP, Mr. Baumann?" Maxime didn't think he would survive the ordeal. Anybody who knew anything about the mechanics of navigation through the antiquated emergency-room triage system would know it was better to stay home unless you had had a massive stroke or a cardiac arrest. Bloody inconvenience.

Donna received her coffee at seven, after Columbus received his pellets, at 6:55 precisely. It had taken some time to convince Donna that her cat could thrive on pellets and water alone. That's right, no milk. The cat also did not require special "wet" cat food— from a special can—costing goodness knows how much. Costing more than fresh organic food for humans, for crying out loud. Anybody who knew anything about brand-name cat pellets with hairball-removal formulas knew that. Bloody wet-cat-food money grabbers.

Maxime told Donna nothing about the recurrence of the swelling. He phoned the urologist's office at ten from his cellphone, after having stepped outside. He had to listen to the plump receptionist's voice: "You have reached the offices of Dr. John Williams, Urologist, Nephrologist and Infertility Specialist. These offices are now closed and will reopen on Monday at 8:30 a.m. If this is a physician calling, you can page Dr. Williams at the following number. If this is a medical emergency, please go to the nearest emergency room for treatment. Thank you and have a great weekend."

Maxime snorted. *How does one have a great weekend with a painful lemon in one's scrotum?* He added another mental note to his list of discussion topics with Dr. Moller when he saw the man again. Imagine: sending him to an infertility specialist. *Lieber Gott, I have two sons.*

On Monday morning, Maxime phoned Dr. Williams's practice at 8:31 sharp, from his office. Donna was still none the wiser. It was better this way. Rule ten on page two stated: *If possible, don't hurt other people's feelings.* This morning the swelling was the size of a large orange.

Maxime was worried.

"Dr. Williams's office, how may I help you?"

Maxime explained his dilemma to the pudgy receptionist, the voice on the weekend message system. She remained adamant: "Sorry, Doctor Williams is booked this entire week."

Maxime explained again. The receptionist wouldn't budge. She remained professional but firm.

Maxime closed his eyes as he held onto the receiver and remembered something he had read only the previous afternoon, in a book Donna had given him on his birthday. She had hoped he would someday heed the advice of Mr. Carnegie.

Maxime changed the tone of his voice. In no uncertain terms, using words inundated with flowers, he told the lady that he understood how hard she worked and how underappreciated receptionists often are, and how busy her poor doctor is—totally overworked, both of them. Then he added how much he, being just one in a crowd of pestering patients, would appreciate it if she could squeeze him in for only five minutes, nothing more, on Friday afternoon, since Dr. Williams already knew the full story. If that could at all be possible, it would give life so much more meaning.

The receptionist paused, then relented. "Okay, Mr. Bowman. I'm going to make an exception, only because you've said so many nice things about us—we don't often hear that we're appreciated. You're a sweetheart. Be here at three p.m. sharp on Friday. And only five minutes."

"*Danke schön*. I'll be there. Thank you, dear lady!"

Maxime slowly crawled through his week as the swelling grew. He didn't go to the gym. How does one exercise with a cantaloupe in one's pants? He didn't have relations with his Donna; this required tremendous effort on his part, as well as ingenuity from him for her not to see it. And he had to inform Mr. J. Johnson that his problem had returned.

"Maxie, I'm worried about you. Should I be?"

"Mr. Johnson?"

"Yes, Maxie. You're a full fifteen years my junior, and now you seem to be falling apart—literally at the seams. What *is* it with you?"

"Mr. Johnson, this is the nature of the condition—it can recur. The hydrocele disappeared, but now it's back, worse than before."

Mr. J. Johnson raised his hands as if in self-defense. "Not a word more, Maxie. I don't want to know the name of the dreaded illness and spare me the gory details. Your task is to get yourself sorted out—once and for all. Do you get that? Perhaps you should consider a second opinion." He gave Maxime a penetrating glance. "I want you to regain your health. But don't waste too much time in doing so. The company needs you. Remember, nobody is indispensable."

This last comment gave Maxime food for thought for the remainder of the week until he saw Dr. Williams at 3:05 Friday afternoon.

Dr. Williams was sympathetic and listened without interrupting. Then he had a quick look.

"Well, my dear chap, it seems we're not winning this bugger," he remarked as Maxime pulled up his pants. "Mr. Baumann, I'll drain the thing now and get Marcia to get us a date for the surgery. We'll have to change tactics. Be a good fellow—there's a questionnaire that you're supposed to complete if we're planning on surgery."

Dr. Williams picked up his phone and passed instructions to his front desk. Then he explained in greater detail to Maxime how they would perform the operation, the possible complications, the possible anesthetic procedures, the consent form and postoperative care. Maxime zoned out long before the urologist started on the consent form, and what he agreed to.

This is serious business, Maxime Baumann. Focus.

It took Maxime nearly fifteen minutes to complete the four-page questionnaire. *So many questions,* he thought. *Why do they have to get so damned personal?* Marital status. Do you live in a house or an apartment? Do you have any other medical conditions? Do you use a wheelchair? *Most certainly not.* Do you make use of home care or require assistance with activities of daily living? *I'm not an invalid. I'm not senile. Neither am I going for a bloody heart transplant.*

By the time he handed Marcia the completed questionnaire, she had a date for him: Tuesday, October twenty-ninth, at nine a.m. The final OR time was subject to change. He had to fast from the midnight before and check in two hours before the scheduled time.

"Do you have any other questions, Mr. Bowman?"

Any other questions? Maxime shook his head—he had a thousand things he wanted to ask the doctor. He shook his head again and waved goodbye.

Maxime considered going to the coffee shop for some down time—for some deeper introspection. But as he turned down the side street he realized with a pang that Donna would be waiting for him at home. She would most certainly be in the kitchen, watching the driveway, ready with the coffee. Waiting. He couldn't do this to her. He circled the block and headed home. Donna would know what to do next.

Maxime's structured world was threatened. He was standing in no man's land. He could feel the searchlight burning into his back, waiting for the siren, heard the guards yell, "*Halt! Wer ist da?*"

Maxime turned into the driveway, waited for the stammering door, watched the cat in the window and inhaled slowly. He should find a new overhead door company. It was a bloody disgrace—half a horse.

They would have coffee. Go for a walk. Talk. Donna would listen.

Donna will know what to do. She always knows what to do.

6

The Boys Are Informed About Their Father's Ailment

Maxime was wrong.

Donna, for the first time he could remember since 1978, did not say what she thought he should do. (And his memory seldom failed him.) Not about having the surgery on the twenty-ninth—she was fully supportive in that regard, especially when he showed her the surplus loose skin where the hydrocele was, and how it was already filling up—but about letting the boys know. She didn't *want* to tell him what he should do about Sandro and Simon.

Sandro was thirty-three and lived in Vancouver. He had left years earlier, soon after learning how to design spaces for people to live. Found a sweetheart there, and they were expecting their first. He phoned Maxime and Donna religiously—every weekend—and visited at least once a year, usually around Christmas. He took after his mother in stature.

Simon, Maxime and Donna's youngest, lived in London, England. They hadn't seen him in two years—much to his mother's concern. She worried that the eternal fog and rain had affected his common sense. There always seemed to be a reason he couldn't make it back home. He used to Skype them once a week; in the beginning. For the past year, they had had little word from him.

Simon was in software development. *I'm building platforms for online entrepreneurs, Dad,* was what he told Maxime when he tried to pinpoint exactly how his son made an honest living abroad. Maxime had thought Sandro was the one building platforms and foundations. He was apparently wrong again.

Both boys had had their first operations at a young age: circumcisions when they were preschoolers, their tonsils out before they were ten. Sandro lost his appendix in grade nine. The boys had little issue with people in white coats—unlike Maxime. They, so to speak, grew up inside the halls of the houses for the infirm.

Maxime shivered. *Hospitals.*

Sandro remained the more responsible and reliable of the two, Maxime thought the next evening as he dialed his son's number.

They shared pleasantries, and Maxime told him about his upcoming surgery on the twenty-ninth. "I want you to come home, Sandro. For a few days, at least. Please."

"Isn't it only a minor procedure?"

"There's no such thing as a small operation."

"Oh, Dad. You know what I mean. They're not doing a bypass or a heart transplant, are they?"

Maxime didn't know what to say to this.

"Dad? Are they?"

"Sandro, you're right that they're not transplanting anything, but this is my *first time*. It's serious. Please come home." He added, hoping it would mellow Sandro, "You know your brother has long since written us off. He's maintaining radio silence."

"Simon is a little caught up in his work. He's okay. I spoke to him the other—"

"So he talks to *you?* We haven't heard from him since before Christmas."

"Dad," Sandro said in a soothing voice. "You know he has issues."

Maxime felt as old as Mr. J. Johnson. "Why is he so angry with us?"

"He's full of BS. He's more upset with the country, with *Canada*. He feels the government could have supported his business better, prevented him from having to declare bankruptcy. He also blames Mother and you for his misfortunes—because he *can*. He believes it's his right. Plus, I think he made some weird friends in London, who recommended he cut ties with his parents."

Maxime flinched. "Why does he *hate* us? We miss him."

"He doesn't *hate* you, Dad. He's confused, even at twenty-nine."

"So why does he phone *you?*"

"That's ... complicated. I'm his brother. It's different, according to Simon. Sorry, Dad."

Maxime sighed several times, wiping his gleaming forehead with his ironed white handkerchief. He tried again to convince his eldest to fly over and visit his parents.

Sandro insisted it would be impossible to come; he had several complex commitments. He was working on a large project—they were trying to get the outside work done before winter hit. Michelle would be working until her seventh month; her due date was in late April. He claimed it was going to be tough for them.

"Sandro, it's going to be tough for *me*. Don't you feel a little ashamed? You guys in Vancouver have no appreciation for what winter is, what *cold* is. You have a few cold spells with frost in February, and you dare call it *winter*. You probably can't recall where your mitts are."

Sandro only laughed. "Dad, your surgery is barely three weeks from now. It's too short notice for me."

"It's exactly three weeks and five days. Almost an entire month."

Sandro laughed again. He could hear the stress in his father's voice. The pitiful perfectionist. He tried to remember which one of his dad's *Lebensregeln* he was in danger of making him break. Probably half of page two and all of page one. He would have to phone his mother the next day and get some clarity on the gravity of the situation. *Poor Mother. I'll have to soothe the dear man.*

"I'll see if we can make it the weekend *after*," Sandro soothed. "I can't promise more than that. I'll have to discuss it with Michelle."

———

Maxime was worried.

For several minutes he sat without moving a muscle. He was more than worried. Had he been that naive, that unaware of how his children had grown apart from him? It had started years ago. But still, it was as if they had drifted apart during the night. Like survivors of a shipwreck, each huddled in their little life raft, attached to the other boats with pieces of string. Only to wake in the morning as the sun inched out above the horizon to find themselves separated and abandoned on an empty ocean. No land in sight, no other boat, no ship. Nothing.

Pull yourself together, Maxime Baumann. It's a silly, small operation. You've heard Sandro. He should know: he lives in Vancouver. He designs spaces. He's an expectant father. He knows things.

Early the next morning, Maxime phoned Simon, hoping to synchronize with a decent hour on the British Isles. There was no answer. Maxime left him a message: "Please contact me—home or office. It's urgent."

Perhaps Simon would respond *this* time. He hadn't heard the boy's voice in eleven months.

The next day, during Maxime's lunch break, Simon called Maxime at the office.

"Dad! What's going on? Is something the matter with Mother?"

Maxime cringed. Simon was never a man to mince words. Maxime had, after all, said it was urgent. He hurried to reassure his youngest and explained that it wasn't his mother.

"Then what's so *urgent? You* sound okay."

Maxime sighed. Didn't anybody get it? Doesn't anybody care? What had happened to compassion in the world? He,

Maxime Bastien Baumann, prided himself for having spent all those years—when his sons were still at home—teaching them compassion, how to care and show empathy. They were aware of his Life Rules. Although, if he was frank with himself, he could recall countless times when the boys, along with their mother, rolled their eyes at his persistence.

Compassion. *Lieber Gott,* that was the seventh rule on page two, one of the big ones: *Do not close your heart to your fellow man.* He had always thought that included one's parents.

"I'm going for an operation, Simon." Maxime explained the procedure. "I've never had surgery before."

"So? Mom had *two*—each time she had us. Sandro has had three, I think, and I've had two. Did you *forget?*"

What Maxime heard was: *Sorry, Dad. We've had our share— now it's your turn. There is justice, after all.*

"That has nothing to do with it. Anything can go wrong— you know that. I'm not twenty-nine anymore. Please come home. I need you guys."

"You don't need me, Dad."

"I'm sixty-four-and-a-half."

"You're *tough.*"

Maxime was not one to give up easily. He gave his son a lecture on the many risks associated with anesthesia and surgery, even in the twenty-first century. What Simon apparently did not appreciate was that the surgeon and anesthetist could always screw up. Anything was possible. Maxime was not one to plead. He pleaded with his son to come home.

"It's safe," Simon insisted.

"What's safe?"

"Dad, they don't use chloroform anymore. Surgery is safer than driving a car."

"That's hearsay."

Simon took after Maxime, big-boned and even more muscular. The last Maxime knew, his son worked out two hours a day, five times a week, and drank whey protein shakes—but he was stubborn like Maxime. Simon explained in greater detail, his voice clipped as if he was annoyed, how numerous studies had shown how safe anesthesia could be.

"How do you know all that?" Maxime asked. "Don't tell me you've started taking medical classes in night school."

His son's sigh vibrated over the line. "Dad, I have doctor friends. We talk."

"Okay. Never mind all that. Please come home. Only for a few days."

"No."

"Why not?"

"Because it isn't a *real* emergency. Do you have *any* idea what went through my mind when I listened to your message? *Do* you? And then I discover that my father lied to me. You're only having a minor procedure."

The line went quiet.

Maxime felt a pang of guilt. Perhaps he shouldn't have used the word "urgent." But it was his sons' duty to be at their father's bedside. He had thought they would be thrilled to be with him, like when they were little—when they looked up at him with admiration, at this big strong man in rubber boots.

"It's not minor," Maxime persisted.

"Dad, I have commitments. I am working myself out of debt—*serious* debt. I'm working like a slave in a coal mine. I can't get out on such short notice. You're scared—I get that. But Mom is there. She'll go with you."

"Simon, I'm not going to keep on pleading."

"That's fine, Dad, you don't have to. But I am *not* coming. You don't need me. You *never* needed me. You never needed *anyone*. Not with your bloody rule book and all."

Another sigh rattled across the line. "Why do you think I left Canada? You're like the government—millions of rules and regulations but zero compassion. Zero. Let me *be*."

The line clicked and went dead.

Maxime stared at the receiver for an indefinite time before returning it to its base.

"Simon, oh, Simon," he muttered.

Maxime was never one for cheap sentimentality. Crying didn't come easily to him. The tears now stung behind his lids.

My boy.

Maxime Baumann felt as old as his boss, Mr. J. Johnson, who was born in 1936. He could not recall when last he had experienced such great sadness, such vast emptiness.

No compassion. Simon had cut them off and out of his life. But why? Anybody who knew anything about elective surgery and pathos and being sixty-four-and-a-half knew that when a son did not feel compelled to rush to his ailing father's side and accused him of being a heartless bastard, the world was going to the dogs. That much was bloody obvious.

7

Maxime Calls His Brother

Maxime was miserable.

No. If he was perfectly honest with himself, he was pissed off.

He buzzed Mrs. Long and asked her to reschedule his clients for the next hour. He had to phone Gunther—immediately.

His sons would shine during their absence. They had more important things to do than come and help hold Moses's hands in the air to win the battle with the Amalekites. The one was too busy, and the other thought his father was a moron.

Maxime couldn't comprehend how they could live their lives without harboring any clemency, and say what they did without choking on guilt. Simon had made it crystal clear: his father was a failure. Sandro, at least, had a grain of compassion left, but he only planned on coming when it was all over.

Maxime dialed. It wouldn't be too late in Basel-Stadt.

"*Guten Abend. Es ist Baumann.*" Gunther's voice was as crisp as if he stood next to Maxime.

"*Hello,* Gunt."

"*Maximus!* How are you, my little brother?"

The joyful voice soothed Maxime's melancholic heart. The sun broke through on his face. Gunther had never got it into his head to call him childish names, like Mr. J. Johnson, not even when they were children. Although, Maxime was convinced that "Maximus" was intended to imply the opposite. They bantered, and he had to give detailed accounts of how everyone in his immediate family was doing, including the boys. He winced again when he talked about Simon.

Gunther had moved back to Switzerland in the 1990s, back to Basel-Stadt, where Maxime and Gunther had once lived with their parents. He had lost his wife and only child twelve years ago, in a boating accident. He had studied mechanical engineering and was now unofficially retired, having made his fortune with patents on devices used in orthopedics and general surgery— endoscopic clamps and graspers. Money wasn't his brother's biggest concern at this point in his life: it was loneliness that gnawed at his soul.

"Gunt, how would you feel about visiting us—Donna and me—for a couple of weeks, or for as long as you'd prefer?"

"When were you thinking, Max? Around Christmas?"

"No …" Maxime hesitated. "How about two weeks from today?"

"Maximus?"

"I'm having surgery."

"*Lieber, Gott. Was ist loss?* Your heart? Why didn't you phone me sooner?"

They had lost their father to a heart attack when he was seventy-one. Their mother passed away a month later from a broken heart. She stopped living—too much love could kill you.

"No, no, Gunther. Nothing as dramatic as that—I have a silly swelling in my scrotum that requires surgery. The doctor has drained it, but it has re—"

Gunther's bellowing laugh made Maxime yank the receiver away from his ear. Maxime frowned. He did not find the present state of affairs amusing—neither the swelling nor its drainage.

"Gunt, do you think it's funny waddling around like a duck because of a cantaloupe in one's boxers?"

"Max … oh, Max. Waddling … cantaloupe …" The laughter from across the Atlantic started afresh. His brother gasped for air, snickered like a schoolboy laughing at a fart joke.

"What's it called, Max?" and he erupted again in shrieks of glee. "What's this cantaloupe called?"

"It's a *hydrocele.*"

Maxime explained what had transpired the past several weeks and about the scheduled surgery.

"Gunt," he said when he was done, "I would appreciate it if you could come. Stay with us. Donna would love it. Stay for a month, or longer. I'm taking time off. We can travel after—"

"Max. Max. Hold it, boy. Sorry, but I'm on a cruise that week. I can't be there, not then. But I *will* come. After. How about *after?*"

Maxime's heart sank. Betrayed yet again. The anger surged from his stomach.

"*What* cruise?" Maxime yelled. "I thought you don't go on ships? You don't get on boats of *any kind*. Not for the past twelve years. Not since Carla and Heidi—" Maxime stammered as his brother sucked in his breath. "Oh, Gunther. Forgive me, brother. I'm sorry. I'm such a heartless idiot."

Gunther laughed softly. When he spoke, there was no resentment in his voice, only sadness. "No harm was done, my friend… I'll never forget them, my girls. Never. But I'm lonesome. I'm nearing seventy. We don't live forever. I met someone, a few months ago—a widow. She made me laugh again. I want to *live* some more. I think this trip will accelerate the healing. It's a river cruise, down the Rhein. It will be quite safe. As long as I can see the shore on both sides, I'll be fine."

The brothers made tentative arrangements for Gunther to come by the second week in November.

"Why don't you bring your lady-friend along?"

Gunther laughed as if embarrassed. "I dare not impose. I don't want to frighten her away with too much, too soon."

"What's her name?"

"Mary."

"English?"

"One hundred percent. Mary McDonald. Well, Scottish, or Irish—I'm not sure. Let's see how the cruise goes. If she behaves, I'll bring her along."

"Promise?"

It was a done deal.

As he hung up, Maxime realized in a panic that he was going to rely entirely on his Donatella for his operative experience—for the excision of the excess *tunica vaginalis* in his nether regions. There would be no Sandro, no Simon, and no Gunther.

Rule five, page two, clearly stated: *Be grateful—every day.*

Maxime started counting his blessings. *Stop being such a damned asshole, Maxime Baumann. Donna will be there. That's more than enough.*

8

Maxime Baumann Receives A Call To Attend A Pre-Anesthesia Clinic

The following Monday, Mrs. Long gave Maxime a strange message. The hospital had called—he was to report to the anesthesia clinic. It was for a so-called PAC appointment, on Thursday, one week before the surgery.

Maxime was not one to be stumped. He took the note from his receptionist, read it, flipped it over and plopped down at his desk. Then he leaped back up. "Mrs. Long. Hang on, please. What on earth is a PAC appointment? I've seen my GP. I've seen the surgeon. What *more* do they want? Mr. J. Johnson is going to have *a fit.*"

"They said it's a pre-anesthesia clinic, Mr. Baumann."

"What? I don't need a *clinic.* I'm not ill—not in the usual sense of the word. So why do I have to see the anesthetist as well? Both doctors said I'm fit and healthy. Now they probably want me to see the *whole blooming team*. Next thing they'll be lining up the nurse, the orderly, the ward clerk and the housekeeping staff. Oh, I forgot—*and* the guys from maintenance and the employees in the hospital's glazed-doughnut-and-coffee shop."

Thinking about coffee shops reminded Maxime, to his shame, that he hadn't seen the inside of the gym for the past ten days, which was unlike him. He had never skipped the gym, at least not for so long. Instead of heading to the gym, he had hidden in the coffee shop, reading and eating banana bread and drinking skinny lattes. He was too ashamed to tell Donna. He wondered whether she suspected. She wasn't entirely stupid. He'd had to move his belt one notch wider. His BMI must have crept up two points.

"Mr. Baumann?"

"Never mind, Mrs. Long. I'll be there."

———

Maxime arrived half an hour early for his appointment. Just as well that he had listened to Donna and left early—they struggled to find a parking spot. "Idiots," he mumbled, the moment he saw the PAID PARKING ONLY: 24/7 sign. He could forget about parking oblique across two stalls in the corner now.

"Max?"

"I can't believe one has to *pay* for parking at a hospital. Inconceivable."

"Oh, Max, they make you pay for the parking, but at least they treat you for free. Unlike in the States." She laughed at him, his Donnatella. It was a hearty laugh, though.

It had required much convincing on his part to get Donna to accompany him this morning. She fervently objected because she had to request time off from work the following week when he was to undergo his surgery.

Maxime, however, remained obstinate. He knew how to play the guilt card. The boys "bluntly refused" to support their ailing father, and Gunther was "courting a new sweetheart, gallivanting" down the Rhein. Donna only rolled her eyes as he explained. Because he was in such an emotional turmoil, he insisted, it would be unloving and unsupportive of her, to the point of being callous, not to come along. The sweet angel he had married all these decades ago would *never* consider abandoning him.

Donna had conceded, again rolling her eyes.

After collecting his folder from Admitting, they went in search of the clinic. Three inquiries for directions and two flights of stairs later, they located it. By the time Maxime dropped into a seat, only ten minutes had remained before his appointment.

No sooner had he sat down than the clinic assistant commandeered him to follow her.

She was a slender lady. His staring at her with great concern made her smile. "Oh, it's only for your height and weight, Mr. Baumann."

He followed her to the end of the short hallway, where she took his measurements and scribbled it on a Post-it note.

"But you measured me with my clothes on." Maxime wore his navy blue suit with subtle stripes, with a turquoise tie and socks.

She held his gaze. "Would you prefer that I weigh you *without* clothes, Mr. Baumann?"

Maxime broke eye contact, grinned and shook his head. He had done some reading the previous day. "Why don't you measure my waist as well?" he asked.

The clerk laughed at him now. "We don't do that." Then she added in a whisper, "Some patients take exception. Although, it *will* put the BMI in perspective." Then continued in her normal voice. "The doctor is quite happy when we provide these two values."

Maxime was called in twenty minutes after his scheduled time. He tried to remember how much parking he had paid for and failed. That's one thing he hated about these long waits—it forced you to hunt through dated magazines, and as soon as you were halfway through an article, something intellectually stimulating, they called you. Bloody inconsiderate.

A petite lady in a long white coat with a stethoscope draped around her neck picked up a folder and stared at the few patients. "Mr. Bowman?"

Maxime snapped to his feet, wondering how she could be a specialist—she looked five years younger than Simon. He gestured for Donna to tag along.

The doctor whisked them into a room. "Please sit down. I'm Dr. Froese, from Anesthesia."

They each found a seat.

"What is Dr. Williams going to do for you?"

Maxime's heart missed a beat. *I thought this was only a formality, to meet the team. She* can't *be a specialist—she doesn't know why I'm here.*

Maxime flushed. *There goes my blood pressure.* "He's removing my hydrocele."

She held his gaze. "That's how I have it. He's doing a hydrocelectomy—a week from today?"

Maxime nodded in affirmation while the doctor slipped the automatic blood pressure cuff on his arm, clipped the pulse oximeter on his finger and scanned the questionnaire. He recognized his handwriting.

"Any allergies?"

Maxime shook his head.

"Medications? Only the sildenafil and multivitamins?"

"Sildenafil?" Maxime croaked.

Dr. Froese laughed. "Oh, sorry, Mr. Bowman. Viagra."

"Oh. Yes," he mumbled.

"Why did you want to come and see us at the anesthesia clinic?"

Maxime's suspicions were confirmed. *In the first place: it's Baumann. In the second place: this lass knows nothing.* He stared at her. "*Entschuldigung?* I did not *want* to come. I came because I was *instructed* to do so."

He repeated over and over: *Rule ten, page two; rule ten, page two.* It stated: *If possible, don't hurt other people's feelings.* He could feel Donna's eyes burning into him, willing him to watch his tongue.

Dr. Froese gave a charming smile. "Not to worry, Mr. Bowman. You seemed to have marked a couple of medical conditions here, and you're sixty-five already. So just as well—"

"Sixty-four." Rule three on page one stated clearly, *Don't ever tell a lie.* He wouldn't—no, he *couldn't* lie about his age.

She mellowed and laughed again, like the tiny bells the goats carried in the hills near Davos where he had grown up. "You marked 'High blood pressure,' and you also wrote, 'Concerned about the proposed surgery and anesthesia,'" she said.

Maxime blinked and looked at the doctor with fresh eyes. Perhaps she wasn't entirely stupid. He listened attentively to her questions and allowed her to perform a focused examination. He relaxed. *She may look young, but she must have done this before.* She was beautiful—not voluptuous like the Vision at Dr. Moller's office, but fit and trim. Her brisk, sure movements spelled "spinning-bike instructor and hot yoga enthusiast slash MD" as if stenciled on her forehead, but in soft pastel pink.

She pressed the PB monitor's button again and made the cuff inflate on his arm a second time. Maxime didn't need to look at his hand. He could feel it turn blue.

"Not too bad, Mr. Bowman. It's coming down: 152 over 90. I'm sitting here with my starched white coat—enough to give you the creeps." Again the Swiss-goat-bells laugh.

Maxime's eyes misted over. He was on the mountain with Gunther and Father, the lake far below them; he was ten and Gunther almost fourteen. Even at fourteen, Gunther was already as tall as Father. Below them, out of sight, Maxime could hear the bells and bleating goats, their herders coaxing them along. Maxime had always wanted to herd goats, from the first time he laid eyes on them as a toddler. Father, who was ten steps ahead of him on the mountain, scaled higher up—with caution—while

Gunther formed the anchor at the back. It was the first time they were going this high, tied in with ropes.

Maxime remembered how he had glanced back down, one last time, to try and see the lead goat, an imposing ram. How he had leaned far back. The next moment there was only sky under his feet. His feet must have slipped, and he started falling, yelling for dear life. He went over the edge and lost sight of his father. Had Father and Gunther not been paying attention that morning, had they not been tied in with ropes and anchors, things could have turned out quite differently for the Baumann family. There would only have remained a bereaved Mrs. Baumann.

Father had gripped the rock face and uttered only one word: "*Gunther.*"

Father never hollered. Maxime had never, in all his life, heard his father scream. Father had never felt shouting was necessary. Didn't he, after all, have three pages of life rules to guide him? That morning on the mountain they were faced with a dire situation—perilous—but no screaming was required.

As Maxime dangled in midair, he could see the herd before they disappeared into the valley. The lead goat even looked up at him, intrigued by this weird human who had dared to yell with so much angst, dangling high above it with funny ropes wrapped all around him.

Gunther and Father had known what to do. Maxime was pulled to safety. The three of them rested on the spot for a long, long time, peering down at the valley. Father sat between him and Gunther. It was an excellent opportunity to have an early lunch.

That morning, sitting next to Father, Maxime decided he would also have two boys, and he would teach them the importance of paying attention to all the members of your team. Make them understand the importance of every little carabiner—especially the weakest link.

"Mr. Bowman? *Excuse* me."

Maxime snapped back to Dr. Froese. "I'm sorry."

"What were you concerned about?"

"Everything," Maxime blurted.

Donna laughed this time with Dr. Froese. Maxime grinned, embarrassed. Donna took his hand and squeezed it, mouthing, *I love you.*

"*How much* did Dr. Moller and Dr. Williams explain to you?"

Maxime told her everything they had discussed and some of what he had read. She briefly discussed the surgical procedure and touched on the anesthesia options. She asked him a little about his work and interests and activities but didn't probe.

"So," Maxime said, "I have *options,* insofar as the anesthesia is concerned?"

"To a large extent, yes, Mr. Bowman. A local block will be a bit tricky, so that leaves us with a spinal or a general anesthetic."

She succinctly outlined the differences between the two as well as the particular advantages of the spinal. Maxime tried his best to remain focused, but her physical vicinity was distracting, and her subtle eau de toilette wafted around him—jasmine—and he kept hearing the goat bells. He claimed later that she did mention something about a 0.2 to 2 percent chance of a severe headache after the spinal, but he wasn't certain. The one thing that spooked him still was the harpoon—a long needle in his back—in his spine.

Maxime cleared his throat. "*Doktor* ... This needle-in-my-back thing. How big is it? And does it go *into* the spine?"

She touched his arm. "It's a 25-gauge needle—very, very thin. We can even use a 27-gauge, which is thinner. The only thing you'll feel is some stinging when we infiltrate with the local, after which there will only be the sensation of pressure in your back." She met his eyes and quickly added, "The needle doesn't remain there, and it doesn't *enter* the spinal cord—it follows a narrow path between the bony parts until it reaches the spinal fluid, on the *outside* of the spinal cord. Then we lie you down, and your legs go numb, from the belly button down."

Maxime nodded. He was numb already, listening to her—from the belly button up.

It seemed that she was done, as she shuffled her notes together. Maxime moved to get up. He suddenly remembered the PAID PARKING stall. *Damn. These bloody parking police. I'm not planning on putting another dollar in that machine. Time to go.* He beckoned to Donna.

"Just a moment, Mr. Bowman. I just noticed something—your vital signs. Did you put on twelve pounds in the past three weeks, since you saw Dr. Williams? I note here on the questionnaire that you listed all the activities you do and how often and for what duration, including going to a gym. You seemed like a fit man for sixty-four." She smiled warmly at him. "What happened?"

Maxime felt naked, but only briefly so. She was such a sweetheart, touching his arm again in gentle encouragement. It was better to confess. He could feel Donna's eyes on him, and he faced her for a moment. Donna's eyes were soothing. *Lieber Gott, ich liebe diese Frau.* He told Dr. Froese about the coffee shop and the lattes and banana bread and staying away from the gym—all because of his fear of the upcoming surgery. He had gone into hiding.

Maxime began to understand why the doctor had been twenty minutes late in seeing him. There was something like being *too* thorough for a medical practitioner. Or was there? She wasn't preaching, but she passionately explained to him why he should return to the gym, ASAP. Today, if possible?

See, she explained, even in only seven days, especially with his previous excellent fitness level, he would quickly pick up and get some of his "breath" back. He should concentrate on his resistance exercises and continue with his whey-protein shakes and eat cleaner. He'd feel better, it would help with his anxiety and the fact was, the fitter and stronger he was, the quicker and faster he would heal and bounce back after the surgery. It would also do his blood pressure good.

Maxime could see the stern face of Mr. J. Johnson scrutinizing him. *Maxie, what is this I hear about you neglecting yourself? Did you dare stop going to the gym? Dr. Froese called me. Should I be worried about you, Maxie? You don't want to be a disappointment to the firm, Maxie.*

"See, Mr. Bowman? A win-win-win scenario."

Maxime beamed at Dr. Froese. Both Simon and Mr. J. Johnson would be so impressed with his performance. Then he remembered Simon's withdrawal. Maxime's face fell.

Dr. Froese accompanied Donna and him to the front desk and gave him a firm handshake, showering him with the Swiss bells as she turned to call her next patient.

See what happens when you follow the rules, Maxime Baumann? Things start looking up. Rule seven on page one states: Show respect for other people. You've been blessed by this gorgeous pipsqueak of a doctor.

Maxime wasn't certain how he would exercise with a cantaloupe in his boxers, but he was willing to try.

9

Maxime Baumann Arrives At The Hospital

Maxime was worried.

Oh, he had followed Dr. Froese's recommendations. He had immediately purchased an extra-large scrotal support at the local drugstore, strapped himself in and had gone to the gym—faithfully, every single day, after work, as well as over the weekend. Donna went too, exercising alongside him. He was certain she only did it to ensure he didn't stray to the coffee shop. It worked. He regained some of his previous vitality and vigor. He even lost five pounds. He felt great. But as he tucked his shirt, he was worried.

A 25-gauge needle in my back.

Maxime was profoundly worried. He had made a list of things that could go wrong: twenty-six of them.

It was just as well that Sandro had phoned yesterday during Maxime's lunch hour.

"Love you, Dad," he had said. "You'll do just fine. Mom told me how you buffed up this past week. I'm proud of you. Enjoy the experience. You might even be able to kick Simon's ass one of these days."

What do the children know anyway? Nothing.

Easy for him to say "I'm proud of you" and "You'll do just fine." But for him then to add, "Enjoy the experience?" *He* wasn't getting a needle slammed into his spine. The next generation was going to the dogs. Him kicking his mesomorph son's ass. Imagine.

Sandro had continued. "Wish I could be there to hold your hand. But Mom is more than capable of performing that duty."

He had added as an afterthought, as if it justified him not showing up, "Anyway, they won't allow us into the OR with you, not even Mom. But we're still planning on coming the weekend. Should be there on Saturday morning, around ten."

That was beside the point—it was all about him going *solo* into the OR. There were principles involved here.

From Simon's side, there was only radio silence—not a call, a text, a tweet, or a single post. Damn it, not even a postcard. Maxime flinched.

Donna called from the mudroom. He had better grab his wallet and go.

At the hospital, Donna made him put money in for eight hours' parking.

Eight straight hours. Twelve precious dollars.

"Daylight robbery," Maxime muttered as he fed the coins into the machine.

He knew he would now be worrying for the next many hours about some asshole slamming his car door into his well-preserved 2003 Mercedes 300E. The twelve-year-old tan sedan still looked like new, all because of his owner, Maxime Bastien Baumann, who took great pride in and care of stuff entrusted to him. He had made a commitment back then, and he was damn well planning on keeping it this way.

In the surgical center, the nurse led them to a curtained-off cubicle, number 12, one of an infinite row of cubicles, and showed him the attire he was to put on. There was a printed fabric gown, paper shoes and a paper cap for him, and a chair for Donna. The nurse said to call her Sylvia. She was a stout lady with a lovely face—all smiles and giggles.

"Everything off, Mr. Bowman." She established eye contact. "I mean *everything*. And the gown goes with its opening facing the back. Please."

"But ... but can't I keep my underwear on at least, Nurse Sylvia?"

"Not if you don't want them to paint it orange with their disinfectant solution. I recommend you take it off. It'll be okay." Another encouraging smile.

Maxime didn't think it was okay. Neither Dr. Moller nor Dr. Williams nor Dr. Froese had said *anything* about him going to go to the OR in the buff. *Lieber Gott.*

Donna was a sensible person. "Max, dear, why don't you slip out of your street clothes and put the gown on as the kind lady requested? I won't be far—I'll stand guard on the other side of the curtain." When she saw his tight-lipped face, she added, "*Bitte.*"

Maxime mumbled, "Naked I came into the world and naked I will depart." But Donna had said please, and he busied himself with folding his gray suit with the stripes and placing it in a symmetrical stack at the foot of the stretcher. His shoes went into the large white bag Nurse Sylvia had given him first, followed by his dove blue socks, underpants, the folded white shirt and rolled-up tan belt, then the suit and, on top, the patterned dove blue tie. Anybody who knew anything about undressing behind a curtain in a hospital, standing in the buff with a breeze caressing your behind, knew that this is how clothes are put into a giant plastic bag with a purse string. Bloody close to indecent exposure.

Five minutes later Nurse Sylvia returned and took his history (again) as well as his vital signs, made notes and then inserted a cannula into a vein in his forearm, secured it with tape and connected it to an infusion set.

As she tidied up, she added, "An orderly will be here shortly to shave you. The surgeon and anesthesiologist will also come around and say hi."

Maxime realized he had not been worried enough after all. "But I *have* shaved this morning," he piped, and rubbed his chin.

Nurse Sylvia laughed. "We're talking about your groin area, Mr. Bowman. You didn't shave *there,* now, did you?"

Maxime's face flushed as he shook his head.

"Not to worry, Mr. Bowman, we do it every day. It'll be chop-chop. No problem."

Maxime could feel his pulse soaring, his heart thumping inside his chest. He felt dizzy. Nauseated. *Exactly. If that blade slips—chop-chop—I have only the one. Bloody disaster.*

Maxime Baumann was a private man.

They have no idea.

Donna—dear Donna—read his mind and pulled her chair closer, taking his hand. "Max, sweetheart, *look* at me." He reluctantly followed her instruction as she leaned forward and kissed him. The thumping inside his chest slowly abated.

Minutes later another female—young, slim and busty, this time in green scrubs—wafted into his cubicle. "Good morning, Mr. Bowman! How *are* you?" she bubbled, effervescent like overflowing champagne. "I'm Sally, an orderly. I'm here to shave you." She brimmed at him and smiled at Donna. "Mrs. Bowman, it you could wait outside the curtains for us? It'll only take a few minutes."

Maxime was soon alone with Sally behind the drawn curtains. He was grateful that he hadn't taken a little blue pill the previous night. He had found that the effect could last well over four hours. He started reciting the twenty-third psalm in Romansch, an ancient language he had learned when he was growing up in eastern Switzerland, alongside the German that surrounded them every day. It was much like conversational Latin. It should take his mind off of matters at hand, he thought.

Maxime could feel Sally handling the electric shaver, starting from his bellybutton and descending south—touching him—shaving in rapid waves with alarming confidence. Maxime, blessed with a fine coat of red-blond fuzz over most of his body, recited harder.

The Lord is my shepherd. Down, boy, down. He leadeth me in green pastures.

Maxime listened to the buzz of the shaver as he recited the entire psalm, before commencing with the hundredth psalm. There was a jersey of hair to be removed. Sally shaved the delicate areas with finesse, and Maxime recited with shut eyes.

Dr. Williams was next to show his smiling face. Maxime was astounded that everybody seemed so glad to see him. The doctor stayed only thirty seconds, checked the correct side as well as the consent forms, then wished him well.

A new face appeared, also clad in green scrubs: a lanky man, stethoscope around his neck, sporting a slow smile.

"*Herr Baumann. Guten Tag. Wie gehen es ihnen?*" He grasped Maxime's hand and gave it a firm shake.

Maxime's face broke into a grin so wide, it hurt. "*Sehr gut, danke, Herr Doktor.*"

"I am Dr. Harry Hill—I'm with Dr. Williams. I'm doing the anesthesia."

That couldn't be right, Maxime's expression pleaded.

The doctor was quick to add, "I see you've met Dr. Froese in the PAC clinic. Well, she's doing another slate today, but I've read her detailed notes. I'll take good care of you. Oh, I'm not German—I lived for two years in Berlin after completing my pre-graduate studies. I don't use the German as often as I'd like to. It's a bit rusty."

His gaze shifted from Maxime to Donna and back. "It seems as if you and Dr. Froese had decided on a spinal anesthetic, correct?"

Dr. Hill proceeded with discussing the options and the plan for the day while doing a brief examination. The thumping in Maxime's chest returned.

"One more thing, Mr. Baumann. For men your age, we usually insert a urinary catheter, which we remove as soon as the spinal has worn off. As men grow older, their prostates enlarge, which can make urinating after a spinal problematic. Usually it stays in only for a few hours. Any *other* questions?"

The thumping intensified as Maxime added three more questions to the existing twenty-six. A *catheter.*

He snapped upright. *"Herr Doktor. Bitte…"*

Dr. Hill turned back, the smile still in place. "Herr Baumann?"

"Who exactly will insert the bladder catheter? Is that *after* I'm asleep?"

Dr. Hill chuckled. "Usually one of the nurses. If they have trouble with it, Dr. Williams will do it." Dr. Hill reached and patted Maxime's leg, covered with a flannel blanket. "Please don't worry. You'll do just fine—you'll be drowsy by that time."

Maxime's heart attempted to pound out his throat as Donna scraped her chair closer and took hold of his hand, not letting go this time. He was considering rule six on page one: *Consider all your options. Always.* Should he make a run for the exit? There was still time.

Donna gripped his hand with both of hers, pressing it against her lips, kissing it with fervor. She must have read his mind, again.

Anybody who knew anything about innate modesty and Maxime Baumann's take on it would know that no woman other than Donna had ever touched him there. (Except for Sally, the orderly, when she had shaved him.) Not one. Not even briefly. *Bloody inconsiderate veterinary-medicine-minded people—did they forget I'm not a bull-calf to be clipped?*

10

Journey To The Operating Room

Ten minutes later, Sally pulled the curtains aside.

"Righty-oh, Mr. Bowman. It's time for your tune-up. Let's get on your fancy blue party hat. There we go. Any dentures, hearing aids or piercings we need to remove?" she asked, buzzing around Maxime and Donna.

Maxime shook his head, grim-faced.

"Not even a belly button ring, Mr. Bowman?"

Maxime cracked a smile. "Silly girl."

Donna let go of his hand and planted a fleeting kiss on his lips. *"Ich liebe dich,"* she whispered.

Maxime waved and waved until his stretcher rounded the corner and Donna disappeared.

This is it, Maxime Baumann. He recited rule twelve on page one: *Never be found without faith. You need it now—and lots of it.*

Sally chatted incessantly about her day and the multitude of things they were expecting her to do. She, a female, was supposed to do the work of two men. Could you believe that—two grown men? Seriously. The administration just wasn't what it used to be. They dared call this progress—this gender equality crap and job demarcation—but had apparently never heard of women's suffrage. There was so much red tape and bullshit these days if he understood what she meant. Maxime nodded in sympathy, momentarily forgetting about his racing heart.

The arctic breeze that met him as Sally pushed him through the OR doors knocked his breath down his throat. And he had thought Chinooks were found only in Alberta. All he could think of was the increased hammering behind his breastbone. Why did they need so many lights hanging from the ceiling, and all those machines on wheels? It reminded Maxime of the time he watched the mechanic change his 300E's alternator—having surrounded himself with an assortment of carts on wheels and diagnostic computer screens. Maxime was immediately grateful for the absence of an engine oil aroma; the operating room welcomed him with a hint of disinfectant and anesthetic gas.

Maxime grimaced. *Anybody who knows anything about operating rooms and disinfectants and sleeping gasses knows that smell can only be that of chloroform. Bloody opportunists—thought I wouldn't know that they're stuck in the days of Louis Pasteur, with ether and what not.*

"*Willkommen, Herr Baumann.*" Dr. Hill called out as he helped the now shivering Maxime from the stretcher onto the OR bed. Dr. Hill explained the function of each device as he connected the monitors to Maxime and covered him with several warmed flannels. As the cuff inflated to a death knell on his arm, Maxime winced. *We're working again on that blue color in my hand.*

He craned his head at the anesthesia monitor behind him, trying desperately to locate the source of the rapid beeping. A number in green blinked on the screen: 128. *Settle down, Maxime Baumann.* The next moment a relaxing wave washed over him—as if he had downed three shots in quick succession.

"Not to worry, Mr. Baumann—I've given you something to calm those frolicking nerves. We'll get your heart to settle down; *then* we'll let you sit up for the spinal."

By the time Sally returned to the OR to help with holding him in the correct position, Dr. Hill was satisfied with Maxime's heart rate. Even Maxime could feel the thumping easing off. They sat him up lengthwise on the bed and, after explaining to him how to properly arch his back, lowered the foot-end. Sally was quick to add that he should curve his back like an angry cat, or a shrimp if he understood what she meant. She demonstrated the proper posture to him with a wink.

Maxime rolled his eyes—he was not a complete idiot, contrary to popular belief.

Grinning, Sally handed him a soft pillow to hug.

Lieber Gott, what else are they going to make me do?

Still not satisfied with his angry-cat-stance, the anesthetist and Sally attempted to get him to slouch more. Sally piped up that he should imagine the worst posture possible. The sooner he conquered the concept; the faster Dr. Hill would be able to find the spot. Maxime yelped and giggled when Dr. Hill's fingers palpated his iliac crests and pressed on the bony parts of his lower back.

Dr. Hill laughed. "Ticklish, Mr. Baumann?"

"*Bist du fertig?*" Maxime inquired.

"No, Mr. Baumann—that was only the positioning. Next, I'll paint your back with a disinfectant, which will be cold."

Maxime sighed and struggled to hold his pose as they painted his back—it was one thing to slouch and arch one's back, but a different thing entirely when they rubbed your back with liquid ice. Sally explained that although he now had a bright, hippie-pink spot that looked like a severe sunburn or an allergic reaction, it would eventually wash off. As long as the missus, Mrs. Bowman, didn't get too concerned when she noticed the odd skin color.

"Okay, Mr. Baumann," Dr. Hill instructed. "Position again. Hold still—a pinch and a burn. Hold *still*, please."

Maxime swore in Romansch. Sally whispered in his ear, demanding that he translate that—she was desperate to learn new words. The spicier, the better. Maxime grinned at her through his discomfort, shook his head and mumbled.

"Don't hold your breath, Mr. Baumann," Dr. Hill said. "We're done with the freezing. Now you'll only feel me pressing. You shouldn't feel any pain."

How did he know I was holding my breath?

While the anesthetist busied himself with the 25-gauge needle, Sally resumed, in a hushed tone, her discourse about the challenges of her job and her resultant inability to achieve work satisfaction. How the low priority given by the administration to structured channels for union members' grievances was getting the better of her, being above her comprehension, and apparently above her pay grade. How could anyone from admin, with a shred of common sense, not realize that they were making complete assholes of themselves? Anybody who knew anything about loyalty and esprit de corps knew that. "Bloody authoritarian bastards," she mumbled.

Maxime's chuckling only made her rant faster. She shared her latest plan of enrolling in an evening course—then she could make it into the ranks of administration and become something of a Trojan horse, infiltrate the System and work on reforming the culture from within, like a bloodless coup. Give the bastards in the ivory tower a run for their money, if he understood what she meant.

Maxime nodded, still grinning.

"*Wir sind fertig, Herr Baumann.*"

At last.

They made him lie down, covered his upper body with a warm blanket, wrapped an oxygen tubing around his ears and blew fresh air up his nostrils. Anybody who knows anything about oxygen tubing and nasal prongs would know that he, Maxime Baumann, was in need not of paired oxygen molecules through a plastic tube, but of a generous glass of sherry.

Maxime could feel another flood of carefreeness wash over him. *Wunderbar.* His legs started feeling weird, all pins-and-needles.

MAXIME

The blood pressure cuff continued its endless cycle of inflating and deflating on his arm, and the monitors behind him beeped incessantly. He drifted into a carefree world.

Sally whispered in his ear, "Good luck, Mr. Bowman. See you in forty-five minutes."

11

The Hydrocelectomy

Maxime entered the twilight world.

For a moment, he had forgotten all about the twelve dollars for the parking and the bladder catheter. Those things didn't matter where he was.

And yet Maxime was uneasy—he could not believe that his overwhelming sense of dread had evaporated. He was in unfamiliar territory: a worry-free zone. It had to be the result of Dr. Hill's potent cocktail. What had Dr. Froese called it? *"They'll take you on a legal trip." They're making an addict of me. Donna—where did Donna say she was going? She would know what to do.*

Maxime could not recall who had inserted the catheter and only noticed, as in a haze, when they clipped the sterile blue sheets to the IV posts, to separate him from the surgical field.

His mind became airborne. Far off, he could hear Dr. Hill talking with Dr. Williams and the scrub nurse. Tunnels of light and fading voices surrounded him—it was what he had imagined heaven to be like, except for the sterile blue drapes and the absence of singing choirs. The odd thing was, the angels and everyone else was dressed in green OR attire.

Maxime didn't feel a thing as Dr. Williams made the skin incision and was startled when Dr. Hill tapped him on the shoulder.

"Mr. Baumann, take a few deep breaths, please."

Maxime floated higher above the multitude in their green scrubs. A single spotlight zoomed in on him, increasing in intensity, blinding him where he lay immobile—as if tied to the tracks. A steam engine barreled down at him. He tried to yank his arms free.

"Mr. Baumann, lie still!"

Maxime blinked and squirmed. How could he lie still? The light drew him closer and closer, like a vortex, reeling him in—unrelenting.

There was a firmer tap on his shoulder. "Mr. Baumann—stop fretting and take another *deep* breath."

It was hopeless. The searing light hauled him in like a magnet—he was in the center of a celestial black hole—soon it became a whirlpool of light and darkness. Maxime began to fall. The spinning became chaotic—the dizziness overwhelming. He felt sick and attempted once more to scamper upright.

Dr. Hill must have decreased the sedation, for Maxime could now hear Dr. Williams asking what the hell their patient was doing and instructed the nurse to pass him a sturdier needle holder and hold the patient's legs on the table for goodness sake. Maxime experienced no pain.

Dr. Hill's voice had a sharper edge to it. "*Herr Baumann! Was ist loss? Bitte.*"

Maxime also wondered what on earth was going on as hands pressed on his shoulders and legs. Another wave of nausea hit him. Without warning the spinning light ejected him as suddenly as it had sucked him in.

"Herr Doktor ... I feel like *fomiting.*"

Maxime could hear his anesthetist speak in foreign tongues before he switched back to English. "*Cough,* Mr. Baumann. *Again. Harder!*"

Maxime could swear someone had slammed a fist on his chest. People in the heavenly zone were negotiating with those in the OR-zone about whether Maxime should become a permanent member of the eternal hereafter.

Dr. Williams leaned across the blue drapes. "What's the matter with our patient, Harry?"

"He's developed a high spinal block. He's semi-conscious, his BP is gone, and his pulse is too slow. Everything was one hundred percent only *seconds* ago."

The monitor alarms sounded.

"Shall we call a code?"

"No, oh no. It'll take only a few seconds for the drugs to kick in."

"Don't worry, Mr. Baumann!" Dr. Hill called out in a thin voice. "It's your blood pressure that's dropped a bit. We're fixing it."

The alarms continued their cacophony. The heaven-bound people were more successful in the negotiations, it seemed.

In the OR everyone scurried around with intense purpose.

Maxime wasn't worried about his BP or the panic around him. He was busy manhandling an upturned canoe. He had to worry about remaining on his feet. He was in lake country with his two boys. It was the summer of '95. He had to call out to get Sandro's attention—Sandro was assisting Simon at the opposite end of the canoe, which the three of them were carrying. The boys almost made him lose his grip. In spite of Simon being two years the junior, he towered above his fourteen-year-old brother.

The shortcut and portage had been Sandro's idea—it would give them practice for the real thing when he and Simon were ready to tackle the Churchill River all the way to Hudson Bay one summer in the future. When and if that would ever happen, was up for debate. But Maxime also firmly believed, as rule ten on page two stated: *If possible, don't hurt other people's feelings.* And he told himself, *Let the boys dream, Maxime.*

The boys each carried a small backpack, and Maxime, of course, the biggest one—and the heaviest, since he brought what they needed to drink as well. He didn't trust the lake water. Never had and never would. It was good to row on, but not to swallow. Not a single drop. Not without filtrating or cooking it.

"Careful now, Sandro. Fall back half a step. Steady as we go."

"Can't we rest? I'm *exhausted*," complained Sandro.

"We're almost there, boys. Only a few more boulders."

For a moment Maxime thought Dr. Hill had pulled his eyelids apart to glance at his pupils.

Maxime yelled at Simon to not run down the narrow footpath leading to the water's edge. The boy was too impatient—he got it from his mother. They were free of the rocks at last. Strapped into the upside-down craft was their three-man tent, for a single night on the island. They already had two hours of rowing behind them, from where the truck had been parked. According to the map, it was a mere two hundred feet of land, but Maxime had his doubts. It felt as if they had to carry the boat for two miles. It didn't help that Maxime was taller than the boys—the realization grew stronger by the minute that he was carrying the canoe all by himself.

It had become an annual thing, this canoeing with his boys—away for a weekend, without Donna. She was the one who encouraged her sons to drag their dad away from the city, from his über-structured life, from his two-page rulebook. Faint chance of *that* was ever happening. Inconceivable. Didn't page one, rule one state: *Stick to the rules?* And rule two reiterated the same sentiment: *Be true to yourself.* Exactly. He, Maxime Bastien Baumann, was a rules man.

Donna had never cared for canoeing. He could get her into a kayak, but a more open vessel gave her the heebie-jeebies. It was one instance where Maxime had to roll his eyes at his spouse. When he had suggested as the boys grew up that they buy two double kayaks, she had said it was "an unnecessary expense." Imagine. Anyone who knew anything about vessels on open water knew that three people couldn't fit into a twin kayak. A canoe's purpose was exactly that: to carry more than two humans, plus cargo. It was that bloody simple.

"*Herr Baumann, öffne deine Augen, bitte.*"

Sorry, doctor, but I can't look at you—I'm keeping an eye on the boys. This portaging business is bloody tricky. I'm teaching the boys.

They're still irresponsible with handling the boat, and a few boulders popped up out of nowhere, right in our footpath.

"*Boys*. Watch out for those *rocks*."

"We're not blind, Dad."

His sons held their grip until they reached the shore. "On my count of three, we'll lower it on Simon's side. Steady, steady ..."

"Can we rest *now*?" Sandro implored once they had laid the canoe down.

The boys didn't wait for permission. They dropped their packs and plopped down. The sun was three hours above the tree line. Maxime conceded to a short rest. They still had an hour of rowing to the island and then had to make camp before nightfall. He hated to set up in the dark, even with the help of headlights. *That's why the dear Lord made the sun disappear only at nine thirty—to give us little more daylight time.*

Maxime fished out the bag of mixed nuts and dried fruit— his power food, as he liked to call it. He gave the teenagers each a handful. They chewed and gulped it down like starving wolves.

Everyone was exhausted; it took almost an hour and a half to reach the island. Simon's attempt to feed each common loon they came across on the water did not make for rhythmic or effective rowing. Maxime wasn't worried: they still had more than an hour of light. As soon as they had carried the canoe to higher ground, he sent the boys to find firewood—nice thick, but dead pieces—for a bonfire that would burn all night. One had to keep the beasts at bay.

Maxime was putting up the tent when Dr. Hill leaned over him and called out, "*Wir sind ganz fertig, Herr Baumann.*"

Done? Bummer. Maxime panicked: he'd better call his sons before these operating-room people took him to the Recovery and left the young boys behind. *There could be black bears on the island.* Anybody who knew anything about the Canadian Shield knew that those large black animals could not be trusted, especially after dark with food in one's backpack.

He would have to get the anesthetist to promise to keep an eye on the boys—Maxime couldn't see his sons anymore. *"Herr Doktor,* my boys ..." Maxime sat up halfway and hollered in a panic, "Sandro! Simon! *Boys.* Where are you?"

"Mr. Baumann. *Maxime.* Settle down, please. We're all done. All went well. You'll see the boys, your family, once you get back to the surgical center. Come, settle down. Please keep your arms on your chest. We're going to tilt you and slide you back onto the stretcher."

"How *are* you, Mr. Bowman?" asked Sally. "There we go— keep those arms on your chest. One, two, three—*bumpy ride.*"

Maxime grinned at the orderly through the shifting fog.

In the recovery room, the mist slowly cleared from Maxime's mind, and the freezing descended his legs—reluctantly slow. However, the spinal was in no hurry to stop interfering with his "hemodynamics," as Dr. Hill called it. The staff had to call Dr. Hill back twice to give a helping hand with a sudden drop in his heart rate, and when his blood pressure bottomed out a third time.

"Mr. Baumann," Dr. Hill laughed, "Seems to me we should just have done a simple GA? The spinal wasn't kind to you." Then added in a serious tone, "This happens, for a small percentage of patients, but it's rare to have such a *labile* hemodynamics. Particularly in healthy individuals such as yourself. Don't worry, though—things are finally settling down. You're out of the woods."

Maxime nodded, but inside he seethed. He was grateful his anesthetist couldn't read minds. *Shame on you, Maxime Baumann. The poor doctor couldn't have predicted your system would go on a rollercoaster ride. But still.*

Anybody who knew anything about hemodynamics and spinal anesthetics and spinal needles knew this about statistics: it was one thing to quote a statistic and an entirely different matter to become the statistic. Bloody medical number crunchers.

12

Maxime Fails To Empty His Bladder

Maxime was worried.

He was back in Bay 12, where Sally, the orderly with the plight of working for the draconian administration, had shaved him. The spinal had worn off, he could move his legs, and the numbness had subsided. It was only reasonable to remove his catheter.

There was a new problem, however.

Maxime couldn't empty his bladder. He first tried it with the plastic urinal bottle, and nothing happened, so he had the bottle promptly returned to the slush room. What would people think if they came into his cubicle and there stood the blue urinal in all its glory?

He had to try the washroom—he'd have more privacy. Maxime collapsed next to the stretcher, saving himself only by grabbing the linen and the side railing. In place of his legs were two rubber stubs. Thank God, Donna was there to support him. Maxime wasn't certain whether he imagined things, but the moment he stood upright before his legs gave way, he experienced a jabbing headache—right in the back where it joined his neck. It disappeared as soon as he scuttled back onto the stretcher.

Maxime never got headaches.

Maxime was always worried, he was seldom late, he lived his life according to the thirty rules, but he did not suffer from headaches.

He pressed his alert button and asked Nurse Sylvia in a honied voice if she could bring him the blue bottle again. Please? His legs were not following commands. He would like to try again. Could he also have two Tylenol tablets?

Donna slipped out and pulled the curtains behind her, and he tried again. They could hear him bearing down. The staff wouldn't let him go home until he was able to pass urine.

What a silly arrangement—to earn your discharge you had to pee in a bottle.

The urinal remained empty.

Damn. Emptying one's bladder was a personal matter, and should remain that way. *Lieber Gott,* what was it with these medical people? Was there nothing left of a man's dignity?

People said he was obsessive. Maxime was aware of this—although he disagreed. His life was structured by a set of sensible rules—mere guidelines—and only two pages when double spaced. Father had had three.

Anybody who knew anything about Sir Isaac Newton would have agreed with Maxime and not accused him of being anally retentive. Newton not only explained his individual rules, he went further and called them *laws*—laws of physics, which governed all physical matter on earth. And nobody who knew anything dared call Newton anal or a liar or an imbecile. They called him brilliant.

Maxime only had silly rules. Newton had *laws*. Maxime was convinced Newton's laws had something to do with his compromised body functions.

Maxime had never been urinary retentive in his life.

As the hours rolled by, Maxime's worry intensified.

But not about his bladder, which was up to his bellybutton. He wasn't worried about not being able to use his legs, becoming constipated, or having a splitting headache or that he couldn't go home.

Maxime was worried about the size of his prostate.

That was what Dr. Williams had told him only minutes ago when he dropped by—the reason for his apparent inability to empty his bladder. He had *BPH*. Men of Maxime's age (whatever that meant), all suffered from BPH: benign prostatic hyperplasia. At age eighty, apparently, eighty percent of men had it. Imagine. He was only sixty-four-and-a-half. He was miles away from eighty. That should apply only to Mr. J. Johnson and his late brother, Mr. C. Johnson.

The spinal anesthetic, Dr. Williams explained, had knocked the nerve supply to the bladder senseless, so to speak, for a couple of hours. The guardians of his bladder-neck were taking exception to the rough treatment and refused to cooperate. Simple.

Dr. Williams was on his way home after his surgical slate. Dr. Hill, however, was still tied up in the OR; he was on call. It was, after all, already four in the afternoon.

The surgeon's last words were, "If you can't manage with the bottle, Mr. Baumann, we'll just slip the catheter back in. No biggie. *Then* you can go home."

Maxime was petrified. Being petrified was being worried times seven.

Another catheter. *No biggie.* He counted the thumping inside his chest: one hundred and twenty-two a minute. *It was a big deal. It was blooming monumental.* Donna had her work cut out for her, clinging to his hand, squeezing it, kissing it and cajoling him.

"Max, it will work out fine," she soothed. "Look on the bright side. The silly hydrocele is gone. You don't have any pain where they operated—"

"Sure, honey, I don't have pain in my groin, but they must have put so much freezing in the wound that my lips are still tingling. And now I have a headache, it hurts where the spinal went in, I can't pee, and my bladder stretches up to my breastbone." He sighed. "And, I apparently have BPH."

Maxime jolted upright but cried out from the blinding headache and dropped flat on his back again.

Donna snapped to her feet and leaned over him. "What *is* it, Max?"

"I know what's wrong with my *bladder*."

"*What?*"

"It's following Newton's first law: his law of *inertia*."

Donna slapped his arm and sighed deep; hers was a moan of despair. *That's what one gets from too much reading.*

Maxime remembered his first rule on page two, which stated: *Accept what you cannot change.* He couldn't change the fact he had had a spinal. So he said out loud, "The first Newtonian law states clearly, 'The object... tends to remain in that state of motion' (in this case, inertia) 'unless an external force is applied to it.'"

He rolled onto his side to face Donna, but with greater care, remembering his headache. "I want you to press hard on my distended bladder, above my belly button in the direction of my pubis—be the external force. Then we'll overcome the inertia, the obstruction."

Donna leaned closer. "You talk rubbish, Herr Baumann. Utter nonsense. The cocktails they gave you in the OR are still messing with your head. You *need a catheter. That* will overcome the obstruction—not me jumping on your tummy. Such action might even rupture your distended bladder. Newtonian law, my foot. I'll call Nurse Sylvia. You know what Dr. Williams's recommendation was." As she hurried away, he could hear her mumble, "Silly Swiss man."

Maxime rolled back. The missus was right—but just. He was convinced that she had not pondered his suggestion about the Newtonian law long enough. If she had, she would have been more agreeable.

Five minutes later, Maxime received a second bladder catheter.

By the time Dr. Hill wafted by, he was full of apologies about Maxime's tribulations. The doctor was ready to discuss some new options. Maxime sighed. There it was again: the concept of choices—alternatives. He hated this vague medical talk.

As soon as Dr. Hill started explaining what a "blood patch" was, Maxime held up his hands. No more poking in his back, thank you very much. He opted for the conservative route. If the headache did not improve by seven that evening, they could admit him. Not that he didn't have faith in his Donatella, but he'd rather make the nurses upstairs work for their money. Donna might not jump for his every whim at home. That much he knew. He hoped it would be possible to bribe the nurses.

———

The headache did not improve.

Maxime was one who enjoyed his coffee—and Donna knew that. It required little to sweet-talk his darling into bringing him four coffees at a time, one after the other, from the glazed-dough-nut vendor in the hospital foyer.

By that time Nurse Sylvia had gone off duty and was replaced by a Nurse Louisa, a long-legged lady with a ponytail—eight extra-large empty paper cups were stacked in Maxime's cubicle.

As soon as she discovered the coffee cups, Nurse Louisa exploded. Gorgeous or not—she lost it. Maxime thought so at least—she was overreacting. He couldn't understand why she ranted on about caffeine toxicity and having to explain to the unit manager why her patient was now peeing liters of obviously filtrated coffee, his eyes twitching like yo-yos and a heart rate that had gone through the tiled ceiling.

A storm in a teacup, that's what his dad used to call such fusses over trivial technicalities. After all, Maxime was only following his physician's instructions. Because they didn't have intravenous caffeine, he, Maxime Bastien Baumann, had opted for the oral route.

Anybody who knew anything about the conservative treatment of post-dural-puncture headaches knew this: caffeine could be beneficial—and a double-double dark roast contained vast amounts of caffeine. It was bloody well common knowledge.

A 0.2 to 2 percent chance of a headache—what were the odds of that? Maxime wasn't certain whether he should feel special that he had become part of a small elite statistical minority. According to Dr. Hill, the headaches, in most cases, dissipated within five to seven days of strict bed rest. *Strict bed rest.* That would be hard. He *had* to get back to the gym. He had just started to regain his life and body.

Maxime wasn't certain how soon he would outstay his welcome in the hospital. They were waiting for the orderly to take him upstairs to the surgical ward. Sally and her colleagues had all gone home.

Around him, the surgical center was emptying itself as the day cases were discharged home. It felt like the mall at five minutes to nine on a weekday evening in summer—desolated. The only life left was that of the cleaners, with their yellow carts stacked with brooms, black plastic bags, mops and spray bottles; tidying up behind the departed shoppers in silence.

Donna had gone home to pack him an overnight bag. For the first time that day, Maxime felt lonely. He wasn't worried anymore—he was too perplexed to be worried. It had been an unusual day.

He wasn't entirely satisfied with the light tunnel he had seen in the OR, the angelic voices, or how he had ended up on a portage with the boys, only to be whisked away from the island without much ceremony. That canoe trip had happened in real life, almost nineteen years ago.

The past several months, he had taken to writing in a small notebook he kept on his nightstand at the end of every day. He would write down at least three worthwhile things that had happened during his day. He had managed to write down something almost every evening. As the orderly pushed him into the elevator, Maxime thought about the notebook and about rule five on page two: *Be grateful—every day.*

He would share his three items with Donna when she returned with his overnight bag: (1) Dr. Williams's knife hadn't slipped. Maxime had just checked: everything was still attached. (2) The hydrocele—the cantaloupe was gone. (3) He and the boys had managed to reach the island before sunset and he had gotten to spend time with the boys, especially with Simon. That was no small blessing.

13

The Conservative Treatment Of A
Post-Dural-Puncture Headache

Maxime ended up in a private room.

Not because he was special or because he worked for Johnson, Johnson & McBride; neither because he knew the CEO and president of the hospital or the mayor or the chief of police. The private room was empty, it was close to the nurses' station, and that was that.

By the time they discharged him from the hospital, Maxime had come to appreciate how unequaled nurses were. They were a special breed of people.

Nurses were also sensible individuals. They had to be, Maxime realized, when they dealt with the sick, with demanding patients, with demanding patients' relatives, with the administration, with physicians, with other nurses, with the lab, with housekeeping, with the kitchen, with the pharmacy—well, with blooming everybody. They had to have their ears consistently nailed to the ground—and still walk around with a smile. Anybody who knew anything about nursing knew that.

Maxime knew many things—he was not entirely stupid—but he had to learn these truths about nurses the hard way. He was a residential property lawyer who avoided appearing in court if he could help it. And his rule book had made no provisions for interactions with nurses—from afar or at arm's length.

His room had a view of the entire roof of the lower section of the hospital and the parking lot at the back. *The view one gets for twelve dollars, Herr Baumann.* He remembered that he had only put money in for eight hours. *The parking police!* Maxime jolted upright, only to fall back flat from a pulsing headache and remembered that Donna had taken their vehicle and would have to find a new spot when she returned.

"Bloody daylight robbers," he mumbled as he mused about paying for parking at a hospital—in effect, 24/7. Preposterous. Inconceivable. Maxime thought of how perplexed his father would have been by the apparent philosophy of the day: *We'll tax you to your eyeballs, treat you in hospital for free, feed you glazed doughnuts and make you pay for the parking.* Anybody who knew anything about the world today would understand that this made perfect sense. The entire place was going to the bloody dogs.

Minutes later, Donna brightened up his room as she floated in with his overnight bag slung over her shoulder and carrying two paper cups of coffee balanced in a cardboard tray. She had showered (her hair was still damp) and had changed into a clingy dress— showing off a hint of cleavage. The dress matched her eyes. She knew he was ogling her; he could tell from her subtle blush.

When she leaned forward to kiss him, Maxime clung to her for a moment. *"Ich liebe dich,"* he murmured. He inhaled her warmth. Then added, "Welcome back, sexy."

Donna pushed him away, as if embarrassed, and sat down at his side, beaming. She always basked in his appreciation. Maxime was not an ignorant man, in spite of his anal retentiveness. She was familiar with his ninth rule on page two: *Go through life with open eyes—behold the world's beauty.*

Donna stayed until almost ten when the night nurse's body language hinted that it was time for decent visitors to go home They wanted to get the unit ready for the night. Mrs. Bowman wouldn't mind, now, would she?

Donna gave Maxime a lingering kiss before she disappeared out the door, but only after she gave the nurse a once-over that said, *You'd better be nice to my hubby, sweetheart.*

Maxime, now on nurse alert, would have to play his cards well and wisely if he had any hope of cajoling the staff into obtaining him more caffeine-laden beverages—lattes, preferably—especially this late in the day.

He bided his time as the nurse took his ten-o'clock observations at a quarter past the hour. I'll do the first talking, he decided and voiced how appreciative he was of all the hardworking nurses bustling about on the ward. It always amazed him that a group of people—an entire profession, actually—could be so unselfish, looking after, he was certain, often grumpy patients who could be a pain in the behind.

The same nurse who had made Donna understand that it was time to go home now turned to him with genuine concern and interest. Her face softened into a reluctant smile as she thawed under his honey-coated words.

Maxime kept talking, kept praising, his eyes never leaving the nurse's face—waiting for the final breakthrough, for her to speak her mind.

"Why didn't you take the blood patch, Mr. Bowman?"

Maxime was ready and explained how, after the anesthetist had described all the possible side effects, especially some of the rarer long-term ones, he had declined the invasive option. Within six days, the headache should be history anyway. He would rather be uncomfortable for a week than potentially struggle with chronic discomfort along some of the nerve roots, thank you very much.

For a moment he considered whether he should introduce her to his two pages of *Lebensregeln*—especially rule thirteen on page two: *The good Lord gave you a head—so use it.*

"How many of you are on the floor, Nurse Lorna? I need to determine how many lattes I have to order."

Nurse Lorna laughed and stood hands on the hips. "Where do you think you're going to find coffee this time of the night, Mr. Bowman?"

"The doughnut shop?"

"They close at eight-thirty."

"The kitchen, then? The cafeteria?"

"Sorry, Mr. Bowman. The kitchen has closed for the night, and the cafeteria is gone. The administration replaced it with the doughnut shop."

Maxime wasn't one to give up so easily. He laughed amiably. "There must be a vending machine which sells pop? Most carbonated drinks contain caffeine, don't they? Please? Here's a twenty."

"Sorry, Mr. Bowman. It's breaching protocol. We're not allowed to do that."

"Oh, please, Nurse Lorna? I would have gone myself, but the moment I sit up or stand, this headache kills me." To make his point he sat up and immediately clutched his head—he groaned like a mortally wounded soldier.

Nurse Lorna lunged to his side. "*Don't* get up, Mr. Bowman! I can see the headache still tortures you."

Maxime watched her through slanted eyes. He wasn't entirely faking it. He *did* have a throbbing headache the moment he sat upright. He croaked, "Dr. Hill suggested I should increase my caffeine intake."

She hesitated.

Maxime was quick to add, "Intravenous caffeine is not available in Canada—oral is my only option. My only *hope*. Don't bother with getting it now. You're too busy—I can see that. When you take your *tea break* in a little while? *Bitte?*"

Maxime held out the twenty-dollar bill. "Anything with caffeine in—Coke is fine—as many as you can get." Maxime coughed and added, "As long as it's not root beer."

Nurse Lorna giggled as she took the bill and gave Maxime a fake scowl. She whispered as she left, "Not a word of this to anyone, Mr. Bowman, or you'll be a dead man."

Some time later, Maxime, who was half asleep, was roused as Nurse Lorna entered his room. The roller blinds were open, allowing the parking-lot lighting to illuminate the interior. Maxime glanced at the clock: it was past eleven. He pulled the cord for the wall light behind him and leaned conspiratorially forward on one elbow.

"Here's your booty, Mr. Bowman," Nurse Lorna whispered as she handed him a shopping bag in which several cans clanked together. Maxime was certain he heard a touch of sarcasm in her voice but chose to ignore it.

He took the bag and gave her his biggest ever Maxime Bastien Baumann smile. "*Danke schön.*" He quickly counted the ice cold cans—ten: two dollars apiece.

"There are three of you?" he asked.

The nurse nodded as he counted out three cans and added two more. "*One* for the night orderly and *one* for the housekeeping lady."

Nurse Lorna took her part of the spoils, shaking her head, as she mumbled, "and *five* for the little girls who live down the lane." She cocked her brow at Maxime. She was, she muttered, already regretting her participation in the acquisition of said pop cans. Maxime had better pray with her the night super would be late for her rounds. First, she had to hide the evidence. Tonight was not the time for a lecture on the code of conduct.

She paused at the door. "Don't tell me you're going to drink five carbonated sodas over the next few hours, Mr. Baumann."

Maxime bestowed upon her another MBB smile. "No, *never.* Just think of my poor teeth. My dentist would develop acute chest pain if he saw me drinking all of these."

"Okay, then, Mr. Bowman—time to settle down. We don't want to bother the other patients now, do we?"

"I'll be as quiet as a mouse." He was fast to add, "Thank you again, Nurse Lorna. You *are* the best."

"Good *night,* Mr. Bowman."

After drinking one can of soda, Maxime turned out all his room lights and lay, propped up just a little bit, watching the parking area, beyond the now blackened hospital roof, its ventilation-flue silhouettes, gaping upward like rows of sea lions. He could see a few figures yonder, clad in scrubs in an assortment of colors, entering and leaving their vehicles. The night shift, he thought.

Maxime was worried.

He was worried about his headache. He was also worried about Donna, alone at home. It was the first time since 1978 that he wasn't at her side at night. Would she be safe? Would she manage? But he was also worried about the fact that he couldn't sleep.

Maxime drank the second can. It had to help with the headache. He turned his light on again and scrambled for his reading glasses. "Let's see: 34 milligrams of caffeine per 355 milliliters of soda. Didn't Dr. Hill talk about a thousand milligrams or more per twenty-four hours?"

He drank a third can, burping all the way. *I'll have to polish off more than twenty of these.* He burped again. *This is going to be tough. She should have brought me some of those proper sports drinks—the ones with the blood-colored ox-design on it. They have real caffeine inside.*

The decision had been made by the evening staff, earlier, to leave his bladder catheter in till the morning. *No harm done— I won't have to worry about going to the bathroom,* he decided as he drank the remaining two cans. *This headache has to give.* He belched long salvos of carbonated gas into the darkness of the room.

Soon Maxime wasn't certain which was worse, his headache when he sat up or his now violent abdominal cramps. He was close to becoming airborne. *She's going to kill me;* he thought as he pressed the call button minutes later.

Brisk footsteps reached his room, followed by a whispering voice at the foot of his bed. "You called, Mr. Bowman?"

"Yes, yes, I did. I can't sleep. Sorry to be a bother. I know it's two fifteen, but I have these horrible stomach cramps. Do you perhaps have something like Pepto-Bismol, Nurse Lorna?"

He burped again—long and drawn out—totally at the mercy of the vast volume of gas inside him. "Excuse me," he said, now in a little-boy voice. He recalled rule thirteen on page two, the one about using your head.

There was a reason Nurse Lorna was in charge. She glanced around and inspected his garbage can like a trained private investigator. "Mr. Bowman! Tell me you *didn't.*"

She was livid. She took his wrist and felt his pulse. She sighed as her hurried footsteps took her from the room, only to return seconds later with a BP machine and pulse oximeter.

"A pulse of 124, and a BP of 168 over 104." She clicked her tongue. "What shall we do with you, Mr. Bowman? Don't you realize that each can is full of caffeine?"

"Only 34 milligrams per can," he piped bravely.

"That's not what your sixty-four-and-a-half-year-old heart says, Mr. Bowman."

"Sorry. I've been an asshole. Please, some Pepto-Bismol?" Maxime squawked, still in a small voice. He felt the idiot he had been.

"Yeah, yeah, okay. I should report you to the night super, you know."

When she saw his face, distorted in discomfort from a headache and now the cramps, her face softened. "Okay, I'll get you some. It's your lucky day, Mr. Bowman—I'm *still* in a good mood."

She stomped from the room, and he was certain she had mumbled, "I would rather put a bloody garden hose down to your stomach and pump it empty of that pop garbage."

14

Going Home

M axime was relieved—but with caution.
He had always been cautious.

Whether it was the Pepto-Bismol, the continuous burping until his throat cramped or a combination of both that did the trick, by eight in the morning, Maxime was headache- free. He had reclassified himself: he was off the Critical Case list and onto the Convalescing list, ready and fit for discharge home.

He was aware that the caffeine content of the sodas was only within the homeopathic range—incapable of having an actual therapeutic effect. On his insistence, the bladder catheter had been removed at seven. He was willing to take his chances. Since then he had been scraping courage together to walk the twelve paces to his en-suite bathroom. He was prepared to drop flat on the bed or floor, the instant the blinding headache attacked. He sat up and waited, then cautiously stood up and walked the twelve paces. Nothing happened. He had his hand on the bathroom doorknob. The truce was lasting. In the en-suite, with some straining, he managed to empty his bladder, gave his hands a lick and a promise, brushed his teeth and made a beeline back to bed.

There was still no headache.

Maxime wasn't superstitious, but he waited for Newton's third law to take effect. It stated: *For every action, there is an equal and opposite reaction.* He had been upright for fifteen minutes. He had had to almost strain his brains out to get past that BPH prostate-thing, and he was behind on caffeine. He was certain the headache was on its way back—sneaking up on him like a cougar on a fawn. It was a matter of time before it jumped him.

He sat upright like a tin soldier. Waited. Dared the headache to reappear.

There was nothing.

Maxime Bastien Baumann, stop acting like an asshole. Your idiotic stunt with the five cans of pop frightened the unwanted headache into oblivion. Pay attention to rule five on page two: Be grateful— every day. Now is such a day.

He pressed the call button. A lady from Housekeeping popped her head into the room.

"Could you please call me the nurse?"

It was a new nurse who showed up, all smiles and effervescence, with an aroma of cherry blossoms wafting around her. "Mr. Bowman? You're sitting up. What happened to the headache?"

Maxime decided to play it safe. "It's a little better."

The nurse chuckled. "I'm Nurse Steffi. I heard you had quite a party last night. You're famous now—Nurse Lorna is your latest fan."

Maxime turned crimson. He wasn't proud of his stupidity, but it had paid off. He shrugged and knotted his brow. Nurse Steffi was lying—Nurse Lorna must hate him. Then again, perhaps he should suggest this new ten-dollar soda cure for post-dural-puncture headaches to Dr. Hill. They only had to remember to combine it with Pepto-Bismol. The two of them could patent the cocktail—call it the Pop-and-Pepto protocol.

"I would like to go home, Nurse Steffi. If you could be so kind as to contact Dr. Williams and get the okay for me to go— as well as from Dr. Hill?"

"Sure, Mr. Bowman. Let me first take your vitals; then I'll contact the physicians."

The moment the nurse left, Maxime phoned Donna on his cell. By the time she showed up, he had shaved and changed into his gray suit, his white shirt and burgundy socks and matching tie, which Donna had brought him the previous evening.

When he requested a wheelchair for going down to the car, Nurse Steffi rolled her eyes at him. "Shame on you," she whispered but fetched the chair. Maxime only pulled up his shoulders and blew her, and the rest of the staff kisses as the orderly pushed him toward the elevator. Donna shook her head and said nothing.

He felt a tinge of guilt playing such a baby, but in his defense, it was four stories down, followed by one kilometer of hallways, and that was only to the main foyer at the front. He hadn't been telling a lie. It was called taking precautions. What if the head-ache snuck back on him? And, he had to make sure Donna appreciated the gravity of his situation.

Donna couldn't carry him, now, could she? Anybody who knew anything about the ability of a fifty-eight-year-old woman weighing in at a hundred twenty-five pounds to carry a one-hundred-ninety-pound, sixty-four-and-a-half-year-old man would know that it was an improbability. Blooming well was never going to happen.

As they waved the orderly goodbye at the car, Maxime turned to Donna—who had insisted on driving, much to his chagrin—and told her about his unique cure for spinal headaches—the pop and Pepto. His Donna had an excellent sense of humor but was never one to laugh out loud.

Maxime looked at his spouse in alarm, because for a moment, he thought she was crying—but she was catching her breath from being in stitches. It reminded him of his phone call with Gunther when Maxime had informed him about his upcoming surgery.

"Keep your eyes on the road, woman!" Maxime called out as he deftly took the steering wheel and held the car on course while Donna composed herself.

"Max ... oh, Max." She gasped for breath and continued. "And you *never* drink soda ... Just as well that it happened to that sexy nurse, who sent me home so early. I'm glad you gave her a run for her money."

"That wasn't funny, Donnatella."

"*Max*. It's hysterical. *Ich liebe dich.* Silly old man." She continued giggling and snickering for much of the way home.

Maxime had little doubt that it would not be long before Sandro and Michelle had every intimate detail of his twenty-four-hour ordeal at the hospital.

His son and his spouse were expected to touch down a quarter after ten, the next day—on Saturday. Work commitments made it imperative for Sandro to return on Monday evening again. Just as well—Maxime wouldn't dream of keeping the children a day longer. All this, Donna had told him in his hospital room as he was getting into the wheelchair.

Maxime had to give Sandro credit—the boy was, after all, not entirely irresponsible. At least he had the decency to come and check up on his ailing father and pay his respects. Anything could have happened to the sixty-four-and-a-half-year-old patriarch.

Simon, his youngest, couldn't care less—he might still break his mother's heart. He would have to have a man-to-man conversation with the boy. London wasn't exactly on the other side of the civilized world. There was no excuse. It was a bloody disgrace.

See how rapidly things had changed the moment the doctor injected the medication into his spinal fluid? The more Maxime pondered his experience, the more he was convinced it had been angelic voices he'd heard in the OR, at the same instant when he had ended up on the portage trip with the boys, carrying the canoe.

As soon as he laid eyes on Simon, his youngest, he would remind him of rule fourteen on page two. The rules were all crucial, but this one stood out: *Life is short—make it count.* This rule didn't give one the license to do damn stupid things, or make a gigantic asshole of oneself, but to make every day count, by involving oneself with worthwhile and responsible actions.

For instance, visit your papa when he begs you to, three-and-a-half weeks before his first ever surgery. Damn it, take your old man seriously. Precox feelings are actual psychological phenomena. Premonitions are real. He, Maxime Baumann, Simon's Papa, had almost been a goner.

Maxime would have to tell him: Learn to pay attention, my son. It will serve you well some day.

Simon still had to learn to stop thinking with only the left half of his brain. Anybody who knew anything about the left and right hemispheres of the brain knew that one couldn't pay attention only to logic. One had to learn to use both halves—think with the heart as well. And, on top of that, learn to forgive oneself and others, and not nurse grudges. Life was too short. That much was bloody well common knowledge.

15

Mr. And Mrs. Baumann Meet
Their Son At The Airport

Maxime had a spine.

Having a spine at times made him refuse to back down.

He was known to be a private person and to worry beyond measure. However, sometimes he would take a stand—when principles were involved. Anyone who knew anything about principles should be aware one can never back out, never not stand up—it would be bloody treason—an act of spinelessness. And the last time Maxime checked, he still had thirty-one vertebrae.

Saturday morning became such a time. Donna—his beloved Donnatella—was of the public opinion that he, Maxime Bastien Baumann, should stay home, wrap a blanket around his knees, sit in the sun, and soak up the last rays of late fall before the earth got covered in white powder. Donna, on her own, would drive to the airport and pick up the children.

Maxime had a different take on the matter. He refused to be among the feeble, sitting on the deck with throws over their knees. He was even accommodating in his rebellion—he agreed to let Donna do the driving. He failed to see what her concern was, given that the surgery was two days ago. His wound was healing, there was no cantaloupe in his boxers, and the headache was gone.

Well, that's what he told Donna. The headache was gone—for the most part. It was not dishonest. Pain is real but remains a subjective experience. Whether or not to inform her was about self-preservation. If he gave her the slightest indication that something was amiss, she would take him straight back to the ER for reassessment.

Unbeknownst to her, Maxime had been gulping down two double-strength coffees every four hours. He took care to wash and dry the cups to hide the evidence. He had to sneak to the bathroom ever so often and was aware of a buzzy feeling—an urge to walk up the walls. It was blissful. He felt invincible, conscious of his heart galloping in his chest. If anyone had told him he would feel so on top of the world, forty-four hours following his surgery, he would have said it was preposterous—complete bloody nonsense.

The closest parking spot was in the annex parking garage, a kilometer from Arrivals. Maxime pondered the wisdom of his insistence of being counted among those *with* spines. He sighed. He had to be dead before he would sit on a deck with a colorful blanket draped over his legs. He clenched his teeth and kept up with Donna—in spite of the scrotal support pinching him. It hurt like hell.

As soon as they had passed through the revolving doors and reached a flight arrival's monitor, Maxime took his time verifying the flight number and arrival time of Sandro and Michelle. His groin was on fire, the back of his head throbbed and the sweat poured down his back. *You can be such an asshole, Maxime Baumann. Why do you constantly forget rule eleven on page two? Don't be smart aleck.*

The air-conditioned Arrivals hall was cavernous—the white noise and human traffic swallowed them whole. Maxime found it tempting to lie down as the effervescent coolness hemmed them in; prostrate himself on the floor. It would immediately soothe the pounding in his neck and groin.

Donna pulled on his hand, but he remained planted, glancing around. Security personnel was scattered throughout the hall. Maxime calculated the odds. They would pounce on him the moment he did something out of the ordinary—like lying face down on the cool marble floor.

Maxime was worried.

He wasn't worried about the security guards, but about Dr. Williams. What if the wound became infected, or worse, tore open? What with all this walking and the support grazing his inner thigh; it burned like a raging fire.

He followed Donna with trepidation. Sandro's connecting flight from Calgary was delayed—fifteen minutes. *A saving grace.* He hastened his shuffling and caught up with her. *There will be sufficient time for a caffeinated hot beverage. It might just save my silly ass.* Maxime took Donna by the elbow and steered her toward the coffee shop. He murmured in her ear, "Allow me to treat my sweet heart to a small coffee."

Donna went ahead to keep a table for them and waited for Maxime to bring the two coffees. It took Maxime several attempts to find a comfortable position. Donna reached for his hands and gave a gentle squeeze, forcing him to look her in the eyes.

"*Was ist loss, mein Schatz?*"

Maxime tried to break eye contact. She squeezed harder.

"Maxime? You can't fool me. You're in pain."

"I'm *fine*. It's *nothing*." He yanked his hands free and brought his cup to his lips.

"You could have been sitting comfortably in the sun."

"You *know* I could never have stayed behind. What would the children have thought of me?"

"That you're smart?"

"It's bad enough that Simon has written us off." He gave a self-deprecating laugh.

"At least Sandro and Michelle are coming. They *know* you had an operation."

"Donna ..."

She jumped to her feet. "I'm going to go find a wheelchair."

Maxime raised his hand. "Donna, *wait*." He had his pride. "Donna ..." he pleaded.

Donna turned back.

"About the wheelchair," he mumbled, red-faced. "Why don't you find out where we can get one but allow me to at least walk toward Sandro and his wife when they arrive?" He swallowed. "I don't want him to see me in a chair—it might alarm him—there's nothing the matter with my legs. Only with my pride. I was stupid."

Fifteen minutes later, Maxime and Donna stood at the bottom of the escalator and watched as Sandro and a visibly pregnant Michelle descended. Michelle was only five months along, but because of her petiteness, her tummy stood out all over the place.

Maxime was worried.

He watched his slender daughter-in-law run to meet them. She looked stunning—glowed with happiness.

Maxime wondered about the wisdom of his insistence that his sons pay him a visit—all because of him, Maxime Baumann, being such a baby. He had had a small operation, yet demanded that the entire world pauses and take notice. Anyone who knew anything about pregnant women knew that you shouldn't listen to your smart-aleck father-in-law if he wanted to make you travel by air when you were five months pregnant. Blooming selfish old man.

Sandro grinned from ear to ear. "*Dad.*" They bear-hugged and patted each other's back.

"Why are you *here,* at the airport?" Sandro pulled their two carry-on bags behind him as Donna and Michelle walked ahead, arms linked, laughing and talking.

Maxime pulled up his shoulders. What kind of question was that?

"Didn't you have the surgery?" Sandro asked. When Maxime nodded, Sandro added, "Shouldn't you still be in bed?"

Donna cleared her throat.

"Sandro," Maxime said, "it was only a small operation, remember? You said so yourself. It's okay. It only hurts a little." He swallowed. "I'm *glad* you came."

Sandro laughed. "Oh, Dad. Michelle insisted. She was so excited—perhaps to show Mother and you." His gazed remained fixed on Michelle's abdomen. "You're the only parents she has."

Maxime ruffled his son's hair, took a bag from him with a bemused grin, and bit on his teeth as they kept pace with the ladies.

Donna stopped at the exit. She instructed Michelle and Sandro to wait and strode off to the side.

"Where's Mom going?"

"She's getting a wheelchair for this silly old goat who forgot he had surgery."

"*Dad.*" Sandro hugged him with greater care. "Sorry," he whispered. "I've been inconsiderate."

Michelle elbowed her husband in the ribs.

Maxime grinned. "No, he's right. I refused to stay home and bask in the sun, as your mom had suggested. You know how well I listen to advice."

Donna and Michelle pulled the carry-ons as Sandro pushed his father toward the tan-colored 300E, parked in the annex garage one kilometer away.

Anybody who knew anything about hydrocelectomies knew it was not the smartest thing in the world to try walk two kilometers through a busy airport building, forty-six hours after your surgery, not even while wearing a padded scrotal support. Some sixty-four-and-a-half-year-old men were so thick in the head you could teach them absolutely nothing. Bloody nothing.

16

Entertaining Visitors Is Hard Work

Maxime was exhausted.

He was exhausted on top of being worried—a potentially lethal combination. (He had long since accepted that being worried was part of his DNA.)

He excused himself the moment they had returned from the airport, under worried glances from his family. He needed a power nap. For the second time in his life, he felt like Mr. J. Johnson, the man who was born in 1936. Maxime was used to the afterburn from a hard workout at the gym—being so spent he had trouble walking—this weariness was different.

All he needed was fifteen minutes of shut-eye, and he would be a new man. Donna knew his habits.

Maxime darkened the bedroom and tried to analyze this physiological breakdown. It was crucial he got to the bottom fast—nip any toxic thoughts in the bud. Maxime recounted all the conversations he had had with the physicians, the reading he had done, even the opinions of his family members on all matters hydrocele, and he still came up wondering why he felt so under the weather, so beaten, so empty.

Stop this malignant introspection, Maxime Baumann—you haven't had a blooming coronary bypass. It was a silly fluid-bag removal.

He closed his eyes.

Twenty-three minutes later, Maxime combed his damp hair with his fingers as he rejoined his family on the patio. His shock-back-to-life two-minute-ice-cold shower has never failed. For a hundred and twenty seconds he had danced and yelled under the pelting ice water like someone escaping a snake pit.

Donna, who had Columbus on her lap, gave him an encouraging smile, but Sandro lurched to his feet. "Dad, are you okay?" His son had him by the elbow.

Maxime brushed him off. "Sit down. I'm no bloody invalid. Why should there be anything the matter with me? I often take a power nap on a Saturday afternoon."

Sandro ignored his father's brusqueness. "You had us worried."

Maxime deflected the ball to Donna. "Ask your mom."

"For all we knew," Sandro said, "you could have had a blood clot—in your brain or your lungs. You *did* have surgery. You're not twenty-five anymore, Dad. Perhaps that's why you're so deadly tired."

"Thanks for reminding me."

Donna and Michelle shrieked and scampered out of the way as Maxime planted himself on his son's lap, ruffling his hair. Sandro was too shocked to say a word. Columbus gave an unhappy meow as he escaped with his mistress, out of the way of this weird old guy who usually wore suits with matching socks and ties.

"You're full of BS, Sandro Baumann," Maxime muttered. "Like your father. If I had a blood clot, I'd be dead or paralyzed, or coughing blood and be blue in the face. So, *no*." Maxime slipped off Sandro's lap and plopped into an open chair. "I was exhausted. Not because I'm old, or ill, but because it's Saturday afternoon."

He mumbled under his breath that anybody who knew anything about previously fit sixty-four-and-a-half-year-old men would bloody well know that being tired on a weekend afternoon, fifty-two hours following surgery which had been complicated by a spinal headache and a near-death experience, was entirely reasonable. Nothing to get one's knickers for in a knot.

Michelle turned to her in-laws. "Daddy, we don't want to be any trouble to you and Mommy. Not with you still recovering from everything." She gave Maxime a concerned look. "Sandro and I can *easily* find a room at the Best Western. I told Sandro that's what we should have done in the *first* place."

Maxime leaped to his feet, signaling with his arms. "Donna— and you were worried about our youngest in England. Seems to me, our older son and his pregnant wife are complete nut cases. Must be the lack of blooming sunlight on the Pacific coast."

He stomped his feet and planted himself in front of his visitors. "Listen, you crazies. Stop talking nonsense. Now is not the time to be worried about it being inconvenient for us etcetera, etcetera. Best Western, my ass. This facility"—he waved his arm around to indicate the entire property, "is a four-star establishment, not three—and that's official. Donna and I discreetly insist that you stay. And that is *that*."

Sandro and Michelle were on their feet and bear-hugged Maxime from both sides until he pleaded for mercy.

Maxime muttered, "*I* was the one insisting you should come."

He faced Donna. "I'm famished, sweetheart. Let's get these Vancouverites something to eat." He ushered them toward the house. "Chicken kebabs?"

Donna beamed as she ran ahead and pulled Sandro through the patio door. "I've got everything ready. I was hoping your father would suggest that. You haven't forgotten how to put chicken breasts on a stick now, have you, darling?"

Maxime busied himself around Sandro, who laughed in surrender as he laid out the utensils he needed on the kitchen island. Michelle and Donna took to the little breakfast table to put a salad together.

"Sandro, time out!" Maxime hollered. "How are you going to prevent contamination of everything else if you're going to handle the raw meat with your bare hands?"

"Dad, *please*."

Donna snuck up behind Maxime and kissed him in the neck, dragging him away. "Come, Herr Baumann, stop harassing our son. He's a big boy. Have some faith. He can sear your kebab to ensure all the bacteria are killed."

"I'm not hassling him. You know very well, charring your meat increases the presence of toxic polycyclic aromatic hydrocarbons, which cause cancer and—"

She hauled him further away, begging Michelle to give her a hand. "*Enough*, Mr. Baumann. Help us start up the barbecue."

Maxime followed Donna and Michelle outside, mumbling that anybody who knew anything about PAHs would know that this was no light matter. For a moment he was uncertain whether this applied only to red meat, but decided it was better to play it safe. Chicken should be included. There was a reason for rule eight on page one: *Never eat charred meat.* It was blooming common knowledge.

17

Maxime Returns To Work And
Stresses Out Mr. J. Johnson

Maxime's worry spells underwent a change.

Donna was the first to notice. She pointed it out to her husband, who only shrugged his shoulders since he wasn't someone who often rolled his eyes at his spouse. Since Sandro and Michelle's return to Vancouver, the intensity, frequency, and duration of Maxime's worry stints had decreased. Oh, they weren't absent, Donna pointed out—they had become more nuanced, easier with to live.

Maxime wasn't convinced. He dared not consider the possibility—it could spell disaster for his future state of mind—enough to make him lose sleep at night. He refused to part with his *Lebensregeln*. The rules defined him: they *made* him. Worry was the driving force in his life.

Mr. J. Johnson was relieved to see Maxime back at the office, even if only temporarily. He had much to say however about Maxime, who had barely had the stitches removed from his private parts before preparing for his *second* leave of absence. Preposterous, Mr. J. Johnson called it. In the history of Johnson, Johnson & McBride, back-to-back sick leaves were unheard of—it has never happened.

"Maxie, I'm more worried about you this time. Your commitment to the firm, Maxie, is it compromised?"

"Mr. Johnson?"

Mr. J. Johnson has never used that tone with him, not in twenty-five years. However, Maxime wasn't too worried. The two junior colleagues had held the fort quite competently. Mr. J. Johnson never showed up at the office before ten a.m., and it was evident that the business was running on oiled wheels, without either senior partner. It could only mean that Mrs. Long kept a short leash on the junior colleagues. Maxime was agreeable with anything she did as long as it made the old man, Mr. J. Johnson, happy.

The receptionist for Dr. Williams's office called Maxime on Tuesday to remind him of his follow-up visit that Friday afternoon at exactly three p.m.

Maxime arrived at 2:50 and found two adjacent vacant spots in the back of the parking lot. He performed his oblique-parking act with ease. Stepping away from the faithful 300E, he was satisfied it would stymie any vehicular perpetrator. He thought of

Donna, who always chided him for this egotistical habit—she called it: "selfish and silly."

Maxime disagreed. It was a matter of self-preservation, and of following rule thirteen on page two: *The good Lord gave you a head—so use it.* He was only using his brains. Anybody who knew anything about patching up damaged paintwork on thirteen-year-old vehicles knew that it was close to impossible to buy matching paint after more than a decade of a car being exposed to the elements. Who in his right mind would want his car to look like a box of Smarties? It would be bloody ridiculous.

Dr. Williams was satisfied with his findings and scheduled Maxime for another follow-up in four weeks' time. "Be a good chap now, Mr. Baumann—be gentle in the gym. These buggers sometimes recur, so we'll just make sure, a month from now."

On Sunday afternoon, Maxime and Donna waited for Gunther in the Arrivals hall. For a change, the flight from Montreal was on time.

Maxime did not recognize his brother. The towering figure stood two inches taller and thirty pounds of muscle bulkier than Maxime. The last time, two years earlier, Gunther had sported a goatee and a ring of silver hair. He was clean-shaven now, both face and scalp, and had on bright turquoise-framed glasses.

"*Maximus.*"

Maxime was a strong man, but when Gunther Baumann bear-hugged him, his feet lost contact with the floor. Gunther thundered, "*Mein Bruder und sein Frau.*"

He dropped the speechless Maxime and immediately swooped the grinning Donna in an equally enthusiastic hug. He softened the embrace and kissed her full on the lips.

"Donnatella. As *radiant* as ever."

"You're a terrible liar." A blush had crept up her neck.

"Welcome home, Gunt." Maxime patted his brother on the back. "Where's Mary?"

"She had to stay behind. Her mother, who's eighty-eight, had a heart attack the night before our departure. The old lady was in a bad state, and the doctors weren't confident she would make it. Mary refused to leave her side."

"That's a pity," Maxime said. "I *have* to meet this wonder-woman who had bewitched my brother."

"*Nonsense.* She's only a good friend."

Maxime snorted as he pulled Donna along on their way to the baggage carousel. He faced his brother. "Donna's right. You're a pathetic liar. You're desperately in love. For Gunther Baumann to shave his beard *and* his head—plus the glasses—it's unthinkable. She must be *some woman.*"

Another laugh rumbled from Gunther's chest as he ruffled Maxime's hair. It was uncommon for the big man to show his tender side in public. As they waited on the carousel to come to life, Gunther unlocked his cell phone and showed them photos of his new friend.

Maxime whistled. Mary was a well-groomed lady in spite of only being in workout clothes. "You've always had an eye for beauty."

Gunther shrugged. "I appreciate her mind even more—she's a smart lass."

"Smart lass with a *tight* ass." Maxime laughed and side-stepped Donna's mock attack. "Honey, be fair. Look at her, all trim and über-fit—like you." Maxime ducked for a second swipe from Donna. He grasped Gunther's arm. "You must have met her in the gym. She's probably your personal *trainer*."

"Maximus, she's fifty-nine. She can't *be* a trainer—"

"She can be *anything* she wants," Maxime mumbled as he stepped forward to pull Gunther's bag off the carousel. Gunther was faster than the sixty-four-and-a-half-year-old real estate law-yer who recently had had a hydrocelectomy. He had the bulky piece of luggage at his side in an instant.

Maxime, bemused, insisted on pulling his brother's carry-on at least. They started the trek back to the 300E.

Maxime, keeping to himself, chewed on the puzzle of Mary with the ponytail. Anybody who knew anything about quinqua-genarians and gymnasiums and fitness and toned bottoms knew that to look like that was no fluke. It required hard work, disci-pline, and buckets of sweat. That much was for bloody certain.

Maxime was convinced, deep inside, that Mary was indeed a personal trainer. Gunther was lying—he must have been afraid Maxime and Donna would think less of him because he had focused on physical attributes in his choice of a new companion.

Gunther surprised his brother when he flung an arm around his shoulders. He bellowed. "I read minds, Baumann. You're *wrong*. Mary's *not* a trainer. She's a master athlete—runs track and field. Mary has a Ph.D. in cell biology. I told you, she's smart. She teaches at the University."

Maxime doggedly sauntered along his brother, mumbling, "Well, damn me. A brilliant cell-cloner who has a love affair with a pair of running shoes and a cantankerous old Swiss."

Gunther bumped Maxime with the shoulder. "You're the *silly old man*. The permafrost has screwed with your common sense."

Maxime snorted and stepped ahead.

"Why does she compete at her age?" Donna asked.

"She's almost your age, Donna She's not old." Gunther winked at his sister-in-law. "Mary loves it. She says *someone* has to do it. Next year, when she turns sixty, she hopes to break a few records—she'll be the youngest in her age-bracket."

When they reached the car, Maxime turned to Donna. "Shall we stop at the mall and buy ourselves high-end running shoes? We can't allow these geriatric athletes to kick our asses like that."

Gunther's laugh thundered over them as Donna shook her head. "No thanks. I don't need to impress people."

Maxime locked eyes with Donna before he got behind the wheel. He agreed with her sentiment. He glanced at Gunther and shuddered at the thought of his brother's reaction once he saw what Maxime had in store for them at the house. He had his doubts about how far Mary's influence had reached into Gunther's life.

18

The Brothers Prepare For A Road Trip

Maxime was worried.

Worried like in the good old days—much to his relief. He was worried whether Gunther would play along. The first thing Donna had said when he'd told her his plan was, "Maxime Baumann, I love you dearly, with all your quirks, with the thirty rules—but this? It's *madness*."

"This" referred to the twenty-eight-foot RV that Maxime had rented the day before. She had added in a whisper, "You forget two things. One, you had surgery barely two weeks ago. And two, what happens after Halloween?"

"*What?*" Maxime couldn't think of any other event scheduled for after Halloween.

"*It snows.*"

Maxime had thought it would be a splendid idea for the four of them—Donna, Gunther, Mary and himself—to travel south until they reached a place where there was no snow or winter—wherever that was. He had planned to show his visitors the southern United States.

Perhaps it wasn't such a brilliant idea.

As they got into the car at the airport, Donna had whispered, for his ears only, "If Mary's not here to go along, then *I'm* not going." She was quick to add that it was an ideal opportunity to bond with his brother.

Maxime said nothing as they approached the house. Donna had insisted on sitting in the back, claiming Gunther's legs were too long to be squeezed in like that. Gunther had immediately objected, but Donna had learned with the Baumanns: you don't give in.

Maxime took extra care turning into the driveway—the RV was twenty-eight feet long, and there were only twenty-six feet of curb between his entrance and the next-door neighbor's driveway. (He had measured it the day before the RV was dropped off.) He dared not infringe on that particular neighbor—the man was troubled by a strange concept of personal rights and property boundaries. The result: the RV stuck two feet across Maxime's entrance.

Gunther laughed as he turned to Donna and pointed at Columbus, sitting in the front window. "You still have the Devon Rex watchdog?"

Donna smiled. "Faithful as ever, Uncle Gunther."

Gunther faced his brother. "What's with your neighbor? Are they allowed to park their camper in front of your driveway? They're going to store it someplace else for the winter, I hope?"

Maxime coughed as he waited for the garage door to stutter open. He realized he was turning crimson. He avoided his brother's eyes burning into the side of his head. "It's not my neighbor's," he said. "The RV belongs to *me*—or rather, I rented it."

"To do what? *You're* going *RVing?*" Gunther slapped Maxime on the thigh as he doubled up in mirth. "You're kidding. You did *not* forget we're halfway into November in the northern hemisphere?"

Maxime turned off the engine once inside the garage. "Don't laugh, Gunt. You're going to help me pack that thing tomorrow, and we're heading south—as far down as Texas. I originally planned the trip for the four of us but plans change, so now it's only *you* and *me*. Two brothers on a road trip."

Once outside the car, Gunther leaned across the roof. He wasn't laughing. "Maximus?" He turned to Donna for affirmation. She struggled to keep a straight face before breaking down in giggles, shaking her head as she walked into the house.

She called over her shoulder, still snickering, "Welcome to Canada, Gunther Baumann!"

Gunther's return flight was scheduled for four weeks later. Maxime's plan was to enjoy a fortnight of blissful summer in the far south and top it off with two weeks at home, in and around the city. Granted enough snow, they would go cross-country skiing, every single day. Gunther, he knew, would love that.

Anybody who knew anything about RVing and campgrounds and triple hook-ups knew that one could tough it out in the great outdoors with a backpack and a two-man tent, almost freezing to death overnight, and share one's lunch with a black bear. Or, one could enjoy much of the same in a civilized manner, with a flush-toilet and hookups for gray and black water, protected from rain and snow and misery. RV-ing could be a blooming life-saver.

Maxime allowed the coffee cups to grow cold before he dared share the particulars of his plan with Gunther. They sat in the kitchen, at the small breakfast table, with Columbus vying for the attention of the visitor since his master and mistress did not jump fast enough at his persistent meows.

Maxime was not stricken with madness, as accused by Donna. Perhaps he was only a little over ambitious. He had done his homework and had reserved a triple hookup site for fourteen nights, in Corpus Christi—at the Colonia Del Rey. Fourteen nights, to be on the safe side. He realized they needed at least two days to travel there, plus two days back. But first, he would have to convince Gunther of the merits of the endeavor and then taking turns at the wheel.

Gunther pushed his chair back and leaned across the table, a broad grin in place. "Luckily for you, Maxime Baumann, I have become a daredevil-in-training. You can thank the cell-biology lady one day. I'm learning to enjoy surprises. Want to introduce me to our home on wheels for the next two weeks?"

That was all Maxime needed. He knocked his chair over and made Columbus scamper for safety.

He grabbed the keys in the mudroom and called from the door, "You want to come along, honey? Please?" He could do with some moral support.

On his way through the garage, Maxime grabbed two orange cones from a hook on the wall. These he placed in the street, next to the RV. He unlocked the RV's side door, turned the engine on, then the generator, and pressed the slide-out button. It was important to demonstrate all the features of the camper to his brother—it could swing the balance toward a more enthused companion.

Gunther whistled as he made his way up the steps, short on the heels of his sister-in-law. "Maximus, have you come into some money recently, or are my eyes deceiving me?"

Maxime pursed his lips. "Nonsense. It costs nothing more than a three-star hotel room per night."

"Most hotel rooms sleep, four adults."

"This one sleeps six."

"Only a three star, Maximus? This thing looks more like a four." He whistled as he poked his head into every closet and cupboard. "*Mein Bruder.* A full-size fridge, and a stove with an oven, air conditioning, a shower *and* a separate toilet. Maxime, this is a *five*-star establishment."

Gunther wiggled in at the table to make room for Donna. "Count me in, *Maximus!*" he thundered. "This has the potential of becoming one grand adventure." He patted the bench on his other side. "Come, sit down. Show me the route we're taking."

As Maxime unfolded the large map, Gunther grinned conspiratorially at his hosts like a pubescent schoolboy. "Maximus, do the Americans *know* we're coming?"

19

Two Swiss Men Invade The United States

Maxime and Gunther left with the RV at sunrise. It followed a long day of stocking it with provisions and utensils—all necessary items, as per Maxime's lists.

Maxime not only was a rules man, but he was also good at lists. He had made two: one for him and one for Gunther. The lists were substantial.

During the stocking up Maxime had to listen to several reprimands from his beloved Donna on why it was preposterous for him, Maxime Baumann, an almost sixty-five-year-old real estate lawyer, to take bicycles along. Had he forgotten that Dr. Williams—nephrologist, urologist and infertility specialist—had warned him about the possibility of developing a hernia if he overdid things? Wasn't this what he was busy doing—overdoing things?

Maxime had kissed her complaints away each time, rolling his eyes. Gunther had strapped the bicycles onto the bike rack under Maxime's hawk-like supervision. It had made no difference to Donna when he pointed that the bicycles were not a spur-of-the-moment thing—they were a legitimate item on his list.

"See for yourself," he had said, waving the list.

Anybody who knew anything about hydrocelectomies and going RVing and the development of a hernia following such surgery knew that was impossible. What Dr. Williams had said was that if he overdid things, he could develop a *seroma,* a reactive fluid collection, not a hernia. It was evident that Maxime had done a much better Wikipedia and Google search.

Donna was prone to whining and over protectiveness. Maxime in turn—to being anally retentive and rule-obsessed. Not that he loved her any less.

A final hug for Donna, a lingering kiss, and they were off.

Maxime took the wheel for the first leg of their journey. They headed southeast on Route 39 and planned to cross the border at Portal, into North Dakota.

Gunther played with the radio, desperate to find something, *"anything"* other than "bloody hip-hop-and-rap rubbish." He mumbled that he couldn't understand how people—radio hosts in particular—couldn't get it that quality music had a profound effect on listener's mental well-being. *Proper* music, like Baroque or Classical or Romantic pieces. "I would even settle for Latino dance music." He paused, remembering where they were heading, "Damn, even *country* music."

Maxime decided to keep Gunther out of the driver's seat for as long as they were in Canada. Once in the States, Gunther, with his Swiss passport and thick German accent, should have fewer problems explaining to the officer why he was driving a twenty-eight-foot vehicle in a foreign country in a reckless manner—especially if he got the kilometers and miles per hour mixed up. Maxime realized, he too then, could claim ignorance as a foreigner.

The Customs officer at the border was a pleasant enough fellow, in a talkative mood, and waved them through without any hiccups, calling after them as he handed back the passports, "Enjoy showing your guest our beautiful country, Mr. Bowman!"

Maxime mumbled under his breath that that was the entire purpose of the visit, thank you very much, sir.

The brothers switched places on the outskirts of Portal. It became Maxime's task now, according to his older brother, to find *decent* music. Maxime was fast learning to roll his eyes at people.

Gunther soon made peace with the *feel* of the oversized vehicle and praised the ease of keeping the monstrosity within the confines of the lane markings. He even commented on the significant difference in the road quality south of the border.

"I *like* these Americans. It's like driving on the Autobahn, Max. What's it with those bloody Canadians? They're *stingy*. Their roads are shitty and falling apart. Perhaps because you aren't paying enough taxes?"

Maxime choked with indignation. "You're ill-informed. Our taxes are of the highest in the world. The tax money is sucked up by bureaucracies with little oversight—who squander individuals' hard-earned money on frivolous and poorly conceived ventures. And, it's often done with much contempt and indifference."

"That's too bloody bad. Did you notice, Maximus, even the *speed limit* is higher than in Canada?"

Maxime snorted. "I know, but keep an eye on the signs—they frequently *change* the limit. Remember, they measure in *miles* per hour."

As the miles and the countryside flew past, Gunter kept pressing his brother to turn up the volume—*way* up. He wanted to *feel* the music. One had to immerse oneself in its effervescence.

"How considerate of the Americans," Gunther gushed, "to have a passing lane every seven miles. One can at least then get ahead of these assholes who drive like they're out on a Sunday-afternoon cruise."

"As long as you stick to the speed limit, Gunther."

Gunther grumbled in his corner.

Maxime used reading glasses on occasion, depending on the font size of the printed material, but there was nothing the matter with his ears. "Gunther, do you hear a siren?" He had to raise his voice above the thumping dance music.

"*Nein, mein Bruder.*" Gunther drummed the rhythm on the steering wheel as he sang along in his thundering voice. He made up the words.

Maxime was worried.

It *was* a siren. No question about it. He leaned over and shut off the radio.

Gunther immediately stopped drumming. "*Ach,* no, Maximus. Just when the beat picks—"

"*Listen.*"

Gunther cocked his head.

"A siren?"

"*Exactly.* There's nothing ahead of us. Anything in your side-view mirrors?"

"*Scheisse.*"

Maxime craned his neck to see in the side-view mirror.

"A patrol car!" they called in unison.

"You think they're after *us?*" Gunther sounded less confident. "This guy sits *on* my tail, with flashing lights and everything."

"Perhaps we should pull over, Gunther."

"You think so?" Gunther switched to cruise control, set to the local speed limit of fifty-five.

"Pull *over,* Gunther!"

"Don't you *dare* raise your voice at me, Maxime Baumann." Gunther rasped, but he pulled over and killed the engine.

"Well, bloody well *listen.*" Maximus hollered. "Stay where you are. Wind the window down, keep your hands on the steering wheel where the officer can see them and look straight ahead."

"Why?

"Just *do* it," Maxime hissed. Then he added under his breath, "It's *the drill.* It's what the Americans that build these fancy Autobahn-quality roads expect you to do. Welcome to America."

The two brothers waited in silence as the patrol officer's boots crunched closer. The man halted half a step behind the door pillar, making it impossible to see his features.

"Good afternoon, sir," the officer said in a neutral voice, but with a strong southern drawl.

"*Guten Mittag, Herr Offizier,*" Gunther responded, equally courteous, looking straight ahead, hands on the steering wheel.

Maxime cringed. He realized what Gunther was doing, but it could backfire. *He's making me an accomplice. The bastard.* All Maxime could think of was rule three on page one: *Don't ever tell a lie.* And Gunther was bilingual—trilingual, in fact.

"Excuse me, sir?" The officer leaned forward an inch, his voice rising a notch.

"*Entschuldigung, Herr Offizier. Mein Englisch ist nicht so gut.*"

The officer leaned forward and caught Maxime's eye. "Do *you* speak any English, sir?"

All Maxime could think of was rule thirteen on page two: *The good Lord gave you a head—so use it.* It was not lying.

"*Nur wenig,*" Maxime stammered. Then, feeling sorry for the man, he added, "Only a little, Officer. *Mein Bruder*—my brother, arrived a few days ago from Switzerland. He speaks German. *Was ist loss, Herr Offizier?* What's wrong?" Maxime tried his best to sound concerned.

The officer snapped upright and coughed—although to Maxime it seemed he was choking. The man leaned forward again, this time much closer, his knuckles blanched white from grasping the open window. Maxime could see the man's dark pupils—he read the man's mind: *bloody foreigners.*

"Sir, your brother was driving this recreational vehicle, complete with two bicycles bouncing at the back, at seventy miles an hour. Fifteen over the limit."

Gunther tried to appease the distraught officer, whose face had turned crimson. "*Entschuldigung, Herr Offizier,*" he mumbled.

Maxime gave a nervous laugh. "My brother says he's sorry. He's so used to driving on the Autobahn. He got carried away, I think."

"I thought the Autobahn is in Germany?" The officer sounded irritated.

"Oh yes, it is, but he was enjoying the dramatic improvement of the road surface, compared to the roads in Saskatchewan. He was singing the praises of the high quality of the American highways. Have you ever driven up north, Officer?"

A smile broke through on the man's strained complexion. Maxime jumped at the opportunity.

"Officer, it is *so* easy to get carried away on these beautiful roads. Particularly with these neat passing lanes, which your Roads Department must have constructed to help weary travelers like us. Do you want to see his passport?"

Maxime turned to his brother and held out his hand, took his brother's passport, then fiddled with his wallet and took out his Saskatchewan driver's license.

He fell back to German. "*Danke, Herr Offizier.*"

The officer took the men's ID as if they could bite him.

"Do you think *I* should rather take the wheel, Officer?" Maxime asked in as neutral a voice he could muster. "Perhaps we should give my brother a break? I'll explain to him, in German, how to do things when in the States. I'll get him to understand this is *not* the Autobahn, even though it *is* a lovely road."

Maxime and Gunther beamed at the officer. Another smile forced its way onto the man's face.

Maxime added, "I'll make sure he gets the bloody *message* about American speed limits, Officer."

The official let out a protracted sigh and returned the documents. He straightened out next to the cabin, fists clenched. Then, as if changing his mind, he leaned forward into the window. "Gentlemen, I'll let you go. Don't let me set eyes on you two going beyond the speed limit again. I'll *make* you pay the ticket, even if it's in Deutsche marks or Swiss francs."

As the man crunched his way back to the patrol car, the brothers Baumann called out in unison, "*Danke schön, Herr Offizier!*"

20

Bliss Can Change On Short Notice

Maxime had a new reason to worry.

He had developed hemorrhoids—there was no doubt in his mind. His bottom was numb, similar to when he had had the spinal anesthesia. They had been driving for two days uninterrupted. His behind was not used to it—it alternated between throbbing and feeling dead.

For a moment he considered how the hemorrhoids would affect his BPH—his slowly enlarging prostate. At least his hydrocele was gone, and the incision had healed.

He and Gunther reached the Colonia Del Rey campgrounds in Corpus Christi Bay at 4:25 p.m. on the second day. They had switched places every 250 kilometers and stuck obediently to the local speed limit, whatever that was. According to Maxime, they were now seasoned twenty-eight-foot RV drivers. Anybody who knew anything about RVs and semis knew that once one got the "feel" of the large vehicle, it became a subconscious matter to steer the colossus. Driving close to three thousand kilometers did that to you—gave you confidence. It was bloody common knowledge.

Not once after their initial altercation with *Herr Offizier* did they run into law enforcement personnel. Gunther was not a little proud of how he had handled the stressful situation, eloquently, and with a relaxed flair, many actors would envy. Maxime had only snorted, pointing out how he, totally against his will, was made an accomplice to an act of deception in a foreign country. He insisted on knowing whether Gunther had any idea what the punishment was for such an offense if convicted. Gunther had only scoffed at his concerns.

It took the two of them, under Maxime's supervision, eighteen minutes to complete the triple hookup. They let the automatic awning down, slid the single expansion out, untied the bicycles from the rack and locked them to the rear fender (Maxime was not convinced that everybody in the campgrounds had honorable intentions and wouldn't be tempted to snatch a higher-end dual sports bicycle with disc brakes.) Next, they took the portable barbecue out, made it stand, (chain-locked that as well), set up two folding camping stools under the awning, after first laying down a carpet-like groundsheet. It was 5:15 upon completion of these tasks.

Maxime wiped the thin line of sweat from his brow.

The late hour was because the young man at the park office, Garry, had taken his sweet time signing them in. Maxime had had to bite his lip three times not to ask him if he had a bloody under active thyroid or another reason for a slow metabolism, making him so painfully inefficient.

Maxime reckoned that they had twenty minutes left before sunset, plus another fifteen before it would be completely dark. Since it was probably five to ten minutes down to the beach, they'd better move their asses. Gunther did not sound enthusiastic when Maxime informed him, the moment the last camping stool went up, that the beach beckoned.

"Maximus, you bemoaned the campground clerk's *under active* thyroid. Yours is bloody *overactive. Sit down.* That's why we came—to rest and relax."

He plopped down in a chair, gesturing to the other.

Maxime was schooled in playing the age game. "I thought your sexy Irish girlfriend got you all muscled up and fit. You sound like a hundred-and-ten-year-old man. Shall I ask Garry at the office for a walker with a seat?"

Gunther only laughed.

"Suit yourself." Maxime tossed him the RV keys. "Lock up if you change your mind. I *have* to run down to the beach— feel the sand between my toes and take a quick dip. The ocean is whispering my name."

He strode off, only to stop. "Damn it, Gunther! Get your swimming trunks on. *Bitte.*"

Five minutes later the brothers Baumann strolled toward the beach, each dressed in swimming trunks, flip-flops, a towel around the neck and a T-shirt in hand. Maxime had had trouble not to grab a button-down shirt. There was no reason to look bloody uncivilized at the seaside. What would Mr. J. Johnson think of him? Or Mrs. Long for that matter?

Every few steps the taller of the two let out a thunderous laugh, pat his companion on the back and spoke adamantly. Every American who passed them could tell they were foreigners. Foreigners, with six-packs. It was impossible to make out a word they were saying, for it wasn't English—American, Canadian or British—they were speaking. The passersby knew it wasn't Spanish, so at least they weren't illegal immigrants. Perhaps they were from Sweden, or from somewhere else in Scandinavia?

Maxime and Gunther discovered the next morning that Garry, the park office clerk, had another day job. With a group of friends, he ran a busy surfing school and surfboard rental shop on the beach. It didn't take Gunther long to convince his brother that they should take an introductory course in surfing that very afternoon.

Later, catching his breath after three solid hours in the water, where he had slowly found his surfboard legs, Maxime had to admit that he owed Garry the clerk, an apology. Garry was one hipster surfboard lad. There was nothing wrong with his thyroid—his only sin was that of being laid back. His life was not micromanaged by thirty *Lebensregeln,* double-spaced over two pages. It consisted instead of surfing and teaching people, irrespective of their age, to obtain self-confidence and faith in their capabilities.

Garry's parents, Maxime learned, owned the campground. Garry helped out in the office when they were short staffed.

The young surf boarder's teaching benefitted the poor sods officially classified as the "seniors"—a designation Maxime abhorred. He disagreed. Anybody who knew anything about geriatrics and social stratification and chronological and physiological age knew that there was a world of difference between the two. It was a blooming falacy that growing old meant decrepitude, wasting away and dependency. It was a personal choice. *Declining function as you age, my ass,* he thought.

The two brothers, each with a beer in hand, studied the other beachgoers from their rented beach chairs, pulled high up on the sand. They had more than an hour of sunlight left, and Maxime was satisfied with their performance in the water that day. It had been a brilliant workout. So pumped and exhilarated was he as they had dragged their exhausted bodies from the surf that he had been irresponsible enough to immediately sign up, with Gunther, for the next level of training, Level One Surfboarding, the next morning.

Maxime thought of his second-last rule on page two: *Life is short—make it count.* He lay back, closed his eyes and thought of Mr. J. Johnson. His thoughts soon wandered off to Donna—his sweet, sweet Donna. Before they had left with the RV, she had told him that she had something important to share with him upon his return. When he'd insisted she tell him right away, she had laughed softly, as if embarrassed. She had refused. She promised to do so when he got back.

Gunther coughed, making Maxime's eyes snap open. Two lithe young ladies, clad in skimpy string bikinis, sauntered past, their toned and tanned bodies mere feet away. It wasn't difficult to picture the Vision in Dr. Moller's office. Gunther grinned at him. Maxime shook his head. *Yes, Gunther. Life is good; they're gorgeous, but I'm fine.*

The brothers returned to the RV as the sun set. Minutes later, a hesitant knock sounded on the side door. Maxime, still in his wet trunks, was getting his toiletries together for a shower in the ablution building. He dropped what he was doing and plodded in his sand-covered flip-flops to answer the door. He shrugged, plagued by guilt for not taking his wet sandals off. It was so unlike him. The time in the water had affected him—he was too exhausted to think straight.

It was a young lady—brandishing a flashlight. She took a hesitant step forward. "Are you Mr. Maxime Bowman?"

"Yes?" Maxime recognized her as one of Garry's co-workers in the campground office.

"I'm Allison. I'm from the office, with an urgent message. You didn't respond to messages on your cell phone?"

"Just a moment." Maxime turned back and stormed to the bedroom for his phone. *Damn. More sand in this once pristine hallway.* He and Gunther had decided not to carry any of their gadgets around with them—not when they were out on the water.

He bumped into Gunther on the way.

"*Was ist loss?*"

"I don't know. It's the young lady from the office. Garry's friend. Something about an urgent message." He entered his password as he scampered down the steps to join Allison outside.

As he opened his messages, he glanced at the young woman who patiently stood her ground. "What's the message you have?" he asked, more brusquely than he had intended.

Alison retreated a step and held the piece of paper, her confidence faltering. "The first is from a Mrs. Long, from Johnson, Johnson & McBride? And I think the next is from your son Sandro. Or is it Shandro?"

Mr. J. Johnson had passed away. But why would Sandro be looking for me?

Maxime found the text messages on his phone.

Remembering Allison from the campsite office, Maxime took the page from her. Mrs. Long, discreet as always: *Mr. Baumann, please contact me. It's urgent.* Sent at 4:07 p.m. Then another, written on the same memo paper, sent at 4:16: *Mr. Baumann, you're not answering your phone. I'm contacting your son in Vancouver. It's in connection with your wife. RSVP.*

Maxime tapped his phone—Sandro's text messages were succinct. He had left a message with the campground office at 4:23. *Dad. It's Mom. Contact me.* He had also sent several texts, the last of which, sent at 6:11, read: *I'm flying out to Saskatchewan tonight. You'd better come too.*

Maxime woke from his daze as the young woman cleared her throat. "Mr. Bowman?" she whispered.

"Thank you, Allison … I'll phone them."

Allison spun around and disappeared between the RVs.

Gunther stood at the top of the stairs. "Maximus?"

He bounced down the stairs when Maxime didn't answer.

"*Max!*"

"Something's the matter with Donna."

Maxime pressed the numbers to call his son, then turned his back on his brother. His shoulders slumped. He couldn't let Gunther see the fear that had gripped his heart.

21

Mr. Baumann Sr. Flies To Canada

Maxime stepped away from the RV and allowed the night to swallow him.

"*Sandro.* What's going on?"

"*Dad.* Why haven't you answered *any* of my calls? Mom's in Intensive Care. She's on her way to the OR. I'm flying out in an hour. You have to abort your trip. Oh, Dad ..." His son's voice broke.

"Sandro, listen to me. We were at the beach all day. I'm sorry. I didn't carry the blooming phone with me. The ICU? Why's she going for an operation? She was in perfect health when I left her three days ago. And I spoke to her last night—she was laughing and joking. She only complained of a headache. Was she in a car accident? *Sandro?*"

"Dad ... she had a brain bleed. She was at the hairdresser when it happened, sometime after three this afternoon. I spoke to one of the doctors—she said it was an aneurysm … I think she called it an AVM."

With that, Sandro could no longer speak.

Maxime apologized again, profusely, for not carrying his bloody cell phone with him while he was learning to surf. He attempted anything he could think of to set his son's mind at ease, his own as well—promising to purchase, at the first opportunity, a small transparent waterproof case for his phone for use during future open-water activities. He babbled about the years when the three of them—Sandro, Simon and himself—went on the canoe trips, every year. About Donna who always declined their persistent nagging to come along.

Maxime couldn't stop blathering.

"Dad … please. Stop talking. I'm okay now. It's such a shock. Get Uncle Gunther to help you catch the first plane out of there. I got hold of Simon. He knows—" Sandro coughed. "But I'm not certain that he's coming. He sounded a bit pissed off."

Maxime assured his son he would find a plane somewhere, even if he had to rob, steal, hijack, or charter one. And if there were no plane to be had, he would hire the fastest taxi and head north, ignoring any imposed speed limit or any *Herr Offizier* in a patrol car.

Then Maxime went in search of his brother. He found Gunther in one of the folding chairs outside their RV. The yellow insect-repellant light cast subdued shadows over his features. He jumped to his feet when he saw Maxime's face.

Maxime allowed the smothering hug as he recounted his conversation with Sandro.

Together, the brothers Baumann strode to the campground office. Maxime's LED headlamp bobbed its piercing beam ahead into the darkness. There was no mistaking it—the two men sounded like foreigners—no civilized American could speak German with such an accent.

Allison was still on duty. Maxime leaned close to the small circular opening in the office window, his arms resting on the sill, and related his conversation with his son.

"Allison, I know you guys have wifi here. Is there any chance I can come into the office and let you help me book a flight?"

"Mr. Bowman? I don't know … Garry's not here, and his dad will be upset with me if I break the office rules …"

Maxime, in spite of his anxiety about Donna, remembered Mr. Carnegie's book, as well as his own rule thirteen, close to the bottom of page one, stating: *Be clear in your vision.* His mission tonight was clear: reach Donna in time. And no one, the dear Lord knew—*no one* was going to prevent him from doing that.

Maxime then asked, in a clear, calm voice whether any of the campground guests had ever had a spouse, three thousand kilometers away, who had ruptured an aneurysm in their brain and was on their way to the operating room.

Gunther gawked at his brother—he had never heard him talk like this.

"How *often* does this happen, Allison?"

"Perhaps *never,* sir?" she muttered.

Allison unlocked the office door, and with her help, the brothers Baumann secured a direct flight for Maxime to Calgary, with a forty-five-minute layover before connecting to Saskatoon.

Maxime had fifty-eight minutes to get to the airport.

In their excitement, both Gunther and Maxime gave the perpetually blushing Allison a quick hug and a peck on the cheek, and almost took the door off its frame in their haste to get back to the RV.

A taxi was reserved to pick up Maxime. He had ten minutes. As he rummaged through the narrow closet and drawers, he pressed Gunther about what to do with the RV. Maxime's first thoughts were to lock the vehicle and fly back, both of them, and sort out the logistics from Canada.

Gunther wouldn't hear of it. He would only be in the way, he claimed—there was little place for him in the middle of this family crisis. He would get a few hours' sleep, pack up by daybreak and drive back—even if it took him three days. Maxime remained hesitant. He was contemplating rule six on page one: *Consider all your options. Always.* And the best choice would be for Gunther to come with him.

"Maximus," Gunther said, "it's straightforward. You can't travel by road—it would take too long. You've got your plane ticket. Leave now. You might still reach Donna in time. Besides, I'm older—you *have* to listen to me."

"What if you run into *Herr Offizier* or one of his colleagues along the road?"

"*Kein problem, Herr Offizier—ich bin Schweizer!*" Gunther waved his Swiss passport at Maxime. "I can be very convincing, Maximus. Don't worry. Me no *spreche Englisch,*" he added with a thick accent. Maxime shook his head and rolled his eyes.

On his way to the airport, Maxime dialed Dr. Manie Moller's cell phone number. He had never used the private number before, but the present situation justified being called "an emergency."

Dr. Moller picked up on the second ring. He told Maxime how he had rushed to the hospital to see Donna and went on to explain the neurosurgeon's findings. Since it was an arteriovenous malformation, several endovascular coil embolizations had to be performed to stop the bleeding and cut off supply to the blood vessels feeding the AVM. He explained how they would push a tiny catheter up the blood vessels into the brain without cutting the cranium—the skull bone—open.

Maxime couldn't care less about the technical jargon. He had to know about his darling. "Did she recognize you, Dr. Manie?"

The line went quiet. Dr. Moller only sighed.

"Was she *that* bad?"

"I'm afraid it's a severe bleed, Maxime. The ER physician intubated her and placed her on a ventilator soon after I got there—"

"Was she … was she able to speak, before he… shoved that breathing thing down her throat?" Maxime choked out.

"She was somewhat awake—opened her eyes on command but couldn't move her left side. She deteriorated fast and had difficulty swallowing and breathing, making it necessary to place an endotracheal tube." Then he added, "*Herr Baumann … Mein Freund. Es tut mir leid.*"

The doctor's sympathy touched Maxime's heart, but he was left with one question. "Will she … *make* it, Manie?"

Dr. Moller paused. "I'm no neurosurgeon. It could go either way. Yes, she could make it. The surgeons and anesthesiologist and nurses and technicians are fighting for her life. What you and I must do is *pray*."

Maxime promised to do just that. But first, he tried Simon's number in London. He wasn't certain, but it was probably close to three or four in the morning there. Too bad. There was no answer. Maxime tried again and got through just as the taxi turned onto the airport road.

"Hello, Simon."

"Is that *you,* Dad?" came his son's gruff response.

"Sorry about the hour. Sandro told me he got hold of you. I'm getting out of the taxi. I'm down here in Texas, catching a plane, back home. Are you *coming?*"

"I don't know, Dad."

A shiver ran down Maxime's back. Each word jabbed like spikes in his chest. He paid the driver and bolted into the terminal.

"*Simon,*" he pleaded.

The anguish, incomprehension, sadness, and longing that welled up in Maxime were unfamiliar to him. What was happening? Nowhere in his *Lebensregeln* was there provision for arteriovenous malformations or grown-ups who despised their parents. Anybody who knew anything about parenthood and adult children and love and affection and respect knew that this was plain wrong. That was for bloody certain.

"Please, Simon," he begged. "She's undergoing another procedure—an operation to control the bleeding. She… she's gravely ill."

"*So?*"

Maxime Bastien Baumann was not someone who gasped. He gasped. "*Simon!* She's your *mother*. Since when do you *hate* her?" He added in a whisper, "This is news to me … I didn't know."

"I don't *hate* her, Dad. I'm extremely disappointed in her. She destroyed my trust. I didn't ask for this *aneurysm* thing to happen. I'm sorry about that. I was hoping I could get some *sense* into her."

Maxime stopped in the middle of the hall. "*What* are we talking about?"

There was a moment's silence on the other end. "You have *no* idea, Dad? Oh, then *never mind*."

"I have to run to my gate now, Simon. Whatever she did— please come. If not for her sake or mine, do it for *Sandro*."

"*Sandro?*" Simon snorted.

Dad must think I'm a bloody imbecile.

"Yes, for Sandro," Maxime said. "He may be the older one, but he needs you."

"Dad…"

"Do it for *Sandro*. Oh, and your mother *loves* you. *Goodbye,* Simon."

22

Maxime Baumann Waits Outside The Operating Room

M axime was worried.

He had taken a taxi from the airport to the hospital and arrived minutes before midnight. In the waiting room outside the OR, Sandro ran to meet him, stopping short of knocking Maxime off his feet. They bear-hugged, and Sandro wouldn't let go, burying his head in his father's neck, his body shaking as muted sobs shook his slender frame.

Maxime thought he only had to worry about Donna. He was wrong. Simon, his youngest, had an issue with his mother about a secret in the past, of which Maxime knew nothing. And now his oldest had trouble containing his grief.

Maxime held his son, patted his back and stroked his head. They were the only people in the room. Maxime tried to recall the last time he had cradled his oldest this way, for this long.

Sandro was inconsolable. *Does the boy know something?* Sandro had been in primary school when he allowed Maxime to hold him like this.

Maxime thought about what had happened and about his *Lebensregeln* and about the first and last rules, which both stated, *Stick to the rules.* He wondered how that had played out for him, how it had influenced him and his family. Could his rule book have played a role in whatever had happened between Donna and Simon, or in what had happened to Donna and now what was taking place among his entire family? *You've been an asshole, Maxime Baumann. Time to get your BS together and save the bloody clan.*

He steered Sandro back to the chairs and made him sit, keeping a firm hand on his arm.

"Sandro, *update,* please. What's happening inside?" He gestured toward the OR.

Sandro glanced at him through puffed eyelids and shrugged.

"Okay, it's eleven fifty-five," Maxime said. "Have you spoken to any of the staff in there? Any of the doctors?"

"I got here at ten thirty, Dad." Sandro sniffled. "I ran into one of the radiologists who said they were taking Mom ..." And he choked up again. Several deep breaths later, he continued. "He said they were taking her back for the third time to stop the bleeding with an endovascular catheter ... and if *that* wasn't successful they ... might have to open her skull."

Maxime pulled his son closer and stroked his head.

"Tell me about Michelle." Perhaps that was something Sandro could do without weeping.

"She's fine. She's doing well, almost twenty-six weeks now. I refused to let her come along, in case it hurt the baby, but I've probably made a mistake … I didn't realize Mom … was in such a sorry state." Sandro started shaking again.

"She'll bounce back … your mother. She's a tough one, my Donatella."

"But she's only *fifty-nine,* Dad. She's too young to die."

"No one is *ever* old enough to die."

Father and son fell silent. They were not prepared to put words to the fear that raced through their hearts—breakaway horses without a coachman—heading into the night.

Maxime broke the silence. "I spoke to Simon. I tried to call on his love and loyalty and whatnot—" He sat back and peered at his son. "Sandro, do you have *any* idea what Simon was talking? I couldn't make any sense of what he said. Something about how your mother had disappointed him and destroyed his trust?"

"Dad, I'm not sure …"

"Sandro Baumann. Stop bullshitting me. The two of you talk. I know. What's the *blooming* story?"

"You have *no* idea?"

Maxime stared at his son. Shook his head.

Sandro returned the gaze as if he couldn't believe that this man, for whom he had so much love and respect, in spite of all his quirks and complexes and stupid rules, could have been so utterly blind. So oblivious to the obvious.

"Simon asked me the same question: 'Do you *really* not know?' What did your mother do that was so terrible?"

It occurred to Maxime that it could be the same thing that Donna had wanted to talk to him about once he got back from his trip. Did she have a secret? Did she suffer from a guilty conscience? Did she do something to the boys, or to Simon when he was little? No—that was impossible.

"Did she ... *abuse* him when he was younger?" he whispered.

Sandro shook his head and turned away. He wasn't certain what to say. How was he to tell his father? It was not for a son to tell his father about such matters—it was for a husband or a wife. When Simon, two years earlier, had stumbled upon his mother in the act and confronted her, she had promised to come clean with their dad. But now, it turned out she hadn't. Had he been shedding unnecessary tears? Did his mother live a double life of secrets and lies? She had promised, claimed it was a one-time thing. A fling. Perhaps Simon was not entirely out of line? Still, it wasn't for a son to tell his father.

"*She* has to tell you, Dad. Sorry ... I can't." Then he added as if it would lessen the blow. "It was a *long* time ago."

Sandro rose. He had learned from his father: changing the subject can be a good escape route. "I'm going to check at the OR desk. Perhaps we can get an update about Mom."

Ten minutes later, Sandro returned with a lady in scrubs. She shook Maxime's hand and took the seat next to him.

"Mr. Baumann, I'm Dr. Prinz, one of the neurosurgeons. We're taking your wife to the OR. The staged endovascular embolization attempts were not successful. One of the risks of the technique is a rupture of a vessel, which is what has happened— we have a delicate situation on our hands." She cleared her throat.

"We're facing a crisis. The rest of the team is getting her ready for an open craniotomy. It's her only chance."

Dr. Prinz stood and gripped his hand. She held his eyes and squeezed hard. "Mr. Baumann, we'll give it our *all*," she breathed before disappearing through the double doors.

For a moment Maxime considered following her, then he remembered he couldn't do that. He dropped his head and plopped down. Sandro touched his arm.

It's her only chance the surgeon had said.

Anybody who knew anything about Maxime Baumann and operating rooms and statistical probability knew that it was no small feat to become a piece of data, to become a statistic oneself. It was no shame, but it was no great honor either. He had had a 0.2 to 2.0 percent chance of a spinal headache, and look what had happened. And this was Donna's only chance.

He had so much planned for the two of them, for their journey together. There was so much living still to do. Dying was not part of the itinerary—not now and not later. That much was for bloody certain.

23

Simon Baumann Arrives From Heathrow

Maxime saw him first.

At the far end of the hallway, Simon had appeared. Maxime squinted at the wall clock: 6:03 in the morning. His son's formidable frame was hunched forward like Mr. J. Johnson on a bad day.

Maxime extracted himself from the cluster of chairs. Every part of his body ached.

He and Sandro had pulled several chairs together after the surgeon had left, in an attempt to get some rest. Sandro was still asleep, curled awkwardly in a fetal position, one arm draped over an armrest, his intermittent snoring the only sign he was alive.

Maxime started toward his younger son—indecisive at first, almost careful. Spilled words can bind stronger than ropes. Soon his legs found increasing freedom as the constraints fell away. His brisk walk turned into a trot, then a run, and Simon matched him, pace for pace, until they raced into each other's arms—uncertain at first, until shared pain united them in a rock-solid embrace.

"*Simon!*"

"Dad."

Maxime held on, reluctant to let go. Then held his youngest at arm's length, unable to hide his surprise, his pride, his joy, but also his sorrow. Anybody who knew anything about fathers and sons and standing up for what one believed in knew that acting like a jellyfish was never an option. But demonstrating the presence of a spine implied pain. This hapless becoming-an-Englishman son of his was no exception. Simon had a backbone. That was for bloody certain.

Simon disentangled himself from his father's grip, leaned over his brother and ruffled his hair. "Wake up, you useless bastard."

Sandro woke when the chair his arm was hooked over was pulled away, and his arm flopped down, making him roll halfway off the makeshift bed. He swung his legs down and leaned forward, rubbing both eyes, then squinted at Simon.

"*What* did you call me?"

Simon laughed and hugged his brother, then pulled their unsuspecting and protesting father into a rambunctious group hug. They only calmed down when a chair crashed onto its side.

"Boys, boys! Settle down." Maxime pried himself free and started bringing order to the disarray of chairs and empty food containers scattered around them. He shook his head in dismay.

Maxime Baumann, just because your wife is having critical surgery is no reason to turn the place into a pigsty. What will the housekeeping staff and the doctors and nurses think about you and your boys—that you're a bunch of bloody vagrants?

Anybody who knew anything about hospitals and OR waiting rooms and sleeping your sorry bum numb on a makeshift chair-bed knew that this was the moment of truth. It could not be good news if the operation lasted longer than six hours.

Once the waiting area had been tidied up, Maxime and the two boys marched as one through the double doors. No news is good news, the saying went, but there were limits to that.

The front desk was deserted. Sandro leaned across the counter and pressed the little bell.

A face poked around a far corner.

"*Excuse* me," Sandro called out. "Could you help us?"

A lady came into full view. She had a mop in her hand—she belonged to Housekeeping. She watched them with an impassive face, not moving.

"Could you please call one of the staff in the neuro theater?"

The lady disappeared down the OR hallway, with her mop.

Four minutes passed, and Sandro leaned across the counter a second time and pressed the bell hard and long. "This is *ridiculous*," he muttered.

New life appeared down the OR hallway. Dr. Prinz tore her paper mask from her face as she approached the trio, her gait devoid of the earlier effervescence.

Maxime introduced his son from London. Dr. Prinz shook his hand then steered the three ahead of her back through the double doors.

In the waiting room, she pulled around two of the chairs—chairs Maxime had meticulously put back in their proper place—to form a semicircle. She plopped down in the nearest one and wiped the back of her hand over her eyes.

She was worn out, Maxime noticed: when she lowered her hand, the mouth smiled, but her eyes lacked conviction.

"Sit down, gentlemen." She indicated the chairs around her. "Please."

Maxime slumped down. He had forgotten how to breathe.

"Mr. Baumann, I'm afraid I don't have good news." She paused, swallowed and held his eyes until he resumed breathing. "They're taking your wife through to the intensive care unit. The bleeding was problematic. She has significant brain swelling."

Maxime's legs followed a mind all their own and made him stand. He peered at the exhausted surgeon. "What are her chances, doctor?"

Dr. Prinz's mouth opened to answer when the PA system blared, "Code blue, ICU. Code blue, ICU."

She snapped to attention and touched Maxime's arm. "Excuse me. That could be her. I am *so* sorry—I should go." She squeezed both his hands, gave him a brave smile and dashed through the doors.

24

The Baumann Men Pay Mrs. Donna Baumann A Visit

Maxime's worry shifted.

This was a different misgiving, though. In the past, Maxime's worrying had always centered on himself and his phobias and the factors that threatened his equilibrium. A shift was taking place here in the waiting room. One of the biggest challenges had always been how to maneuver around the idiots and assholes who shared his earthly existence.

Maxime was now worried about Donna. *His* Donatella.

When he grew up, in Davos, his parents spoke German and Romansch. He learned English much later. People from the south of Switzerland, where they spoke Italian, sometimes visited his father. Maxime had loved sitting on his dad's lap, listening to them talking. In later years, he forgot most of the words and their meanings, but when he first laid eyes on Donna, and she told him her name, he remembered some of the forgotten words. She had only laughed, thought he was hallucinating.

"*Donna*. I like it. It means 'lady.'"

She had blushed and mumbled how she had always hated the name. Her parents had done her a grave injustice with their poor choice of a name. It remained a struggle to forgive them.

"*Dónna*." He had placed a different accent on her name. "No, I'll call you *Donatella*. That's even prettier."

Now he had her attention.

"And what does *that* mean, Mr. Know-it-all?"

"'Divine gift; given by God.'"

"You're making that up, Maxime Baumann," she had protested.

"*Dad.*"

Maxime was still in Davos with his sweetheart.

"Dad!" It was Sandro.

Maxime faced his son. The tears were close to the surface.

"What's happening with Mom? What was Dr. Prinz talking about?"

Across the room, Simon answered, "She was trying to tell us it's over." He had been pacing in front of the only window in the waiting room, but now he came over, pulled a chair closer and sat down. "Think a little, Sandro," he said. "What did you *think* that code blue thing was? You heard what the doctor said to Dad before she ran off: *I am so sorry.*"

"Boys," said Maxime, "We don't *know* for certain."

Maxime put a hand on Sandro's arm and leaned forward to touch Simon's knee. His sons allowed the unfamiliar intimacy.

Maxime made an effort to banish the ridiculous rules from his frazzled mind. *Now is not the time, Maxime. You have been weighed and measured, and you have been found wanting. Accept it.* Rule twelve on page one states: *Never be found without faith.*

How could he bear this? How could his "lady," his "gift of God," simply be taken away? He had had much faith. And now? He needed more than faith—he needed a miracle. Anybody who knew anything about faith and miracles and life and death and silly rulebooks knew that rules were of little help or consolation now. That was for bloody certain.

"Mr. Baumann?"

It was Dr. Prinz. Her voice was soft and hesitant. She stood in the door, then stepped closer and took Maxime's hand in both of hers. "I'm sorry, Mr. Baumann. Do you want to come with me to the ICU?"

Maxime shuddered. "It's over?"

Dr. Prinz nodded as she gave both Sandro and Simon a quick handshake. She took Maxime by the elbow and steered him through the double doors, the two brothers forming the rearguard.

She led them to the ICU, to the bed, then stepped from the cubicle.

It cannot be true.

Maxime shuffled closer until he touched Donna's bed.

You look so peaceful, my darling. Are you holding your breath?

Sandro and Simon stood three steps back. The staff had removed any sign of a breathing tube or infusion line from

Donna. The hospital gown accentuated her paleness. A bandage around her head, the only telltale that something could be amiss, hid most of her short auburn hair.

You must still be sleeping, my sweet.

Maxime leaned forward and kissed her pale face. Her lips were cold. *I had so many plans for us. What am I supposed to tell Gunther?* Maxime took her cool hand and stroked it. He kissed her again. *Never mind Gunther. What am I expected to say to that bloody cat of yours? He won't believe me.*

Maxime brushed over his eyes and turned around, carefully hugging each son before steering them toward the bed. Sandro bent and kissed his mother's hands. Simon walked around to the other side, leaned forward and placed a quick peck on his mother's forehead.

"Goodbye, Mother," Simon mumbled as he stepped back, gave his father another hug and stomped from the room.

Maxime and Sandro remained by the bed.

"Gentlemen? Mr. Baumann?" It was one of the ICU nurses. Maxime wasn't certain how long they had been there. Donna's hand felt colder than it had. The nurse guided them out of the ICU. Dr. Prinz was waiting to speak with them, she said.

When Maxime and Sandro entered the waiting room, Dr. Prinz wasn't there, but Simon snapped to his feet and strode closer. There was nothing of Mr. J. Johnson left in his posture. He was a man certain of his mission.

"Dad, I'm returning to London later this morning."

"*Simon?* Your mother?"

"Mom's *gone*. I came—because of Sandro and because of you. I'm sorry for your loss, but I *have* to go." He reached out to give his father a hug, but Maxime scuttled back.

"What are you *thinking*?" Sandro hissed as he grabbed Simon by the shoulders and steered him away from their father. "There will be a *funeral*. What about *him*?" Sandro whispered. "You can't do this to Father, *or* to her."

"She betrayed us. I came and paid my respects. You look after Father now. He'll be okay. His *rule book* will sustain him." Simon freed himself from his brother's grasp and bolted down the hallway without looking back.

25

*Maxime Considers The Possibility That
His Rule Book Is In Need Of Revision.*

M axime was in the doldrums.
A condition and state, unfamiliar to him. He has never
been there—the mopes—a fearful and lonesome place. Being
worried, even being perplexed was part of being Maxime. On a
daily basis, he dealt with exasperation, brought on by the seem-
ingly endless supply of idiots around him. It was part of life,
being surrounded by fools and worry. He could cope with that.
Woebegone was new.

He had never been away from Donna for more than seventy-
two hours. Today was his fourth straight day away from her. It
was also the first day of him being without a wife, and for the
boys being motherless.

As Sandro lead him through the hospital hallways toward the
car, he thought of Gunther.

Dear Gunther, I now understand the hurt you felt when the accident snatched Carla and Heidi from you. Emasculated. Endless waves of pain and numbness washing over one—lifting one high and smashing one into the rocks.

The numbness was different from that of the spinal anesthetic. There was no headache now, only an unrelenting pressure in the chest. No notice was served, no one-minute warning given, no sign in the sky, no voice—no nothing. Just *bam!* And it was over. Followed by silence.

Maxime was aware of a looming silence.

He couldn't remember the ride back home. Only when Sandro turned up the driveway and his eyes caught movement in the front window did he stir. *Columbus. The bloody cat.*

The feline wouldn't believe him. He would hate him. *What did you do to my mistress? You never loved me anyway, Maxime Baumann. You tolerated me because of the madam. It was reciprocal, FYI, but never you mind.*

"Come, Dad."

Maxime was an automaton as he followed Sandro into the house. It was not that different from Gunther's situation. *I've just lost two of my people, Gunther. Simon is as good as dead now too.*

In the kitchen, he picked up the meowing cat, stroking it with a tenderness he had not thought he possessed.

Columbus, desperate for physical contact, allowed the stiff arms to hold him. He was willing to settle for the second violin, but only until the lady boss came home. At least this guy who always walked around in a suit, refusing to pick him up, was now dressed more like a normal human being. He even smelled like the laundry basket, which Columbus adored.

The cat wriggled himself free and bounced to the floor, giving a forlorn meow. *This guy might have been nice picking me up and smelling unwashed for a change, but the poor sod forgot I need my specially formulated pellets.*

Maxime strolled to the pantry, shooed the purring cat away and retrieved the bag with cat food. *It's why I left this annoying animal in Donna's care. She excelled with all the pampering and oohing and ahhing. It's not my style.* Dogs are different—they are loyal on a much deeper level. They can almost talk. They don't purr and they don't require a stupid litter box. Anybody who knew anything about acute onset widower status and neutered tomcats and the need for litter boxes and absent mistresses knew that change was inevitable.

It seemed foreshadowed that the anally-retentive spouse of the cat-mistress might become the next-in-line cat benefactor. That much was for bloody sure, clear even to the hapless Maxime.

"*Dad.*"

Maxime returned to the present—he was sitting across from his son. He glanced at him now with a sardonic grin.

"Sorry, Dad." Sandro patted his father's hand. "Sorry. You were elsewhere. I made coffee. Would you like some?"

Maxime shrugged.

"It's hot and strong," Sandro insisted.

The two Baumann men sat together in the small kitchen nook, elbows resting on the table, steaming mugs clasped in their hands. They sipped unhurried. Father and son looked into each other's confounded souls. It sufficed for now—the silence—the sitting close. Now was not a time for talk. Words were redundant.

The cat, meanwhile, had decided that his new stand-in human was perhaps not so bad after all, not if one needed feet to curl around.

The mugs were empty and cold when Sandro snapped upright, startling his father. He shoved his chair back. "I think we forgot about Uncle Gunther and the RV." He plopped down again, grabbed Maxime's hands. "Have you phoned him, Dad?"

"I've been thinking about him every five minutes ... about Clara and Heidi ..."

"No, Dad. Where do you think he'll be by now? Kansas? Nebraska?"

Maxime gave it thought. "Nebraska, perhaps." Then added with a chuckle, "If he didn't run into *Herr Offizier.*"

"But does he *know?* Did you tell him? About Mom?" Sandro choked up.

Maxime watched his son's stricken face. *How do I tell my brother his sister-in-law is gone, Sandro? How does one do that?*

"Do you have his cell number?" Sandro asked.

Maxime picked up his phone and scrolled through his Contacts. When he found Gunther's number, he just stared at the name on the screen. Should he call him now?

Sandro held out his hand. "May I?"

Maxime handed him the phone, and Sandro made the call. Sandro jerked the phone away when Gunther's booming voice came through. "Maximus, son of our mother!" Maxime could hear from across the table. "I thought the Rapture had taken place while I was enjoying the semi-desert landscapes of the southern United States." He bellowed another chuckle.

Maxime took the phone from his son and walked toward the living room.

"Hallo, Gunt." He tried hard to sound upbeat. "Where are you?"

Again the laugh. "Halfway between Wichita and Salina."

"The RV can't *go* that fast. You'll freak out those conscientious patrol officers."

Gunther Baumann bellowed another laugh and described in great detail how he had just saved two hundred U.S. dollars by using his Swiss passport and sticking to his mother tongue.

"*Ich verstehe kein Englisch, Herr Offizier,* I told the officer."

"Gunther, they'll lock you away this time. They have computers these days which talk to one another. Be careful, please. I *need you* ..." Maxime's voice faltered.

There was a pause on the other end. "Maximus? *Donna?*"

"Yes, Gunt ... she didn't."

"Oh, Max ..."

Maxime gave his brother a clinical rundown of the past twenty-four hours. He had decided he wasn't going to spill the beans about his youngest one's bizarre actions at the hospital. It was still too fresh—too unthinkable. Unmentionable, even. He had mentally dissected his thirty rules, top to bottom and bottom to top. There were so many guidelines among them that he had thought reasonable, if not sensible, which would have steered poor Simon through any crisis.

Perhaps he was wrong. Perhaps a revision of his rules was needed.

Maybe he should scrap the rules.

Maxime tried to steer his brother's cross-examination away from his last born. If he told Gunther anything, he would have to explain to him why Simon was so mad at his late mother.

"Maximus? What are you *not* telling me?"

Anybody who knew anything about the persistence of an almost-seventy-year-old Swiss man driving a rented twenty-eight-foot RV in a foreign country, disregarding the rules of the road and willing to make fun of well-armed U.S. patrol officers, knew that there was no other option. The unadulterated truth was required. Yes, sir. That much was for bloody certain.

So Maxime told his brother.

26

Three Baumann Men Attend A Funeral

Maxime was perplexed.

It was the second time that Sandro had knocked on his father's bedroom door, inquiring whether Maxime was ready.

Ready? Can one ever be prepared for this?

Maxime paced up and down his and Donna's bedroom, glancing at the bed. He couldn't make up his mind. On the bed were five suits, draped side by side.

The choice of the shirt had been straightforward: white. The shirt Maxime already had on—he only owned white collared ones, ten of them. He paced faster, in bare feet, without pants, hoping to find clarity.

He glanced at the bed one more time. Next to each suit lay five ties and five sets of matching socks. Maxime had discovered to his horror that he had no black tie or even a tie which was predominantly black. Wasn't it inappropriate to wear flamboyant ties to a funeral? And flashy socks? *What will people think? That I'm celebrating my spouse's demise?*

"Dad?"

"I'm *coming.*"

Sandro knocked again and poked in his head. "Oh, *shit. Sorry,* Dad." He jerked his head back but didn't close the door. *The poor man,* he thought.

"Are you okay, Dad?"

"Sandro …"

"Do you need help deciding?"

"How did you guess?"

"May I come in? We *have* to get going. Uncle Gunther's pacing has trampled open a footpath on the living room carpet."

Maxime pulled his still hesitant son into the room.

"Which one?" He pointed at the bed and plopped down into the armchair at the window.

Sandro studied the display for a moment and turned to his father. "You don't have any *quieter* colors?"

Maxime shook his head.

Sandro picked the black suit, a tie and pair of socks and passed them to his now silent father, who slipped them on.

Sandro found it impossible, though, not to laugh.

"What's so funny?"

"You should have seen yourself when I poked my head round the door."

"Don't you make bloody fun of me, Sandro Baumann," Maxime grumbled.

While Maxime fixed the knot in his tie, Sandro hung the other suits in the closet and put the socks and ties away. Gunther was calling.

"Coming!" Maxime hollered back.

Father and son joined the almost-seventy-year-old Swiss man in the living room.

"*Max.* You're okay?"

"Why shouldn't I bloody well be okay, Gunther? What *is* it with you and Sandro?"

Gunther and Sandro's eyes met, and they stepped back, waiting for Maxime to indicate when he was ready.

Columbus sat in the window, eyes fixed on the street. The humans apparently didn't understand his predicament.

Maxime stooped down and picked up the protesting cat. "I told you, Sandro. He thinks he's a *dog*. The only thing he doesn't do is wag his tail." Maxime scratched the squirming cat between the ears and tried to bury his face in the large cat's short fur, mumbling, "You miss her too?" But the animal bolted from his grip and returned to his post at the window.

Sandro and Gunther stood at the front door. "Dad? Can we *please* go?"

Maxime didn't move. He stared at the cat. "Sandro, do you think he knows?"

Sandro walked back into the room and took his father's elbow. "Come, Dad," he murmured. "You're right, Columbus is one smart kitty. How does one tell a cat something like this?"

Maxime followed his son. "No need to tell him anything— he's brighter than some people. He sensed it the moment we returned from the hospital."

He paused at the door. "Goodbye, Mr. Columbus."

Sandro drove the three of them to the church, glad they had made it this far. His father had insisted on a proper burial. First, there would be a church service, followed by the burial, or as his father had phrased it, "Laying your mother to rest." He would not hear of cremation. He had fumed at even considering not putting her body back into the earth, "where it belonged." His father had become lyrical about the incomprehensibility, as far as he was concerned, of wanting to place people's remains in a small metal container. "Or in a bloody *urn,* if you wish to call it that," Maxime had hollered when Sandro had tried to convince his father otherwise.

As far as he, Maxime Bastien Baumann, was concerned, the countryside lay wide open—there was lots of room. *Just look around you, Sandro Baumann,* he had demanded. *What do you see? Endless Prairie. Bloody endless frozen tundra. Surely, there is enough room to accommodate one more body?* And the ground wasn't even that frozen yet. Sandro had tried to explain that a traditional burial was so much more expensive. Maxime would hear none of it.

"Sandro, this is the least I can do for your mother. Her youngest wouldn't even attend her final journey. No, we'll do it in a proper way." That was the end of the discussion.

Sandro recalled the one rule even he knew by heart, number one on page two: *Accept what you cannot change.*

As the three of them walked down the aisle, Maxime wondered how the news had leaked out. The church was packed.

The whole bloody city is here. They loved you too, Donna.

He noticed in passing the faces of Mr. J. Johnson, his two junior colleagues, and Mrs. Long. They all raised a tentative hand in support. Mrs. Long gave him a brave smile. Maxime nodded in return. It was impossible not to notice Dr. Manie Moller. The Hawaiian shirt was gone; he was donned in a pristine suit and tie and took up half a pew by himself. A smile adorned his face, and he put out a hand to give Maxime a reassuring handshake. A flurry of movement caught Maxime's eye on the opposite side. The Vision. She had dressed appropriately in black, but the dress did a poor job of concealing her magnificent cleavage. She beamed at him.

Sandro pulled on his father's sleeve, mumbling something, and steered him down the reserved pew closest to the front.

And then, before Maxime knew it, the church service was over.

Maxime, as if unseeing, following Sandro and Gunther out of the church. He was aware of a throng of people around him, pushing and shoving to reach and touch and hug him to sympathize, but they seemed distant.

Lines from "Amazing Grace" ricocheted in his head:

> *Yea, when this flesh and heart shall fail,*
> *And mortal life shall cease,*
> *I shall possess, within that veil,*
> *A life of joy and peace.*

He had no doubt about the veil that had now draped itself over his life; about the joy and peace, he wasn't so certain yet. That much was for bloody certain.

He glanced around with blank eyes, shaking hands and mumbling, "Thank you, thank you. Thank you for coming."

He remembered only the one thing the pastor had said during the service. *All come from dust, and to dust, all shall return.* That much was so. *And that is why I will put you to rest in the earth, my sweetheart, back from where we came.*

It began to snow as they huddled together, close to the grave. Maxime peered at the gray sky, which changed to ivory as they stood there. He licked the flakes from his lips. The black suits, black dresses, and black hats turned white as the wafer-sized flakes drifted down from the heavens, from an apparently endless supply.

Maxime and Sandro took the lead as pallbearers from the hearse to the grave. Gunther positioned himself behind Maxime. Tears, burning behind his eyes, made Maxime stumble over the unevenness of the dirt hidden by the felt drapes as they neared the grave. Gunther steadied the slumping figure of his brother. With precision they maneuvered the casket, first resting it on the frame, then, stepping wide on each side, moved it carefully forward to rest it on the two broad automated straps.

Sandro walked around, opened his umbrella and positioned it over his father's stooping head. He pulled his father close with a firm sideways hug.

The snow blotted out the viciousness and finality of the mound of dirt behind them. Even the symmetrical rows of headstones all around them appeared less grim and inevitable. The green felt-drapes lining the borders of the gaping hole had turned white—a rectangle in white. Virgin blank—pure, without blemish, without stain.

The minister's voice droned on.

Donna, he's talking about you. About us. About the boys. About joy and hope and peace and eternal life. Oh, sweet Donatella.

The handful of earth that Maxime sprinkled on the coffin as it cringed into the earth was damp; dirt mixed with snowflakes.

"Auf Wiedersehen, mein Schatz," Maxime murmured before he turned around and allowed Gunther and Sandro to lead him back to the vehicle.

27

Maxime Receives An Unexpected Visitor—A Tragedy Avoided

Maxime was worried.

It seemed he had lost his influence on humankind. No one paid him any attention anymore. Donna had led this troublesome phenomenon. He had become obsolete.

It was barely ten a.m. He had just turned up his driveway, watching Columbus, who still sat in the front window. The cat might as well be nailed in place. Mr. J. Johnson had sent Maxime home. Maxime had stayed home the previous day, on the insistence of Sandro and Gunther, but had decided this morning to go to the office. "To sort things out," he had claimed.

Maxime dared not tell them he couldn't stand the empty house, the half-empty bedroom. He had never seen Mr. J. Johnson so determined as this morning—he had walked into Maxime's office, took him unceremoniously by the arm and accompanied him to the front door of Johnson, Johnson & McBride. "Go home, Maxime," he had said. "There's a time for work. There's a time for grief. That time is now. Go."

As soon as they had returned from the cemetery, Maxime had tried to convince Gunther and Sandro to return to Switzerland and Vancouver, respectively. Not that he didn't appreciate their presence, but he needed alone time. Both men had laughed at his request—literally laughed in his face. Maxime was hurt.

Anybody who knew anything about losing your life partner of thirty-seven years knew this was not a time to sit idle at home and play with your multicolored socks. That was why he had insisted on going to the office. He could bury himself in work. Escape. Create some distance. That was why he had tried so hard to send the others back to their respective homes. He didn't have the strength to face that sorry cat, who refused to eat, demanding to know what happened to his mistress. Things were *simple* at the office.

And Simon—he was beyond the dead, beyond the reachable. He had driven a spike through Maxime's chest when he had turned and walked away that day in the ICU.

Maxime filled the kettle, turned it on and scooped Columbus into his arms. The feline had entered the kitchen with reluctance, clearly indicating that Maxime was his second choice. Maxime paid his attitude no attention. The cat was losing weight. He might have to force-feed the beast. But they had the house to themselves—Sandro and Gunther had opted to go cross-country skiing. Gunther had become a nuisance, bursting out of his skin with pent-up energy, so Maxime, out of frustration, had suggested this. They'd be at least another hour, Maxime guessed. They would be tired: before they'd left, they had shoveled his driveway, as well as that of old Mrs. Nightly across the street, and had waved him goodbye with great fanfare.

Maxime squatted down at the little kitchen table, coffee in the one hand and Columbus in the other.

Columbus, for the most part, was open to any friendly advance. It did not suffice anymore to lie at his master's feet. Closer human contact was required. This weird guy with the funny socks who always refused to pick him up when he had on a suit, now had to do. And, since his mistress had forsaken him, he had only to meow, and he was in the man's arms. It was better than sitting in the window like a bloody idiot the whole day, waiting.

The doorbell brought master and pet back to the present.

"What the bloody hell?" Maxime muttered. "I don't have time for these fundraisers. I have enough Girl Scout cookies to last me a decade. And I gave to the Red Cross last month." Maxime dropped the cat and plodded to the front door.

He swung the door open, sucking his breath as a frigid wind wafted in—he was ready to give the caller a telling off. Instead, he closed his mouth and took half a step back. It was a man in an expensive suit and winter coat—well fitted—in his early fifties, perhaps even late forties. He was as tall as Gunther.

The man stood his ground, blowing white plumes.

"Can I help you?" Maxime finally offered.

You're wasting my time, buster with the fancy coat.

The man moved for the first time and cleared his throat. "You must be Mr. Maxime Baumann?"

"Yes." Maxime shivered and closed the door on the stranger who couldn't make up his mind.

The man lurched forward. "Mr. Baumann! *Please.* I need to speak to you."

Maxime let the door open again—a hand-width. It was bitter cold.

Have I seen you somewhere?

"Mr. Baumann, I'm Donat Drabik. Your wife, Donna, works at our chiropractic office. Well, I mean … she *used* to work there. Until …" For the first time, his voice faltered.

That's where I saw you.

"I'm so sorry about your wife… about Donna. May I please come in? I *must* speak to you."

Maxime stepped back without a word, opening the door wider. Donat Drabik stomped his feet on the doormat to free it from the snow, then stepped inside and took off his leather boots. Maxime knew a few things about fashionable clothing and footwear.

Italian boots—handmade. Vergelio. The loaded bastard. He must shop in New York or in Rome.

Maxime remembered his manners and ushered the man into the living room, indicating a chair. He didn't take the man's coat. The are limits to manners. He took a chair opposite the man he now presumed, based on his footwear, was the chiropractor. Maxime's back remained board-stiff. The hair on his neck stood erect.

So you must speak to me?

Maxime waited. He had no intention of making it easier for his visitor, in spite of his thirty rules. There are rules, and there are principles. Donat Drabik being here felt like a principles thing.

Donat Drabik leaned forward. He cleared his throat a second time.

The poor man must have a postnasal drip. I should refer him to Dr. Moller.

"Mr. Baumann, did Donna... Did your wife tell you anything about me?"

"I know you're her boss. That's about it."

"Yes, that's correct. But did she tell you about *us?* She said she was planning on doing so..."

"*Us?*" Maxime bolted upright. "*Us,* as in the *two* of you? *My* Donna and *you?*"

Donat Drabik also rose. He stood two inches taller than Maxime. He nodded and raised his hands as if that could explain what had remained unsaid.

Maxime stepped forward.

Stick to the rules, Maxime. Be true to yourself. Don't ever tell a lie. Work hard. Don't take what doesn't belong to you. Consider all your options. Always. Show respect for other people. Never eat charred meat. Your nose does not belong in other people's business. Never be jealous of assholes.

By the time Maxime reached rule eleven on page one, mere inches separated him from Donat Drabik. Never mind the rules. Maxime was pissed off.

He waved with his hand as if to brush off common sense. A wave of fearlessness washed over him: another unfamiliar emotion. Maxime thought of Donna, of Simon, of Sandro, of Gunther and Mr. J. Johnson.

Was *this* what Simon had tried to tell him about? About his mother and this man?

Donna? You and this dandy?

"Did you *touch* her?" he said to the man's face. "Did you *ever* touch her? *Intimately?*"

Don't take what doesn't belong to you. Donna? You knew that rule, darling.

Never be jealous of assholes. Donat Drabik is an asshole.

Donat Drabik scuttled back and kept his hands in front of him. "Mr. Baumann, let me explain, please. It happened over two years ago—"

"So why the hell *now?*" Maxime lurched forward and grabbed Drabik's genuine lamb's wool coat. "She's been in the earth barely forty-eight hours, her body not even cold, and you have the nerve to come to my *house?*"

Drabik ripped his coat free of Maxime's grasp. But Maxime was faster and grabbed the chiropractor again, yanked him down and slammed into his forehead—right above the man's eyes.

Donat Drabik hollered, and the two men stumbled apart.

"Mr. Baumann, let me *explain!*"

"There is *nothing* to clarify!" Maxime shouted. "You … *raped* my wife, then have the nerve to come to my house. With … her barely two days cold."

"Mr. Baumann, I *did not* rape her. It was consensual. I loved her."

"Consensual ..." Maxime choked, then began to cry. Dry sobs shook through him. When he touched his hand to his eye, he saw red: his forehead was bleeding. But that was nothing. He leaned forward, resting his hands on his knees. His breathing came fast. *The asshole. The asshole. Donna? Oh, Donna.* He raised his chin and glared at Drabik, who had backed farther away.

"Did you have *sex* with her?"

"Mr. Baumann, that was two years ago ..."

Donna? He says he loved you? He touched you ... everywhere. This man says he's been inside you. I thought what we had ...

Maxime righted himself, took the ironed handkerchief from his pocket and pressed it against the cut. Then he brushed past Donna's ex-lover and marched into the kitchen, to where the big kitchen knives lived in a sturdy wooden stand next to the stove. He took his time picking the biggest, sharpest one. The knife was well balanced. He was ready. He flung himself around, knife in position.

Donat Drabik had followed him into the kitchen.

Does the man have a death wish?

The inside door to the garage opened with a ping, and the voices of Sandro and Gunther washed over him. Maxime looked at the butcher's knife in his hand.

Mein Gott. What am I doing?

The skiers laughed and gibed as they shook their wet clothes off in the mudroom.

"Dad?" Sandro called.

Maxime glanced at Drabik, returned the knife to its rightful place in the knife stand and stomped over to a chair at the small table in the breakfast nook where he plopped down.

"Dad!"

Maxime gestured Drabik toward the front door. "Go," he whispered. "Just go." Then he called out, "In *here,* Sandro!" He bent down and picked up a frightened Columbus, burying his face in the velvet fur. He pulled the startled animal into his neck.

Sobs shook his muscular frame as the front door clicked shut.

28

Mr. J. Johnson, In His Private Capacity, Entrusts A Letter To Maxime

Maxime wept.

Gunther Baumann had difficulty recalling the last time he had seen his brother cry. It has been, he thought, in primary school. Maxime hadn't cried at Heidi and Clara's funeral. He was sad for Gunther's sake, but that was about it. At Donna's service and burial, the other day, he had solemnly kept to himself, shedding no tear in public—an example of stoicism.

But now this. Perhaps it was what Mother had meant years ago when she told her boys about "delayed shock."

"*Maximus*." Gunther knelt down next to him.

"Dad!" Sandro was ready at his other side. "I thought you were laughing."

Columbus gave an anxious meow and escaped the embracing arms. This guy with the funny socks had gone weird. He'd better retreat to a safer distance until the man had stabilized.

"Dad?"

"Maximus?"

Maxime's glance shifted between Gunther and Sandro. He wiped his nose with the back of his hand. "I almost *killed* a man." He shuddered as he rose. The cut on his forehead had started bleeding again.

Sandro lurched forward. "You're hurt, Dad. What did the man *do?*"

Maxime brushed him off. "It's *nothing.*" He sniffled louder and chuckled through his sniffling. "I didn't realize chiropractors' heads are that bloody hard."

"*Dad.* Did you *head* him?" Sandro whistled. "So the fancy C63 parked on the street belonged to him?"

Maxime nodded as he dabbed his cut with the now stained white handkerchief.

"What did he want?" Sandro asked.

"He came to tell me he was in love with your mother. That he had ... sex with her ... all dressed up in his fancy Italian hand-made bloody leather boots."

Maxime broke down once more. He cried for Donna. He cried for Heidi and Clara. That had been twelve bloody years ago. He cried for Simon. He cried because he had broken so many of his thirty rules during the past thirty years. He cried for himself, and then he cried for Donat Drabik, that he didn't kill the man when he had the opportunity. And then he cried more because that would have been so wrong.

Sandro boiled the kettle, and Gunther rummaged through the pantry until he found a forgotten bottle of whiskey. Only after the second spiked coffee did Maxime settle down. Anybody who knew anything about sharp kitchen knives knew that one could easily kill another human with them when in a terrible rage. Best to put those sharp things away—in a safe place—perhaps even inside a safe. That was for bloody certain.

That same evening, Sandro and Gunther, on Maxime's insistence, helped him wrap each of the six butcher knives in a dishtowel and slip them into a flat cardboard box. The box went straight into Maxime's safe in the bedroom. Once the six knives had found a secure storage space, there was little room left in the steel box. But Maxime was satisfied.

Gunther and Sandro stayed for another week. Every morning, they dragged Maxime out skiing for at least an hour, then to the gym in the afternoon, for a second grueling session. Maxime rebelled at first. Toward the end of the week, he silently rejoiced. He was so exhausted by early evening that he had no energy to think, and he slept like a newborn. He slowly got his groove back. By the fifth day, it was Maxime who raced against and coaxed the others. And, every day, on the way back from the gym, they would drop in at the coffee shop for a fix of hot caffeine (without any banana loaf slices), and long conversations.

Maxime and Gunther dropped Sandro off at Departures at six, Sunday morning. Sandro was now the one to wipe away a tear. He would miss this dogged, governed-by-thirty-rules Swiss man, whom he had never before seen so brittle, so exposed—naked in his sorrow—but also so resolute. The week had filled and cemented the gaping holes that had developed in recent years in their once rock-solid bond. He stepped closer and pulled his father to him with force. He loved this man.

Maxime returned the hug, then patted his son's back and ruffled his hair. He had last done this in public when he had dropped Sandro off for kindergarten.

Both men's eyes were moist.

By six that same evening, the older brothers Baumann were back in the Departures hall. They had just dropped Gunther's bag off at the counter. Maxime gave Gunther his best rib-scrunching hug, and his brother allowed it, grinning, only to, the next moment, lift his newly widowed brother right off his feet, squeezing the air from his chest.

"Gunther, *du bist in Canada.*" Maxime protested.

"Oh, Maximus. What *will* the people say? I'll miss you, Max." Gunther's booming laugh echoed through the hall as he returned the flustered Maxime to a stable upright position.

"Will you be okay?" Gunther held his sibling at arm's length, not laughing anymore. The PA system announced that boarding had commenced for his flight. He shrugged. "The kitchen knives will remain under lock and key, Maximus?"

Maxime grinned. *"Ja, ja. Mir geht es gut. Auf Wiedersehen, mein Bruder."*

"Auf Wiedersehen, Maxime."

Maxime waved until the Security line-up at customs swallowed his brother's lanky figure. He stood there for another five minutes and scrolled through the rules in his mind, giving much thought to number four on page two: *Remember the worthwhile things. Write them down.*

There was so much to write down. How did one write down the thirty-seven years with someone? Donat Drabik was an asshole. He wouldn't write anything else about him. And the past week with Gunther and Sandro had given him so much new material—he would write about that as well. For now, he would go home to Columbus.

The next morning, Maxime returned to work. He had been up half the night, writing.

Mr. J. Johnson immediately stopped by his office. He gave him a handshake and a penetrating once-over. "Welcome back, Maxime. I see you've followed my advice."

"Mr. Johnson?"

"You look more human, much less like a ghost, Maxime. But wait—I'm becoming sentimental. We've both got work to do. Drop by my office before you go home today."

And that was the end of that.

Life goes on, Maxime realized as he ushered his first client of the day into his office. Then he paused for a moment. It was monumental. Mr. J. Johnson hadn't called him "Maxie." He wondered whom he should thank for that.

It was close to five when Maxime knocked on Mr. J. Johnson's office door.

"It's open. Come in, Maxime."

Maxime sat down. "Mr. Johnson?"

"This is not business, Maxime. Well, not strictly speaking. I have a letter for you."

Maxime took the letter. His name was written in pen on the front: Maxime B. Baumann. He recognized the handwriting. It was an official Johnson, Johnson & McBride envelope.

"You're not going to open it?"

"Not now, sir. You want to tell me about it?"

Mr. J. Johnson came from behind his desk and joined Maxime on the other leather sofa. "Donna brought it to me, a little over three weeks ago." Then he paused, as if uncertain of how to proceed.

"Mr. Johnson?"

"She was vague," he said. "I have not read the contents of the letter. She asked me to take it into my safe keeping. Claimed she'd explained everything in the letter to you. She was planning on discussing it with you at the earliest opportunity, in person." He paused again. "Did she?"

Maxime shook his head. "The night before my brother and I left on our RV trip; she was adamant about something she wanted to share with me. I insisted that she tell me, but she refused. Said it had to wait till we returned."

"I am so sorry, Maxie ... I mean, Maxime."

"It seems to me we all carry secrets, Mr. Johnson."

"Do we, Maxime?" Mr. J. Johnson rose, unhurried. "I hope the letter doesn't cause fresh heartache, Maxime."

"I don't think so, Mr. Johnson. Goodnight, sir."

Maxime Baumann was confident the letter was about a certain Dr. Donat Drabik and how he had crawled into Donna's life. Anybody who knew anything about secret letters and secret lives and extramarital relationships knew that a simple letter couldn't hope to explain everything. It could never put things right. If it could be that simple, he would read a hundred letters.

The letter, secure inside the embossed Johnson, Johnson & McBride envelope, went, unopened, into the safe in Maxime's bedroom. He found a tiny spot for it on top of the flat box with the wrapped kitchen knives. The letter would be safe there.

Mr. J. Johnson was wrong. Maxime slept well that night. For the first time since Donna's aneurysm, he did not wake with a fever dream.

29

Maxime Takes A Stand And Visits His Grandchild

Maxime was worried.

Since his earliest childhood, he had dreaded asking permission. That had never changed—not in sixty years.

He felt terrible for thinking this, but Mr. J. Johnson refused to die. To make it worse, he loved the old man. He was so unlike his brother, Mr. C. Johnson. However, it seemed to Maxime, that the elderly gentleman had no intention of giving up the ghost. And as long as Mr. J. Johnson refused to expire, he also declined to stop working, which implied Maxime could never become the senior partner or, more importantly, retire. And that was that. Maxime had accepted this reality resignedly.

He had to approach his senior partner for consent for matters of importance—but also for something as trivial as visiting his new grandchild. Mr. J. Johnson wasn't even his boss—a laughable situation.

There was no question that he *had* to request time off. British Columbia and the Pacific coast particularly was 1600 kilometers away—unsuitable for a one-day road trip. A first grandchild was a momentous occasion. With Donna gone, he now had to play both grandpa and grandma. It *was* a big deal. Even if he flew there, it remained an expedition. That was for bloody certain.

But Maxime also knew that Mr. J. Johnson would be so disturbed by all this; there would be a relapse, and Mr. Johnson would start calling him "Maxie" again.

Maxime could hear him say, "Maxie, how do you think this firm will ever flourish if we all gallivant to our hearts' delight? Why don't you send the children a telegram, or perhaps an email? Or even better, why don't you Skype them? Isn't that what the young people do nowadays, 'virtual visiting?' Have you given the future any thought, Maxie? *Nothing* can replace good old hard work. Not if we want to get *ahead* in life, Maxie."

Maxime dreaded this.

He was convinced that Sandro and Michelle were going to have an Easter baby. He had done his research on Wikipedia, and even when he Googled it, he was left with only one conclusion: the baby was past its due date. Shouldn't they consider doing a Caesarean he had asked his son. Sandro had only laughed. *Dad, the obstetrician has his finger on the pulse. Michelle and the baby are both fine.*

Maxime had to accept this and wait, like everyone else. He wasn't great with waiting.

Then again, being called "Maxie" was perhaps not the worst thing that could happen.

If he had survived Donna's sudden demise and Donat Drabik's house call, stopping short of lethally wounding the man for confessing to the big betrayal, and if he could survive rejection by his younger son, perhaps he could survive being called a silly name by his senior partner.

Perhaps it was time.

Perhaps it was time that he, Maxime Bastien Baumann, took a stand.

It was time to retire.

Time to walk into Mr. J. Johnson's office and not ask permission to visit his grandchild, but hand in his resignation. Or at least give the man an alternative: he would take a sabbatical.

Rule fifteen on page one stated: *Listen to your heart.*

It was time.

On the first of March, Maxime approached Mr. J. Johnson's office. He had made up his mind.

"Mr. Johnson, I'm giving a month's notice. I'm taking a six-month sabbatical."

"A *sabbatical*, Maxime?"

Maxime knew that through all the decades of the existence of Johnson, Johnson & McBride, taking a sabbatical had been an unheard-of phrase—it was a foreign concept. No one has ever done it. Mr. J. Johnson's face said so.

"Mr. Johnson, my older son, and daughter-in-law in Vancouver are having a baby. I wish to be there."

"Maxime? Will our young guys, Foster and Friesen, manage? You've trained them well, I've noticed. But *six months?*"

"It's not only the baby, sir. I'm still getting over Donna. I was fine, initially, but lately … The empty house is spooking me. Perhaps I should also try and make peace with my younger son in England. While I'm there, I'll be close enough to pay my brother in Switzerland a visit."

Mr. J. Johnson was on his feet faster than Maxime had anticipated. He bolted around the desk, surprisingly nimble, and grabbed Maxime's hands. "I owe you an apology, Maxime. I should have been more observant, my friend. Don't worry. We'll keep the fort. I'll read Foster and Friesen their rights. It's about time those two stepped up to the plate." He winked at Maxime, "The training wheels are coming off."

While Maxime waited at the carousel for his bag at the Vancouver International, he received a text from Sandro.

Sorry, Dad. Change of plans. Please take a taxi to the hospital. Michelle's in labor. The baby couldn't wait. Greetings, Oupa!

I'm nobody's Oupa, Maxime muttered—*not yet. These airport people better come up with that suitcase if there's a baby in the process of being born.*

The carousel hadn't even come to life, and already the impatient passengers were pushing and shoving to get a first-row vantage point around the periphery of the luggage disperser.

"Bloody imbeciles," Maxime murmured, keeping three steps back. *Hoodlums. No respect for senior citizens. Just as well I followed Gunther's recommendation of attaching six orange neon name-tags, on every clip and handle of the bag. We'll see who spots their bag first.*

Afterward, Maxime relaxed in the back seat of the Prius cab, his large bag with the six bright name tags on his lap. He had just given the driver his destination when his phoned pinged again.

Dad, she's fully dilated. Hurry. S.

Too much information, Sandro. When you and your brother were born, the nurses wouldn't even allow me into the room, never mind keep me informed about the status of my wife's cervix.

In spite of himself, Maxime leaned forward and tapped the protective transparent shell separating him from the driver.

"Excuse me, sir. My son and his wife are having a baby. It's going to be born any minute. Can you *please* drive faster?"

The driver shrugged. *"Dādā jī?"*

"*Yes*. It's my grandchild. Please *hurry.*"

The driver grinned back. "I know a shortcut. Fasten your seat belt."

The engine whined as the driver accelerated, flinging Maxime with his orange-name-tag-festooned case into the soft leather backrest. Maxime pushed the bag down to the floor and wondered for the hundredth time why he had refused to let Sandro tell him the sex of their unborn child. At least this city council believed in synchronizing traffic lights.

"Sometimes, you surprise even me, Maxime Baumann," he mumbled. So much for your bloody sixth rule on page two. *Don't be late. Never.* As if that would be of any help to him now. *It is what happens when you try to be a smart aleck and fly standby for a cheap seat.* Maxime had missed out on a seat on an earlier flight and had to wait for the next trip. When he had made these financially sound calculations, Michelle had not been in labor. Her due date was in five days' time. *Bloody fetuses that can't wait like respectable citizens to make their appearance.* He or she was probably hollering his or her little lungs out by now, too glad to join the rest of civilization in the big, wide world.

Maxime bundled several twenty-dollar bills into the surprised driver's hand as they pulled in at the Emergency drive-through.

"Thank you, for driving faster," Maxime called out as he extracted his case from the back seat.

"Enjoy the new *grandson,*" the driver beamed as he waved and pulled away.

Grandson? How would you bloody know?

Maxime flung his carry-on over his shoulder and pulled the orange-tagged bag behind him. It bounced along as he strode through the main entrance.

The three floors in the elevator were a prolonged punishment. It reminded him of his garage door.

When he reached Labor and Delivery, Maxime was halted by a clerk with her brows in a knot—she insisted on knowing his reason for being there. Maxime had to wipe the perspiration from his brow, at a loss for words. The young lady, however, wouldn't budge.

Neither would Maxime. "But it's my *grandchild.* You *have* to let me through. He or she must have been born minutes ago. The child belongs to Sandro and Michelle Baumann. Baumann: two *n*'s."

"Sorry, sir. I *have to* get verification from the parents first. Please wait here."

"But *Miss.*"

"*Dad.*"

Maxime spun around. Sandro ran toward him, arms wide open.

"*Now* can I go in?" Maxime raised his brows at the clerk. She pouted her lips in return. Rules were rules.

"Come see your grandson, Dad."

"*Grandson?*"

"Yes. *You* were the one who refused to know. Come and meet Donald Maxime Baumann."

"*Donald?*"

"Absolutely. Mother would have been proud. It's in honor of his grandmother, an exceptional lady he'll never have the privilege of getting to know."

Maxime was getting used to weeping in public—though in a more discreet fashion.

In the room, his glance swept from proud father to proud mother, and back to the purple-pink face in his arms. Anybody who knew anything about being married for thirty-seven years and then becoming single overnight only to wind up holding a little bundle that groaned like a newborn pup knew that it was impossible to keep up a stern demeanor, and not shed a tear. Maxime Baumann wasn't carved from stone. That was for bloody certain.

"Hello, Donald," he crooned. "I'm *Oupa* Maxime."

30

Maxime's Daughter-In-Law Calls Him From Vancouver

Maxime was ticked off.

The phone had woken him. It was in the middle of the night as far as he could tell. First the landline, then his cell phone wouldn't stop ringing. He ignored the calls. Even two pillows over his head didn't help. The caller only tried again. And again.

They are not giving up, Maxime.

He patted around on the nightstand in the dark and scraped his phone closer. Anybody who knew anything about being a law-abiding citizen and decency and a proper time to call people should still be asleep at this ungodly hour. That much was for bloody certain.

"*Yes?*"

"Dad? Sorry for the impossible hour."

Maxime dragged himself upright. It wasn't the boys. It wasn't his brother. The voice belonged to a young woman. He glanced at the alarm clock: 4:04.

"Dad, it's Michelle."

"*Michelle.* What on earth? Where's Sandro? And the baby? Something the matter with the little fellow?" It had been only two weeks since Maxime had left baby Donald with his parents behind in Vancouver.

His daughter-in-law gave a shrill laugh. "The baby and I are fine. It's Sandro. He's ill with pneumonia—admitted to the hospital."

"But he was fine when I left. He only had a cold."

"Your son takes after his father—stubborn as a donkey. Sorry, Dad, but it's true. I had to threaten him to get him to the doctor."

They had thought it was only a result of the lack of sleep with Donald's birth and being new parents and a simple cold that wouldn't go away. It had started with terrible exhaustion spells, even during the time Maxime was still there. "He's an excellent actor, your son. On top of being a brilliant architect."

The night Maxime had left, Sandro had developed a high fever and received antibiotics the following day. For a few days, he got better, and that was when he had the first nosebleed. The coughing only got worse, often ending in him either bleeding from his nose or coughing up blood. It went on and on—for days. She had to put her foot down. She insisted the doctor admit him to the hospital. That was the day before yesterday. They had just moved him to isolation.

"I didn't know what else to do, so I phoned you. I don't know what's going to happen to Sandro—" Michelle's voice broke.

"Why didn't you phone me *sooner*?"

"I thought it was only a bad case of bronchitis. He had it a year ago. And Sandro didn't want to alarm you."

"What does the doctor say?"

"*Doctors.* They're not sure yet. They've done *hundreds* of tests."

"I thought you said it was pneumonia. Doesn't he only need an X-ray? And why the isolation?"

"Apparently to protect *him*." Michelle giggled, half hysterical. "What *he* has is not contagious. It's something to do with his bone marrow. Something with his immune system ..."

"It's not *tuberculosis*?"

Michelle snorted. "*No.*"

"Can I speak to him?"

For the second time, his daughter-in-law lost her composure and couldn't answer. Maxime could hear her quiet sobbing.

"Michelle?"

"I told you ... they've put him in *isolation*. He can't come to the phone."

"Michelle, *listen*. I'm coming as soon as I can book a flight. Does Simon know?"

"I think so. Sandro spoke to him this morning ... Yesterday morning."

"But that was before the doctors knew what was going on?"

"I don't know what he told Simon." She paused, then added, "In spite of everything, the two of them are close. They'll sometimes talk for hours. Contrary to what you may think, Simon misses his mom."

"He hates her."

"No, Dad. Disappointment and hate aren't the same things. Both the boys were close to Donna. I'm sorry—to their mom. I always knew Sandro was, but I only now realize the same was true for Simon."

Maxime sighed. *Yes, she didn't have thirty blooming rules to mess up her life and those near and dear to her.*

Maxime said goodbye to his daughter-in-law, then phoned his son in England.

There was no answer, and he left a message, choosing his words wiser this time: "Simon, it's Dad. Please phone me when you get a chance. I'm flying to B.C. as soon as I can get a vacant seat. Michelle tells me Sandro spoke to you. Talk to you soon."

For a moment Maxime considered phoning Gunther as well, then decided against it. Better to get the story from the doctors in Vancouver before he alerts all the King's men. No need for unnecessary hysteria. Perhaps it was, after all, only a bad case of bronchitis.

He had less trouble flying standby later that morning. For a moment or two, Maxime thought the flight personnel recognized him—he was becoming a frequent flyer to the Pacific coast. But it was only their usual effervescence. The cab driver dropped him off with his single carry-on outside the main entrance to the hospital. According to Michelle, Sandro was in the Internal Medicine unit—the fifth floor.

Maxime found the interrogation less intense this time when he presented himself to the unit's front desk.

Yes, Mr. Sandro Baumann had been admitted there. And no, Mrs. Baumann had gone home. With the baby. Yes, the baby was quite unhappy—he was fussy and cried without stop. Yes, he could visit his son, provided he followed the barrier protocol.

"Barrier protocol?" Maxime asked.

"*Come*, Mr. Baumann. I'll show you where your son is and *how* to do it." It was a new voice. A unit nurse wafted around the desk and took over from the clerk.

Maxime followed the nurse down an endless hallway. They walked for an eternity until they turned down a second hallway and walked for half an eternity before the corridor came to an abrupt end. To their left was the fire exit, and across the fire door, one last room.

He needn't be told: this room housed his son. Outside the door, a gleaming hospital trolley stood against the wall, next to an oversized disposable linen receiver and a similar-sized waste receiver. On top of the cart were various boxes with different sizes of disposable gloves, masks, overshoes and head covers.

Maxime eyed the trolley, transfixed, like Moses in the desert watching the burning bush. Fear prevented him from stepping any closer. It was hallowed ground. For a moment he pondered his choice of footwear. He realized that he didn't have a staff in his hand. He wished he had put on sandals that morning. He waited for the voice to address him from the burning bramble.

Only when the nurse cleared her throat did Maxime stir. "Sorry, Mr. Baumann. I should have introduced myself at the desk. I'm Nurse Ferguson. We'll probably see more of each other in the coming weeks."

Maxime, startled, shook her outstretched hand, then noted her almond eyes—they were gentle. *Weeks?* For the first time, he took in how her flowery scrubs hugged her full breasts. She was somewhere in her late thirties, perhaps forty, vibrant and trim. She reminded him of the Vision—but less intimidating.

"The disposable gowns are in these drawers. 'Large' is in the bottom drawer. You have to put on the gown backward—open end at the back."

She handed him a Large.

Nurse Ferguson noticed his hesitation and looked him in the eyes. "This must be quite intimidating, Mr. Baumann. I'll go in with you. I can check and see that he's okay."

Maxime, following her example, tied the gown behind his back and slipped on overshoes, a mask and a paper head cover. He was ready.

She paused at the door. "Your son may look different from when you last saw him."

Maxime stopped and cleared his throat. "Nurse Ferguson. What's *wrong* with my boy?"

"The doctors are not a hundred percent sure, Mr. Baumann. The bone marrow test was done only a short while ago. You'd better speak to the hematologist."

Maxime had had ample time to surf the internet while he had waited for his flight. "Does my son have *blood cancer?*"

"I can't answer that ..." The nurse lowered her eyes.

Maxime stepped forward and grasped her gloved hands, willing her closer. Her eau de toilette wafted at him as she gasped, her pupils large—inches from his face. He inhaled her warm body. Her chest heaved, almost touching his.

"*Please* tell me ... Does he have *leukemia?*" Maxime croaked the last word.

This is wrong. Nurse Ferguson shuddered and yanked her hands free. Her face was glowing—that was inappropriate contact. He was strong, this distraught father. But he didn't mean her harm. His face was too vulnerable for that. *How could an old man have such an effect on me?*

Nurse Ferguson spun around without a word and entered the isolation room.

31

Maxime Visits His Son

"**M**r. Baumann, you have a visitor."

"Dad!"

"*Sandro.*"

Maxime grabbed the outstretched hand and leaned in to hug his son, careful not to dislodge the intravenous line. The next moment his son's strong arms took him by the shoulders and pulled him in for a proper bear-hug. Maxime, unprepared for the enthused manoeuvre, ended up halfway on the bed as he struggled to regain his balance. Sandro laughed boisterously at his father and the equally surprised nurse.

"Glad you could come, Dad. Once the kind nurses and doctors finish these antibiotics, we'll have the pneumonia kicked in the butt, and I'll be out of here."

Sandro glanced from his father to the nurse, who said nothing but busied herself with taking his vital signs. Maxime looked out the window, scared his son might read the truth in his eyes. It was easier to inquire about the hospital food while peering outside.

He stepped further back to give the nurse room to complete her observations while he observed his firstborn. Perhaps it was the artificial light, but the boy had a distinct pallor to him. It was hard to tell, but it seemed he had unfamiliar red freckles on all his exposed skin. A bruise the size of a child's palm covered his free hand.

Nurse Ferguson was satisfied. She straightened and turned to Maxime. The almond eyes bore into him—they were unreadable. "It was a pleasure meeting you, Mr. Baumann." Then she nodded at Sandro with a smile, "Mr. Baumann." A moment later she was gone.

Maxime pulled a chair closer and sat down next to the bed. He touched his son's hand with his gloved hand.

"Fill me in, son."

Sandro gave his version of the past four weeks, since the arrival of little Donald. For the most part, it kept up with what Maxime had already learned from Michelle. Sandro infused his version with sunny days and happy memories. The unfamiliar signs and symptoms of his illness were only inconveniences, as far as he was concerned. The doctors had to stamp out his chest infection, and that was that. Simple. Similar to dealing with a city bylaw—an inconvenient stipulation. A little pain in the ass. Just a small modification of the sketches, alterations to the plans, and *voilà*.

"What did the *doctor* tell you?"

Sandro looked at him, his brows furrowed. "Dad?"

"Didn't he say *anything* else? Besides pneumonia? What about the nosebleeds? Is there a *connection*?"

"Dad, as far as I know, the official diagnosis is pneumonia."

"Michelle said you coughed up blood."

Sandro laughed, shaking his head, then started coughing. He grabbed the right side of his chest as if to support his ribs. His pupils were large, his breathing fast and shallow.

Maxime was back on his feet. "Pneumonia, my bloody foot! Where's the call button?" He looked about for a cord or lead or anything familiar dangling from the wall behind Sandro's bed.

"Dad, calm down. You know Michelle—she loves making a mountain out of a boulder."

The second bout of coughs shook Sandro's frame. "It's okay. It's *nothing*. I'm fine ... *Here's* the call button."

Maxime pressed the red button with force. "Sandro Baumann," he wheezed, "I won't calm down. You need *help*." Then, more to himself, "If only you knew."

Maxime paced the room, his gaze shifting between his son and the door.

"Where *are* the nurses? They're taking their *bloody* time."

Maxime swirled around to face the door. Nobody. He couldn't make up his mind and turned back toward the bed and snatched the call button a second time where it dangled from the bed's side-railing. He pressed hard and long. Sandro had fallen back against his pillows, exhausted. In an unguarded moment, fear had flashed across his son's face before his eyes had fluttered shut. The smile was gone. His breathing was rapid again. He seemed paler than before.

For a second time, Maxime spun around. He'd find the nurses himself. His son needed urgent care. He barged toward the door, his paper gown billowing in his haste, and yanked the door open.

Immediately, he had to sidestep two incoming blue-clad figures, as if launched at him. The nurse in front must have pushed the door from the outside.

She stumbled forward with a shriek and a muffled curse.

Side-stepping nurse Ferguson, Maxime realized she was crashing toward the floor and reflexively put out his hands, steadying them both. Their bodies made full contact during the convoluted dance to remain upright. Her parted lips were inches from his as they clung together for a second. The voluminous gown was unable to hide her firm contours. As if stung, they jumped apart, but her clean scent lingered. Maxime's hands had unmistakably brushed across her breasts during the rescue effort.

"Mr. *Baumann*?" Nurse Ferguson gasped, her eyes burning into him, her chest heaving.

He stepped much farther away, allowing the second nurse entry. "Forgive me, Nurse Ferguson. I was alarmed by my son's condition." He gestured toward the bed.

The nurses examined Sandro while Maxime stood as far away as possible, against the far wall. He could not afford a third close encounter. She would report him—claim he's a pervert or something.

Anybody who knew anything about being concerned about one's son who had fallen deathly ill and about sudden movements through hospital doorways and bumping into beautiful women knew that he couldn't have helped himself the first time when he took her hands in the hallway. He had to know about the cancer. This second time was her bloody fault. She'd been as good as asleep, barging into a room like that.

Nurse Ferguson sent the junior nurse, Nurse Collins, to find a nasal prong for administering oxygen to their patient. She glanced at Maxime, her brows raised—the mask did a poor job hiding her glowing cheeks. Her chest rose and fell as she swallowed several times before speaking.

"Your son has a high temperature. His chest sounds worse than this morning. I'll get him something for the fever and also give him the additional oxygen. Then I'll page the internist to come see him, again."

Maxime nodded his appreciation and waited until the nurses had the oxygen tubing connected and had given Sandro some Tylenol. Once they had left, he pulled the chair closer again. He grasped Sandro's hand and squeezed. His son's eyes darted open, and a slow smile appeared.

"Dad. I *love* you …"

Maxime leaned closer, brought Sandro's bruised hand to his mask and kissed it.

The internist found father and son in the same position an hour later. The boy lay against the pillows, his breathing slower and more regular. He was asleep. The father, clasping his son's hand, was reluctant to let go.

"Mr. Baumann? Pleased to meet you. I'm Dr. Pauls, internist, and hematologist."

Maxime jumped to his feet and made room for the physician, shaking his gloved hand. Dr. Pauls had to be halfway between his age and Sandro's. He seemed as if he looked after himself. His handshake was reassuring.

"If you'll excuse me for a few minutes, Mr. Baumann? I need to examine and talk to my patient. We got most of the reports, the results back. Why don't you go down to the cafeteria and get some refreshments? Take a break—let's say, half an hour?"

Dr. Pauls waited. Maxime realized the man wasn't asking. It was a friendly instruction.

"Sure … doctor. I'll go find the cafeteria."

Maxime paused at the door. "Half an hour?"

Dr. Pauls nodded curtly and busied himself with his patient.

Maxime freed himself from the gown and other disposable paraphernalia. He took great care to place each discarded piece in the indicated receptacle. He'd prefer to stay out of any nurse's path.

It was a great consolation that these people followed a rule-book. He wasn't the only person in the universe who preferred to surround himself with structure, order, and guidelines.

Mercifully, only the unit clerk was at the desk. She gave Maxime directions to the hospital cafeteria.

32

The Internist Speaks With The Baumanns

Maxime returned to the endless hallway on the fifth floor, struggling to tie a gown behind his back when Dr. Pauls emerged from Sandro's room.

"Why don't you speak to your son, Mr. Baumann? I've discussed our findings with him. I have some documentation to do. I'll be back in fifteen minutes. Then we can review the situation and our options."

The man tapped his forehead in a salute and disappeared down the corridor.

Sandro looked up when Maxime entered. He raised a hand in welcome, but it plopped back down on the bed. His eyes were wet. He sniffled. Maxime was still getting used to people becoming all teary. He crouched down and took Sandro's hand.

"What did the man tell you?"

"He says I have *purpura*." Sandro pointed at his collection of bruises with a brave smile.

Maxime forced a grin. "I know. But did he say *why* you have those blotches?"

"I have the *Rinderpest*, Dad. I'm certain now. I have contracted the *Black Death*." He still smiled.

Maxime sighed. "I think they eradicated *Rinderpest* a few years ago."

"He said it's leukemia, Dad. AML."

"He told you just like that?"

Dr. Pauls and another hematologist, Sandro said, had visited him earlier, in the morning. They had shared their preliminary findings, but only after he, Sandro, had insisted on knowing. The doctor now had confirmed their earlier suspicion.

Sandro grabbed his hand. "*Acute* leukemia. How does one process such a thing? It's a *sentence,* isn't it, Dad? Only brave or profoundly ignorant people can unravel this in twelve hours. I'm neither. I need more than twelve hours ... perhaps twelve years. What about twelve *lifetimes?*"

"What did Dr. Pauls say is the plan?"

"He mentioned a few steps, some for now and some for later... said he needed to speak to you as well. We need to make informed decisions. He'll talk to Michelle tomorrow morning when she comes with Donald." Sandro choked up and wiped his eyes. "Dad... what about my little trooper?"

Maxime cringed and mumbled, "Donna, where are you when we need you? Your son needs you. Damn it; I need you."

Movement behind him made Maxime jump.

"Gentlemen." Dr. Pauls pulled up a chair.

So this is going to be a long story, Maxime thought as he sat back down and tried to find a comfortable position.

Dr. Pauls turned to Maxime. "Mr. Baumann, I've discussed the final results with your son." His glance shifted between father and son. "The clinical findings, lab results, and bone marrow tests all confirm our initial diagnosis. It *is* acute myeloid leukemia."

Dr. Pauls turned his attention to his patient. "This is how we're going to tackle your illness, Sandro. You have to understand, leukemia, specifically AML, is not your little friend. It's a dragon with seven heads. But it *can* be conquered. I'm not going to give you or your family false hopes—it's going to be a hard and long battle, especially the next six months to two years. There *are* individuals with AML who have survived ten years." He paused. "Others only get a few months."

"*Survived* ten years?" Sandro whispered.

"That's what you'll be able to do if we win the first battle, and continue winning. Become a *survivor.*"

"Doctor, what's the first plan of action?" Maxime asked.

"We're still waiting on the results of the genetic mapping of the leukemia cells, Mr. Baumann. So far, everything points to a more favorable picture of his AML cells, which means a better prognosis. He is young and was in excellent physical condition when the disease struck—that counts in his favor."

"And the treatment?" Sandro asked.

"I have to discuss everything with your spouse tomorrow. We prefer to have every team member on board. But we're aiming to start chemo in about forty-eight hours. We'll begin with the induction treatment. It's a course of two drugs, for ten days."

"What percentage of patients make the ten years, doctor?" Maxime had jumped to his feet. Remaining seated was impossible. He paced the room.

"Ten to twenty."

Maxime picked up his pace but glanced at the physician. Anybody who knew anything about Maxime Bastien Baumann and the significance of statistical probabilities knew that a 0.2 to 2 percent chance of a spinal headache had struck him, and this was five to ten times better. But in Sandro's case, it was about living and dying, not about a silly headache. That was for bloody certain.

Maxime halted mid-stride, recalling something he had read online while waiting for his flight. He turned to the hematologist. "What about a bone marrow transplant or a stem cell donation?"

"It depends on the genetic testing. Those *are* options. But it's no guarantee that they will work in Sandro's case."

Maxime sat back down. "Will the chemo be able to do the trick?"

"It usually does, but the drugs are going to make him extremely sick. We have to kill as many of the leukemia cells as possible. It will knock his bone marrow to the ground. We might need to give him transfusions."

"He's already sick."

Dr. Pauls straightened. "Mr. Baumann, I'm afraid this is what we have to do to get him on the twenty percent survivor list."

He opened his folder and handed Sandro a couple of pages. "Please read these, Sandro. It's about the two medications we're planning on giving you. Everything has side effects."

Dr. Pauls turned to go, then paused as if he had remembered something. "Sandro, if we *don't* do chemo, there's almost a hundred percent chance that you won't survive more than a few months. The drugs are potentially lethal, but they *can* increase your survival to between twenty and sixty percent. What I expect and hope will happen is that you will go into remission. We'll reassess a month after the chemo and on a monthly basis after that. The chances are high that you will relapse within three years. But if you can last at least eighteen months before worsening, you will do so much better. Then we'll do a salvage chemo course and prepare you for a transplant: marrow or stem cell.

Think it over, Sandro. I'll see you in the morning. If you consent, a physician will insert a special central venous catheter, through which the medications will be administered. Gentlemen, until later."

After the doctor had left, Maxime resumed his pacing. "Bloody medical people," he mumbled. "What's it going to be? Ten, twenty or sixty percent of surviving, or a bloody one hundred percent chance of dying?" Maxime turned to face his son, his index finger in the air. "I know," he declared. "We should take the *sixty percent* survival option, Sandro."

But Sandro was asleep. His pale body was propped high up on the pillows, his hair, matted to his damp forehead.

It's bloody unfair, Donna. You had a zero percent chance. Then again, with Sandro, we at least have a little fighting room.

33

A Phone Call To Switzerland

M axime stepped from the room, freed himself from the blue gown and unclipped his phone. It was time to inform Gunther. The signal strength in the long hallway was too weak and Maxime wandered down to the foyer where he sunk into one of the sofas. How would Gunther respond?

"*Maximus.*"

"*Hello*, Gunt." Maxime gave an involuntary shiver.

They bantered hence and forth, and Gunther shared how he and Mary had just returned from their ten-day Elbe River cruise, from Berlin to Prague.

"Max, you *have* to see the places we visited. We rented bicycles and cycled through every town where we threw anchor."

"One of these days, my brother… but first I need to find a girlfriend."

"Max, I'm such an idiot, babbling like a schoolgirl. Where are you? Back home?"

"I was, but I've returned to Vancouver. I'm phoning from the hospital."

"*Das Krankenhaus? Was ist loss?*"

Maxime sketched the past twenty-four hours. How it had started with Michelle's early-morning call. How disappointed he was with the children for hiding the seriousness of Sandro's condition. Sandro and even Michelle knew the rules. Didn't rule three on page one state: *Don't ever tell a lie*? Here was his son, in isolation with a terminal illness, and they didn't even tell him.

"Can you *believe* that? Not a word?"

"Maxime, they were in shock, in denial. And didn't you say the doctor just spoke to you and Sandro? It requires time to confirm a diagnosis."

"But still … They could bloody well have phoned me."

"Do you want me to come over, Max?"

"Would you?"

"*Definitely.* I would have loved for you to meet Mary, but she's preparing for a couple of races in six weeks' time. I'll ask, but I know the answer."

Maxime painted the bleak picture of what the coming two weeks had in store for Sandro if they decided to consent to the treatment. He continued with a detailed statistical exposition and explanation of the treatment options and probabilities of surviving the blood cancer.

"Max, do you think they *won't* consent?"

"The chemo can kill Sandro."

"Yes, it *can*. The cancer *will* if they don't treat it."

"*Gunther.*"

"Not to worry, little brother. I'll saddle the horses ASAP, find a plane, and get my ass over there."

"Thank—"

"Don't thank me *yet*," Gunther cut him short, "Before I say a definite yes, you have to swear solemnly."

"Gunt? It's bloody serious. We *need* you. Sandro will certainly—"

"Swear."

Maxime sighed. "Okay, I swear. *What*?"

"Promise you won't surprise me with another twenty-eight-foot RV in your driveway." Gunther's laugh boomed over the tiny speaker, and Maxime yanked the phone away.

He chuckled half-heartedly. "I solemnly swear, Gunther Baumann. Text me the details of your flight. *Danke schön, mein Bruder.*"

"My pleasure. *Wiedersehen,* Maximus."

As Maxime put his phone away, he felt eyes on him. Nurse Ferguson stood ten feet away, carrying a raincoat over one arm— she was on her way home it seemed. She appeared uncertain. It was easy not to recognize her. She looked different; chic, without her scrubs. The mid-thigh dress hugged her slim frame.

"Mr. Baumann." She took a step forward.

Maxime jumped to his feet. It was impossible not to notice her chest. "Nurse Ferguson. I owe you an apology. About… about first grabbing your hands and then later bumping into you like an idiot…"

A soft rose crept up her neck.

"It's fine now, Mr. Baumann. It wasn't my place to give you the diagnosis, and the second time was *my* stupidity." She grinned at him, then added, "I was on my way home. Your son ... Are *you* okay?"

Maxime nodded, not trusting his voice. Why did she seek him out in the foyer where he sat, far to the side? He swallowed and raised his hand.

Maxime Bastien Baumann, get your bloody head together. You're acting like a wimpy teenager, for goodness' sake.

"Can I ..." He swallowed again. His voice trembled. "Will you ... allow me to make it up to you? Coffee, perhaps?" He gestured at the cafeteria behind them.

Nurse Ferguson stepped closer, clutching her purse and raincoat. She reached out as if to touch his arm, then pulled back. Her eyes had turned a dark ebony. She nodded, turned and gestured for him to follow her.

At a cafeteria table, minutes later, they sipped their coffee in complete silence.

Maxime avoided eye contact and wondered what had possessed him to invite her. She was now definitely thinking him a pervert, or worse—a cradle-robber.

She's your son's nurse, you bloody idiot. It's called inappropriate fraternization with hospital staff. Then again, rule fifteen, page one, says: Listen to your heart. So, damn it, Maxime Baumann, perhaps you should pay attention.

When Maxime raised his eyes, he looked straight into two dark pools. He swallowed.

The eyes softened, and she smiled. "Thanks for the coffee, Mr. Baumann."

"I *owed* you."

She took another sip and glanced across the rim. "Do you *work out*, Mr. Baumann?"

Maxime raised his brows. "Nurse Ferguson?"

"I *know* you're not thirty-three anymore, but the sure way you prevented me, stopped *us*, from crashing to the floor could mean only one thing."

He shrugged and smiled.

She started telling him about growing up in the Okanagan Valley with her three sisters. About the fear of wildfires destroying the farm in the dry summer months. How she and her sisters learned to do everything that a male farmhand could do, only better. Maxime nodded, not saying a word, egging her on with his head. After completing school, she had moved to the coast where she started with nursing, and just never left. She married this smart young guy, a lawyer.

Maxime's glance dropped to her hands. She only had on a single ring, with a pearl, on her right hand.

She smiled up at him, pulling a face. "It couldn't last—he systematically suffocated me."

Maxime looked at his hands. He had removed his wedding band weeks ago. A pale ring of skin was still visible on his finger.

She followed his gaze. Their eyes locked.

"What's your first name, Nurse Ferguson?"

"Fanny." Her eyes challenged him.

"*Fanny?*"

"Frances. It became 'Fanny' when I was still little. In Greek, it means 'bright.'"

"And in the States it means …"

Her laughter bubbled over like tiny bells chiming. "Don't *go* there, Mr. Baumann."

"The Americans talk of a *bottom*."

Fanny Ferguson stuck her tongue out at him as a new wave of crimson crept up her neck. She grinned, glanced at her watch, and scraped her chair back, jumping to her feet. "Mr. Baumann, forgive me, talking all about myself. I *have* to go."

Maxime rose. She leaned forward and touched his sleeve. "Thank you for listening—and for the coffee."

Maxime inhaled her lingering scent, pushed his chair in and followed her with brisk strides.

"Nurse Ferguson … *Fanny* … Thank you, for back there." He gestured at the cafeteria. "I'm Maxime. With an *x* in the middle and an *e* at the end."

Again the tiny bells. Fanny tilted her head ever so slightly. "Goodnight, Mr. Baumann."

Maxime watched Nurse Ferguson float through the revolving door. Anybody who knew anything about bumping into alluring ladies inside a hospital doorway knew that it would be impossible to get off scot-free.

A price will have to be paid. The coffee drinking was innocent enough, but he wasn't certain about anything else. He could feel his blood pressure surge. Even his heartbeat had become unsettled. She was an awesome gal, but beyond his sphere of influence—he was an old geezer, like Mr. J. Johnson. That was for bloody certain.

34

Speaking To Simon

Maxime was worried.

Would Simon even speak to him? He dropped onto the same couch where Fanny Ferguson had found him. Clutching his phone, Maxime rested his head in his hands. He wasn't ready.

Stop being such a bloody coward.

Common sense fought a silent battle.

Maxime sighed. Then he dialed. His heart skipped twice—his son had picked up on the third ring.

"*Simon.*"

"Dad."

"Have you spoken to Sandro since he got admitted?"

Simon relayed the conversation he'd had with his brother. His sentences were succinct, staccato-like. But his voice gradually thawed.

"Have you made any plans, Simon?"

"I promised Sandro I'd come." Simon's voice climbed. "How could I *not* come?"

Maxime bit his tongue not to snap at his son, took several deep breaths, then recounted the meeting he and Sandro had with Dr. Pauls. He introduced Simon to the seven-headed dragon which, according to Dr. Pauls, had to be slain. Also to the fact that Sandro had now become a potential survivor.

"Potential?"

"He has a ten to twenty percent chance to survive ten years."

"That's *bugger all*," Simon groaned.

Maxime sighed as he explained that if they didn't start with the chemo soon, it would be zero percent in six months, never mind ten years. They could choose between a little hope and none at all. He and Sandro had marked the *little hope* box. The line went quiet.

Simon gave a dry sob. "Is he going to…?"

"Not on our watch. At least he's been given *some* fighting chance."

"Will it ever be enough?" Simon took several shuddering breaths, then started rambling about how he had met a girl a while ago. She was refreshingly different. A little intense, but during these dark months had become a beacon in his life, a savior. Many times had she dragged him out of the dreary pits. It all started four months ago when he gave a training course for the new program he had developed.

"Does she have a name?"

"Charlotte."

"Sounds English."

Simon gave a sob-like chuckle. Maxime had to meet her, he insisted, and see for himself. She was born and raised in Liverpool and was the VP of marketing at a new firm. A young lady with tons of guts. She was a cycling fanatic, did taekwondo, and was vegan.

"That's not very British, only eating leaves."

"*Dad.* Her dietary preferences have *nothing* to do with her nationality. She's super-fit, extremely healthy and über smart."

Maxime chortled, glad to not be talking about death for a moment. "Sharper than you? You're not too dumb yourself—"

"She's twenty-six and already a *vice president.*"

Maxime mumbled about high intelligence being incompatible with a lifestyle of eating leaves and hugging trees, that vegans were guaranteed to be malnourished.

Simon scoffed. "You're wrong about many things, Dad. She's a sweetheart with attitude—you'll see. Yes, it's a philosophy, but she's not extreme. She's more of a pescatarian."

Maxime choked. "A *what?*"

"She'll occasionally eat fish."

Bloody ridiculous—my soon-to-be-daughter-in-law has an eating disorder. Something has to be done. What will happen if they decide to have offspring? What will the poor little brats get to eat? I'll have to Wikipedia this condition. I've heard of Presbyterian and sectarian, but pesca-what?

"And what does young Charlotte think?" he said out loud. "Did your charm rub off?"

For the first time in the conversation, Simon gave a proper laugh. Charlotte was smitten, he said. Well, the point was, the feelings were reciprocal. The two of them hung out together, and it was fun to be with her. She made him happy. She challenged him, pushed him. He loved that.

The next moment Simon choked up again. "Dad, enough about Charlotte. What's going to happen to my brother?"

"This is *not* the end," Maxime said in as reassuring a voice he could muster.

"What if I'm too late?"

"Sandro's not *that* bad. I can pick you up at the airport."

"Did you rent a car, or did you drive there?"

Maxime chuckled. "I flew. I'll take a cab and come and get you."

"Stay with Sandro, Dad. There are hundreds of taxis waiting at the airport. I'm departing just before midnight, on a direct flight. Should be there before ten in the morning."

"But a direct flight is *double* the price."

"*Now* is not the time to go on standby for a cheaper flight. Not when my brother *needs* me."

Maxime bit his tongue a second time. *When your dying mother needed you, where were you, Simon Baumann? When we laid her cold body in the frozen earth, didn't you think we needed you?*

"But still—" Maxime insisted. *Didn't rule 27 on page two state—*

The phone in London was slammed down.

Maxime Baumann, you're a master asshole. The prodigal son confided in you about his new girlfriend, and you went ahead like a stormtrooper and hazed him about his own bloody money. You need to reread that book Donna gave you about winning friends. Congratulations, caveman.

Maxime dragged himself up to the fifth floor. Then he plodded down the long hallway, castigating himself for his spectacular performance in the father–son relationship arena. Maxime's stricken face was unable to hide the impact of the disastrous conversation.

35

Simon Arrives

Maxime's entire body protested.

He had refused to return to Sandro's house for the night. Instead, he had remained in the chair next to his son's bed, only to surrender during the early morning hours. He had pulled the remaining blanket from the closet and made a bed in a corner, on the floor, rolling his jacket into a pillow. He looked and felt like his crumpled jacket.

In the east, the new day arrived unhurried, painting ochre and gold across a grey horizon, high up into a pale sky.

Sandro's cheeks had more color than the previous evening and enough energy to chastise his father for declining the nurses' offer to have a sleeping chair brought into the room. Maxime mumbled something about how it would have been a bloody shame for the poor nurses to drag a cumbersome contraption into the room for a young man like Maxime. Disgraceful, it would have been. He was no invalid.

Maxime remained fidgety. "I have to run to your house but want to be back in time for Simon's arrival."

Sandro laughed as he waved his father out the door. "He won't be here until noon. Go take a shower and bring my sweethearts back with you."

Three hours later, Maxime accompanied Michelle and little Donald down the hallway toward the isolation room. It was an art getting them dressed in the mandatory barrier clothing—especially the little boy. The charge nurse had made it clear the previous day that an isolation room with access by barrier-clothing was no place for an infant. A comment at which Maxime had only shrugged his shoulders.

Today, when the three of them passed the unit's front desk, the nurse had jumped to her feet, but Maxime silenced her protestations about the child with a promise that the boy wouldn't stay long. Besides, he missed his papa and wasn't a baby anymore. A frowning Nurse Friesen peered at them with intent, particularly at the tiny boy in his mother's arms, a pacifier bobbing between his lips.

Maxime didn't wait for her final blessing. He gave the nurses a half-salute and steered his daughter-in-law and grandson around the corner. A junior nurse tagged along. Maxime missed the sizzling presence of Fanny Ferguson. She wouldn't have been so close-minded—although she would have reprimanded him with, "Rules are still rules, Mr. Baumann."

He returned to the foyer, satisfied—Sandro and his family needed some alone-time.

Maxime picked a couch close to the entrance—with hawk eyes he watched the revolving doors—scrutinizing every person who entered or left the building. *So this is what security guards do all day? Damn hard work, not losing one's concentration.* It required only a moment's distraction, and the person on your wanted list could slip through, undeterred and unnoticed. Although, perhaps their task was not so hard—they had closed-circuit cameras and monitor screens to aid them.

Maxime couldn't remain seated and paced the foyer. It was only a quarter to eleven. *Deep breaths, Maxime. It's still too early for Simon to be here.* He ambled over to the cafeteria for a newspaper. Back on the sofa, Maxime alternated now between reading a few lines and scanning the front doors every time a draft caught his attention. *If he's not here by twelve, I'll return to the ward and make sure he didn't sneak past me. It is possible to pick a different route to get upstairs.*

"Dad."

A man with a trimmed beard and shaven head towered over Maxime. Next to him, reaching his shoulder, stood a slender lady, her blond head cocked to the side. Simon? Charlotte? His son must have joined a motorcycle gang or converted to a secret cult.

Maxime snapped upright, immediately realizing his mistake. He stumbled, momentarily dizzy. Simon and Charlotte lurched forward, each grabbed an arm, steadying him.

Maxime, you imbecile. What will this girlfriend, the Pesca-something, think of you now?

"Dad?"

Maxime straightened to his full height and pushed out his chest, freeing his arms. Charlotte smelled lovely, and there was no doubt about her strength. *She'll whip your ass, Maxime Baumann.*

Maxime laughed as he shook his son's hand, pulling him in for a proper hug. It took several seconds of Maxime's persistence for his son's body to relax; only then did he hug his father in return.

"I'm fine, I'm fine," Maxime murmured. "I got up too fast."

He held out his hand to the girl. "Mind to introduce us, Simon?"

"Sorry. Dad, *this* is Charlotte. Charlotte, my Dad."

Her eyes reminded Maxime of thunder clouds, but lighter. Her handshake was solid. She held Maxime's gaze and grinned. *She's sizing me up, the little minx.* She was tough, but he might get to like her. No bullshit. That's good. The hair was colored, no question. *It suits her. Damn it, Maxime. Stop bloody well staring. You'll give Simon the creeps.*

"Dad, where's Sandro? Why are you down here? Have the doctors decided when they're going to start with the chemo? Is he *okay*?"

Maxime held up his hands, picked up the paper, folded it over and over, only to drop it on the coffee table. "Sandro's sick. He's pale, he has purple bruises all over—but he's okay, for the most part."

As Maxime navigated them toward the elevators, he had to drag information from his still reluctant son. Peace between father and son had not yet been made. The self-inflicted wounds still throbbed. Charlotte, however, filled him in on all matters trivial. She bubbled effortlessly, confiding that she had never been to Canada. But more important, she had come along to support Simon, since they saw each other now every day. It would be unimaginable to be apart for goodness knew how long. And he needed her—she added, turning crimson. Maxime only smiled.

When they reached the first hallway, Maxime turned to his son. "How did you describe her? 'Sweetheart with attitude?'"

Charlotte quipped, "*Careful* how you answer the question, Simon Baumann."

Simon grinned, embracing her. "You know that's why I like you. You've got *guts*."

Once they reached the isolation room, Maxime took the lead. He held out a size small for Charlotte, then scrambled through the bottom drawer for a size large for Simon.

"Remember, you have to put it on according to the book, or you'll have Nurse Friesen, the unit boss, blowing down your neck." Maxime demonstrated how to put it on correctly.

Before they entered the room, Maxime took Simon and Charlotte by the arm and whispered, his eyes moist, "Thank you for coming... Charlotte, thank you for looking after this tough guy, for bringing him back."

Simon murmured, "Dad, stop the theatrics ..."

Charlotte gave Maxime a peck on the cheek. "My pleasure, Mr. Baumann."

36

Sandro Receives His Ten Days Of Chemo

G unther arrived from Switzerland the following afternoon. Maxime, Simon, and Charlotte bundled into Sandro's van to greet Gunther at the airport, but only after father and son had reached an agreement on who should drive.

"Simon, *how* long have you been driving on the wrong side of the road?"

"Dad, that's irrelevant. It's like riding a bicycle. It's not brain surgery—it comes automatic."

"Automatic, my foot, I am *used* to driving on the right side of the road on *this* side of the pond."

"Dad, let's not make a scene," Simon insisted. "I'm much younger than you, I'm more alert, and besides, I've driven here before, and, *in* Sandro's van. Have you?"

Maxime had to surrender. All of Simon's statements were true. Simon knew bloody well that Maxime had never driven in

Vancouver, or in Sandro's fancy van. Rule ten, Maxime, rule ten. *Never be jealous of assholes. Even my son can be guilty of being one.* The thought brought great comfort to Maxime as he listened to Charlotte's chatter.

Maxime heard his brother's booming voice before he noticed him among the surge of passengers.

"*Maximus.*"

Maxime steeled himself for the onslaught and remained for the most part on his feet throughout Gunther's hug.

Gunther didn't recognize Simon, not until the younger man spoke.

Gunther bellowed, "Simon! *Der Junge ist jetzt ein erwachsener Mann.*"

The moment Simon had introduced his girlfriend, Gunther turned to Charlotte. "So *you* are responsible for turning him into a biker?"

She didn't flinch. "No, sir. He's no biker, but I made him join a skinhead club. He's the treasurer. They're a white-collar gang. Sophisticated—think high-class British mafia."

It wasn't often that Gunther Baumann's mouth gaped open in surprise. The next moment he laughed, leaned in and gave her an extra firm older-brother hug. She shrieked as her feet left the tiled floor. "Don't mess with my jet lagged brain, *Fräulein.*"

Sandro's ten-day chemo course started the next morning. For three days, the poison of choice would be anthracycline, followed by cytarabine for seven days.

He waited the first morning, propped up high on his pillows. The nurses would be there any moment. The previous afternoon, one of Dr. Pauls's colleagues had inserted a special intravenous line.

Sandro waited like a man on death would his last meal.

It was nurses, Friesen and Ferguson, who wafted in, gowns billowing. They brought the infusion pumps and bags of fluids and medication.

"Hello, *ladies*. Nurse Friesen—you did something with your *hair*. It looks *ravishing*."

The charge nurse was in her early fifties and subject to mood spells. She had, in fact, taken extra care with her appearance that morning, but it was impossible for the sick Mr. Baumann to know that—not behind her mask and cap and gown. He was taking a chance, she was certain. She still felt herself blush.

"Now, now, Mr. Baumann. We're here on serious business. We have to double check the drug before we administer it. You're a blatant liar, anyway. You can't see what I look like at all."

Ill or not, Sandro Baumann insisted, "Nurse Friesen—it's impossible to hide your beauty. Nurse Ferguson, don't you think Head Nurse looks special today?"

Fanny Ferguson laughed and arched her brows at her patient and superior.

"Ferguson," Nurse Friesen muttered, "don't encourage the man."

"Nurse Friesen," Sandro continued, "out with the truth. Did you put highlights in especially for this occasion? You shouldn't have. How will I get a wink of sleep tonight? I'll be dreaming about your flowing hair ..."

"Mr. Baumann, you'd better only be dreaming about your wife and little boy. Come, we have to *concentrate.*" Her blushing intensified as she primed the pumps.

The two bags, one a background infusion, had to be connected in a sterile fashion to the central venous catheter. This task fell on Nurse Ferguson.

The moment the nurse unclipped the right shoulder of Sandro's hospital gown to expose the transparent dressing covering the catheter port, Sandro called out, "Nurse Ferguson, did you notice I shaved my chest for the occasion? It accentuates my pectoral muscles."

Nurse Friesen mumbled to her colleague, "Get on with it, girl. Perhaps we should take the poor man's temperature. He's hallucinating."

Fanny Ferguson's and Sandro's faces were inches apart. She could feel the crimson rising to her cheeks. Unbelievable. The son had a similar effect on her as his father. With great care, she pulled the sticky covering free and made eye contact. Unlike his words, his eyes weren't mocking her. His dark eyes were warm and trusting, steadfast. The man had such sad eyes, though. His chest had indeed been shaved for the occasion. What was it with these virile Baumanns? Even sick and having lost weight, her patient still had well-contoured pectoral and deltoid muscles. *He must be a handsome man in a swimsuit.* Her blush intensified. *It's not good to be without a man in my life.*

"I don't know what you're thinking, Nurse Ferguson. Please tell. Was it wise to have shaved my entire chest instead of only a small area around the port?"

Fanny Ferguson chuckled.

Nurse Friesen grumbled. "Mr. Baumann, *cut* it out."

On the second day of chemo, Sandro's nausea started. The anti-emetics helped to a limited extent. The taste of bile remained in his mouth. As the days progressed, Sandro became weaker and sicker. Visitors were restricted. Nurse Friesen tightened the execution of her orders, day and night, demanding they were adhered to, especially when she was off duty.

Maxime realized by the fourth day that visitors would soon be *verboten*. He refused to return to Sandro's home, where he and the others from far away, had been staying. He would sit in the foyer watching the revolving doors for hours, then stagger up the stairs and down the long hallway to see if they would allow him to see his son. By day five, Nurse Ferguson had given orders that only the patient's spouse and father were allowed, but only one at a time, once a day.

"Sorry, Mr. Baumann. He's too weak to receive you. His immunity is gone. Please go home and get some sleep."

Maxime refused. He wandered up and down between the waiting room and the foyer.

On the sixth day, Gunther and Simon executed a mini-coup. With ample help from Charlotte, they convinced Maxime to leave his post in the hospital's foyer and join the three of them. They would take him back to Sandro's house in the suburbs where his daughter-in-law and grandson awaited his presence.

"Dad, *these two* also need you—Michelle and little Donald," Simon insisted once he got his dad alone at the house. "They *need* us. The hospital staff doesn't want us in Sandro's room. He's too sick …"

"I can't lose my son as well," Maxime pleaded.

"Dad, Sandro's not gone. Us being there might only make it worse. The nurses and doctors are taking care of him. Let's take care of one another here. We, the *living*."

"How *dare* you?"

"What's your problem, Dad? I love my brother, but us being in his room the entire time is not helping."

"Don't you *yell* at me, boy."

"I'm *nobody's* boy."

Maxime's face was inches from his son's. He could feel his heart pounding. He was light-headed. There was an odd pressure in his chest.

Gunther barged in on the yell-fest. "*Genug. Lieber Gott. Was ist loss?*"

Simon wouldn't back down, but Gunther towered over his nephew. "I *said* back off!" He turned to the still flustered Maxime, led him to a chair and made him sit. Gunther instructed Simon to find his girlfriend. The younger man trudged off like a schoolboy who had lost his first playground fight.

The ceasefire lasted throughout the evening. Before they went to bed, Gunther declared that they would all be going to the beach the next day, one way or another.

In the morning, Gunther summoned his brother, his brother's son, and the son's girlfriend, insisting that formal peace is made—the only way they could enjoy the day.

"Simon Baumann," he said, "*Apologize.*"

"I did nothing wrong, Uncle Gunt. My dad—"

"*Genug.* Apologize!"

Simon mumbled incoherently.

Gunther turned to his brother. "You too, Maxime Baumann. Apologize. Now."

"Sorry, Simon. I've been an asshole—"

"Now kiss and make up," Gunther instructed.

Neither of the men moved.

"Oh, give your father a blooming bear-hug, you bearded *skinhead!*" Gunther insisted.

In the end, it was Maxime who initiated the hug, but without conviction. He was simply too pissed off. It felt like the time his son had walked out on him and Sandro when Donna's body lay in the ICU.

Charlotte stood next to Gunther and made eyes at Simon whose arms hung limply around his father—she pleaded reconciliation. Simon's arms slowly developed tone and he hugged his father with increasing conviction. The tension shuddered through Maxime's torso as he returned the hug. When they broke apart, both men's eyes were moist.

The young man sniffed and mumbled, "Sorry, Dad." He grasped Charlotte's hand and escaped the room.

At noon, everyone was summoned by Gunther to fetch their beachwear and get in the van; no one would be excused.

The visiting uncle from Switzerland had decided, never mind the cold Pacific, they all needed ample fresh air, wind to tousle their hair, some sun, and sand to crunch between their toes. Beachwear was compulsory, he insisted. It would flush the misery from their systems. As a precaution, a couple of umbrellas were packed. One could never be too assured about the bloody rain.

Maxime and Simon packed the picnic lunch.

Simon insisted on driving. Gunther didn't allow that to upset him. He turned to Michelle, who sat with him and Donald in the middle seat. "Where to, my dear? Which place won't be too swamped with people?"

"Spanish Banks, Uncle Gunt. There are miles of open beach. I'm sure we'll find a sweet spot."

Maxime made himself comfortable in the third row; he had insisted that Charlotte sits in front with her beau. Anybody who knew anything about having almost head-butted your incorrigible son and who understood young relationships and driving with a baby and five adults in a van knew that one of the adults would have to sit in the back. It was pure mathematics. Maxime was good with numbers. That much was bloody obvious.

37

Maxime Stays Behind In Vancouver

Sandro completed the ten days of chemo.

The poison that killed his cancer cells stopped short of killing him too. He had turned the same color as his bed linen—typing-paper white. On the eleventh day, he received two units of packed red blood cells and five units of platelets. The transfusions restored a hint of rose to his cheeks.

Dr. Pauls, the eternal optimist, was convinced the ten-day treatment would suffice. Within twenty-one days they would know whether the AML had gone into remission. And since Simon's tissue had demonstrated a match with Sandro's, Simon could be called upon in the distant future.

Simon, whose return flight to London was leaving later that morning, went to greet his brother.

Nurse Collins, the youngest staff member on the hematology wing, accompanied Simon, on Nurse Friesen's instruction.

"Nurse Collins, could you do me a favor?"

Not trusting Sandro Baumann's renewed vigor, she stepped closer with caution. "Mr. Bowman?"

"Nurse Collins, you've witnessed how I've risen from the grave. The chemo not only made my hair fall out, but it has made me weak. I don't dare walk to the washroom. Would it be possible to bring me a basin of hot water, some facecloths, and a towel? My brother will get my shaving gear. I'll remain indebted to you for the rest of my days, and those we know, are numbered."

"One shouldn't make light of such matters," the nurse muttered as she walked to the door. "I'll get the water for you, but *only* because you were so terribly ill."

By the time Simon had the shaving utensils organized, the nurse had returned with the steaming water. "Room service, Mr. Bowman."

This time a soft rose crept up her neck as she placed the items on the bedside trolley.

"You're the *best*, Nurse Collins. But I have a second favor to ask. My brother has to leave. He has a plane to catch and won't be able to help me shave."

The nurse stepped back, her brows knotted. She shook her head.

Sandro persisted. "I've lost considerable weight, much of which was muscle. I'm in danger of cutting myself shaving, and who knows, I might still bleed uncontrollably. Nurse Friesen would take serious exception if I got blood on her bed linen. Could you *please* help me?"

The nurse hesitated.

"We'll leave the shaving of my chest for another day. *Promise.*"

Cathy Collins laughed and eyed the Baumann brothers. She seemed grateful that only one of them was her patient. "Only if you keep your hands where I can see them."

Sandro threw his hands up in surrender. "Scout's honor."

Simon stepped closer and ruffled the few tufts of hair on his brother's head with his gloved hand. They hugged in silence for several seconds.

At the door, Simon turned and gave a formal salute. His eyes brimmed as he groaned through pursed lips, "*Farewell*, Sandro."

Sandro waved as he watched his brother go. He wiped over his eyes with the back of his hand, swallowed several times before he busied himself with the shaving foam and only then passed Nurse Collins the contoured shaver. He met her eyes and stuck out his chin. "I'm *ready.*"

As soon as the nurse had shaved his cheeks and moved to his neck, Sandro piped, "You remember the location of the *carotid* arteries, Nurse Collins?"

Their faces were in proximity as she murmured, "I paid attention in anatomy class, Mr. Bowman."

"Be gentle, Nurse Collins. My skin is sensitive …"

"Stop whining, Mr. Bowman. *And,* stop talking. Your Adam's apple bobs up and down. My hand might slip and *cut* that little vessel."

Her fragrance wafted around Sandro, and he closed his eyes. He inhaled deeply. *Morning Rose. And there's mint on her breath. Oh, never mind, Sandro Baumann. You're pathetic. You need to get home to your wife.*

Nurse Collins was doing the finishing touches when a sudden commotion at the door made her knock the basin—foamy water spilled onto her patient's lap. Her eyes met those of her patient—his irises widened in surprise.

"Sandro, my boy!" boomed Gunther Baumann.

Maxime followed steps behind his brother.

Nurse Collins wiped up the spill, then grabbed the basin, washcloths, and towels. With a nod in each man's direction, she took her leave, her cheeks glowing.

Sandro waved after the nurse as she stepped through the door. "Nurse Collins, you're a gorgeous, sweet angel of mercy!"

She fled the room with a quick, "*Goodbye*, Mr. Bowman."

Maxime's gaze shifted from his son to his brother. What had he just witnessed?

Gunther laughed. He found such situations entertaining. Maxime could be so old-fashioned. Gunther always appreciated beauty and spirit, irrespective of age and circumstance. Sandro demonstrated good taste. His wife was a perfect example of that.

"Sandro?"

"Dad?"

"Were you flirting with the nurse?"

Sandro laughed. "Dad, for the past four days, I've been wandering the hallways of the dying. It wasn't a pleasant place to be. Since late yesterday, I've been able to rejoin the land of the living. I'm celebrating it. She gave me a shave. You guys startled her when you barged through the door. She's young, vibrant, and beautiful. That's all. It's not as if we've had sex, you know? I needed *kindness*, and she showed me some."

Gunther threw an arm around his brother's shoulders. "Lighten up, Maxime Baumann. Your son survived his Mount Everest. He required a tonic. Don't be such a sourpuss."

Maxime plopped down at Sandro's side and reached for his son's hand. "Apologies," he mumbled. "I continue being an asshole."

Maxime closed his eyes. Anybody who knew anything about having lost one's spouse and then watching one's firstborn toil on the border of an open grave knew that none of this was funny. Still, flirting should always be seen in a serious light. Perhaps the chemo drugs had fried parts of Sandro's brain.

How can I not be concerned for my son's sake?

Later that afternoon, after Maxime had dropped off his brother at Sandro's house, he returned with Michelle and little Donald. He took great care as he guided Sandro's van through the midday traffic toward the hospital. Simon had a bloody cheek to think him incapable of driving a van on the Pacific coast during rush-hour.

38

Maxime Invites Fanny Ferguson For Coffee

Maxime was worried.

He sat in the foyer, watching the unending throng of people. Their faces intrigued him: some stricken, some angry, some friendly and exuberant, others silent and contracted with pain.

Michelle and Donald were upstairs with Sandro, who had informed them that the doctors were considering discharging him the next day, pending the lab results. Sandro had beamed when he shared the news with his family.

What will happen to the boy now? What if Dr. Pauls's prediction was incorrect? Maxime had done a new internet search the night before, and he didn't know anymore—he was less certain about everything. To become part of the sixty percent survival group would be asking for a miracle. For the impossible.

Maxime Bastien Baumann, what happened to your rule twelve, page one? Never be found without faith. What's your bloody story, old man?

"Mr. Baumann? *Maxime?*"

Maxime jumped. He hadn't heard or seen her approaching. He unfolded himself from the couch.

"Fanny ..."

She sat down next to him. Maxime plopped back down but toppled sideways in his haste. Fanny reached and grabbed his hands, steadying him.

Maxime laughed as he regained his balance. *Idiot.* Their faces had almost collided. He inhaled Fanny's warmth. *Dear Lord, have mercy.* Fanny held onto his hands, not letting go until Maxime wiggled free.

"You need to be more careful, Mr. Baumann." Fanny rested her hand on his arm. Her touch was light.

"Thank you for saving my life, *again*, Nurse Ferguson."

She giggled, retracted her hand and leaned back against the sofa. "You were deep in thought. I stood there for a full twenty seconds. Only when I spoke—"

"I have *nothing* to say, Your Honor."

"Sandro? But isn't he going *home* tomorrow?"

"Only *perhaps*. But what happens *after* tomorrow? His chances of survival—"

Fanny took hold of his hands again. "Maxime, you still have a son. He survived this crucial first battle."

She rose and pulled him to his feet. "Just think," she said. "He's going *home* tomorrow." She laughed and twirled him around. "We *have* to celebrate, Maxime Baumann."

Maxime mumbled, "We can celebrate *tomorrow*."

Fanny glanced around, took a firmer hold of his hands, pulled him closer and gave him a kiss, smack on his lips. She whispered, "Don't be such a sourpuss."

"Who's sour?"

"*You,* Mr. Baumann."

Maxime touched his lips. "And what was *that?*"

"When was the last time you had a kiss, Maxime?"

He stared at Fanny Ferguson and touched his lips again. "It's been a while."

Fanny reached for his hand. "Are you going to ask me or what?"

"I haven't done this in a long time, Fanny. How... about coffee?"

Her bells bubbled over. "That's all I meant, silly old man."

"Are you working tomorrow?"

"I'm off at four."

"I'll meet you here at 4:05, then. I'll take you somewhere for coffee. But it's not a date."

She laughed. "I'll be here. Good day, Mr. Baumann."

The moment Fanny disappeared through the revolving door, Maxime sagged down into the couch. He'd only noticed now: she had long sculpted legs.

Maxime Baumann, are you a complete idiot? The good Lord gave you a head, and you are not using it. This woman is barely ten years older than your sons. She's feeling sorry for you because of Sandro. Remember, it's not a date.

———

Maxime arrived early the next day, at ten to four, and decided not to sit down. He had been embarrassed every time Fanny had snuck up on him. He paced the foyer, then realized that he could still miss her if he went the wrong way. It was time to change tactics. He took position behind a pillar, close to the elevator.

At exactly five minutes past four, Fanny stepped from the elevator and glanced around. Maxime waited five seconds before he stepped out from his vantage point and caught her eye. She changed direction and quickened her pace.

Fanny laughed. "Are you playing hide and seek?"

Maxime took her hand. He shook his head. "No, I'm a sourpuss. Remember?"

Fanny snorted and gave him a peck on the cheek.

"What? No proper kiss?"

"It's not a date. Only coffee."

"Ah, I forgot."

In Sandro's van, which Maxime had borrowed for the occasion, Maxime turned to Fanny. "I've done my research. I have a list here of forty-five possible cafés, but I don't know which one will be worth our while."

He handed Fanny the printed list. She opened her mouth but swallowed her words when she saw his expression. She scanned the list.

"Okay, Mr. Baumann. Prepare to be impressed. It's not far from here. As soon as we're out of this parking lot, take a sharp left, and left again at the lights."

Ten minutes later Maxime slid in at a table opposite Fanny in a dimly lit café. He loved it.

"*What*?" Fanny asked.

"How did you know I would like *this* place?" It was so similar to his beloved coffee shop back home.

She raised her brows. "Educated guess." Then added, "You're an easy study, Mr. Baumann."

Maxime smirked.

Fanny pushed her chair back. "I forgot. We'll have to go to the counter to place our order."

Maxime cupped his hands around the now empty waxed paper cup and listened to his companion. And he had thought he understood women. He had let Fanny do most of the talking. It was charming how excited she became about everyday life, about everything with which she was involved. A passionate soul. It was refreshing.

"Why did you come with me today?" Maxime asked.

She cocked her head.

"Do you feel sorry for me?"

She held his gaze. "Should I?"

Maxime shrugged. "I'm not good at this," he mumbled. "It's been a long time…"

Fanny reached for his hand. Maxime stiffened but didn't pull free. "Maxime, I don't feel sorry for you because your son has

AML. I feel a deep empathy. But I *do* feel sorry for you, because ... because you're afraid of me."

Maxime freed his hand and scoffed.

"You *are* afraid."

"I'm afraid of *no* one." Maxime's lips tightened into a thin line.

"Why are you so cautious then?"

"Life is serious, Fanny. *Love* is serious."

"Life is *short*, Maxime."

She held his eyes, her mouth pursed.

Yes, Maxime, she has a mind. She is not a rollover. She'll kick your ass if you blink.

"I thought this was enjoyable." Fanny gestured at the café.

This time Maxime leaned across and took Fanny's hands. "*Sorry.*"

She tried to pull her hands free. "No need to apologize. Remember, this is not a date, Mr. Baumann."

Maxime squeezed her hands and chuckled. "I'm known for being an ass from time to time."

"And the rest of the time?"

"Charming?"

She snorted loud, then clasped a hand over her mouth, glancing at the other customers. No one was paying her attention. She shook her head. "Charming you're not. I'd say ... You're a mature male, rather handsome, if not sexy, burdened by a couple of serious hang-ups."

"*Hang-ups?*"

"I bet you have a list—a long list of principles that guide your every day?"

39

Maxime Bids Vancouver Farewell

Maxime remained in Vancouver for two more weeks. Sandro was back home and basked in the attention of his wife, son, friends and various well-wishers who dropped in, most of them uninvited. Maxime moved to the background; he was grateful for all these people but realized he didn't fit into their world.

It seemed Dr. Pauls's prediction had been right: Sandro was healed.

During the day, when too many visitors showed up at once, Maxime went for a run. In the evenings he escaped with Sandro's van, to visit with Fanny Ferguson. By the third visit, he was willing to call it an "official date."

On his insistence, they had met at the same coffee shop, at the same time in the early evening. The baristas now greeted them as regulars. The night before his return to Saskatchewan, Fanny, however, insisted on cooking him a farewell meal.

Fanny buzzed him into the building, and Maxime took a position at her apartment door. Hands behind the back of his sports jacket, he waited. He had come prepared: it was their last evening.

When the door swung open, Maxime gulped, stopping short of dropping what he had in his hands. The woman who held the door for him was one step ahead of the Vision: Fanny surpassed her in radiance. A short summer dress hugged Fanny's lithe figure—four-inch heeled sandals completed the picture. Her entire presentation beckoned.

"*Maxime?* You want to come in?"

Maxime laughed, embarrassed; he had been gawking. He brought out the roses and bottle of wine from behind his back.

"Thank you, *sweet* man." Fanny stepped forward, pulled a speechless Maxime by his lapels into the apartment and pushed the door closed behind them with her sandalled foot. She didn't take the offered gifts from her guest but wrapped her arms around his neck, taking her time to push him against the wall. Her mouth found his lips. It was not the peck that she had given him the first time in the hospital foyer. As her tongue searched his mouth, her breasts crushed into his chest. Her muskiness wrapped around Maxime.

Maxime returned her kiss but soon wiggled free of the close embrace. "Requesting time out, *Ma'am.*"

Fanny trailed him into the kitchen, where he placed the flowers and wine on a counter. Maxime's face glowed. "You look ... *ravishing.*"

Her chest rose and fell, both nipples straining against the thin fabric. "*Thank you,* Maxime," she breathed. "Then why do you need a time-out?"

"You were *different*, back there—intense ..."

"*So?* You're going home tomorrow. You're flying out of my life."

"I *have* to go back."

"To *what?* An empty house? A silly cat?"

"You forget I still have a job. I'm not retired. I've been away for five weeks. Mr. J. Johnson, the senior partner, had no problem with granting me compassionate leave, but he'll wonder whether I'm *ever* coming back."

"Oh never *mind*—let's eat—the food is ready."

Fanny rummaged in a drawer and handed Maxime a bottle opener. Only halfway through the meal, after a tall glass of wine, did her pursed lips soften. Her effervescence returned, if with caution. She wanted to know what on earth he was planning on doing when he got back home.

"Work. Go to the gym. Collect Columbus from the animal hotel. I'll probably have to mortgage the house to pay the vet's bill. There is no doubt the cat will be upset with me for neglecting him so long."

"Poor kitty. Will you at least miss *me?*"

"Not at all." When Fanny made a face at him, Maxime leaned in, took her hand and brought it to his lips. He pressed the back of her hand to his cheek, peering into her dark irises.

With a chuckle, Fanny pushed her chair back and grabbed Maxime's hand, pulling him to his feet. "You're forgiven. Come, *dance* with me."

Maxime protested. He had two left feet when it came to dancing—there was a disconnect between his brain and his dancing feet. Besides, it had been years since he'd been on a dance floor.

Fanny ignored his pleas. She had planned her evening in advance and walked over to the stereo and pressed Play.

"Thou complaineth too much, Mr. Baumann." She grasped his right hand, straightened her left arm, placed his left hand on the small of her back, then placed her right hand on his shoulder, pulling him closer until their chests brushed.

"*Ready*? Now pay attention." She led as the music began. She soon pulled him closer. "Look me in the eyes, Max—forget about your feet."

The tempo increased, and Fanny steered him with expertise, turning and stepping and twirling. Only by the fifth piece did Maxime loosen up, his stick-like rhythm gradually following the smooth movements of his partner.

She soon slipped the second CD in the machine and took off on a faster tempo, her hand now pressing into his back, forcing him even closer.

From time to time her breasts grazed his chest and arms as they glided and maneuvered through the living room and kitchen, twirling around furniture. The livelier the tempo of the tango, the more recklessly Fanny steered him through the apartment. They giggled and laughed and sometimes bumped into objects, which hurled them into each other's arms. There was no stopping her.

By the end of the second CD, Fanny had him dancing down the short hallway, where she pulled him into her bedroom and plopped down on the bed, not letting go of his hand. She rolled onto her side and pulled him down next to her. They were both laughing and breathing fast.

"*Kiss* me."

"Miss Ferguson ..." Maxime cleared his throat.

Fanny sat up on the bed, pressed him flat on his back and straddled him. She leaned forward and kissed him.

"*Maxime.*"

He took his time kissing her, reluctantly at first. His lips discovered her face. He inhaled her almond breath. Every part of her was a sweet revelation. His lips brushed her eyelids, trailed along her nose, lingered at her lips, then found their way down to her neck and up to her earlobes, which he nibbled.

Fanny sighed as she arched over him, pliable like clay.

Then she leaned back, took his hand and placed it on her left breast. Maxime sucked in his breath. His suspicion was confirmed. She wore only a diaphanous camisole under her summer dress. The mount fitted perfectly in his hand. She smiled at him through hooded eyes. She took his right hand and guided that to her other breast. Fanny sighed louder, her breasts straining in his hands. She held his hands in position, breathing faster, then leaned forward, kissing him with more fervor.

Her pubis gyrated across his rock-hard manhood. "Make love to me, Maxime."

Maxime groaned.

"Fanny …" Maxime gave a muffled cry and freed his hands from her heaving chest, pulled her down onto him, burying his face in her hair. "Oh, Fanny."

He pulled her closer and held tight. He held her like this for a long time, until her writhing pelvis quieted down.

When she pulled free, her eyes were wet. "Am I not desirable enough, Mr. Baumann?"

"Oh, Fanny. To the *contrary.*"

She jumped to her feet. "'*Oh, Fanny.*' You're pathetic." She straightened her dress and combed her hair with her fingers.

At the bedroom door, she said, "I think you should leave."

"*Fanny.*"

"Don't 'Fanny' me. It's embarrassing. You must think I'm a cheap woman, throwing myself at you like that. I assumed you *wanted* me, at least a little ..." She gave a sob, ran into her en suite bathroom and slammed the door.

She yelled from behind the door, "Go home, Maxime Baumann! Go back to your boss and your glorious work and your poor love-starved cat. I have *nothing* more to say to you. Please leave."

Then she cracked the door open, poked her head around it and sneered. "Didn't you feel comfortable without your little blue pill, Maxime?" And she slammed the door shut a second time.

Maxime gawked at the closed door. It wasn't bloody fair. "Fanny, please *listen* to reason."

"Just go. It's best if we never see each other again. It was a mistake."

"*Fanny!*"

"I'll phone 911 if you're not gone by the time I come out of the bathroom. You have ten seconds. Take your jacket and leave my apartment."

"Fanny?"

"*One. Two. Three ...*"

40

Sandro's AML Relapses

Sandro's leukemia relapsed seventeen months later.

Michelle phoned Maxime the same evening that her husband was readmitted to the hospital. She sounded upbeat at first, even excited that Dr. Pauls had opted to manage Sandro's treatment again.

Maxime listened, not saying a word. When Michelle took her first breath, he asked, "Michelle, *how* is Sandro doing? I need an *honest* answer."

A deep sigh shuddered across the line. "He's devastated. We all forgot he was on borrowed time—that he was only lent to us the past year and a half."

"And you and Donald?"

She gave a soft sob. "Dad ... I've cried so much since yesterday. Donald wouldn't understand why he couldn't stay with his daddy."

"What's the hematologist's plan *this* time?"

"He's putting Sandro on a new course of chemo. If that is successful, they'll consider a stem cell transplant."

"Which means a matched donor?"

According to Dr. Pauls, Michelle explained, Simon was one possibility, but the hospital had also contacted the local donor banks. The problem was that they hadn't heard from Simon in over three months. It was the longest stretch Sandro had ever gone without speaking to his younger brother. Simon had always phoned, at least once a month. The last they heard, he and Charlotte had gone on an indefinite hiking trip through southern Europe—walking the entire coastline of Italy and Greece, or something similarly spectacular.

Michelle gave another snivel.

"Maybe they're heading back," Maxime offered. "Even the Mediterranean must get damn chilly at night by now. We had our first snow two weeks ago."

Michelle chuckled. "Your poor people on the Prairies with your eternal snow. We've only had a cold drizzle. I don't know about you, Dad, but I never took a liking to her, Simon's girlfriend. She's too intense, too smart, *too* perfect—in a controlfreak kind of way. She's sitting on his *head*."

Maxime snickered. "She seemed sweet enough, tough as she was. But I may change my opinion if she makes him disappear off the map. Don't worry," he soothed, "I'll track them down. Should I fly across tomorrow?"

"There's no rush, Daddy. One of my close friends has come to stay with Donny and me. And there's nothing any of us can do for Sandro. They won't let me stay with him—he's already in isolation. The new IV line is in, and they're starting with the poison in the morning. The cell transplant is supposed to be in eleven days—twenty-four hours after completion of the chemo."

Maxime promised to pack his bags and find Columbus a temporary home. Mr. J. Johnson wouldn't mind too much. The past several months, he had been hinting at Maxime to take the reins. Maxime had chosen to ignore his senior partner's suggestions. He was not ready for or convinced he wished to commit to such a long-term responsibility.

He left messages on Simon's home phone and cell phone and sent him an email as well. Next, he called Gunther. His brother had contacts throughout Europe. Perhaps he could put those to good use to find the vacationing couple.

Such was indeed the case, Gunther confirmed—he knew the director of Search and Rescue in Italy. He would phone the man in the morning and get the word out. He also promised to see if his contact could convince their national TV stations to help locate the two backpackers.

Gunther found the situation somewhat amusing. "What if the two lovebirds don't *want* to be found?"

"Lovebirds? They have some bloody cheek," Maxime fumed. "It's not as if they're on a honeymoon. And if they were, it should never have lasted this long. Gunt, even if it requires us to send a group of Navy SEALs to pinpoint them, then we'll do that."

"Shouldn't Sandro's hematologist be able to track down a donor in Canada?" Gunther asked.

"There's no guarantee. Timing is going to be everything. Please help me find them."

The next afternoon, just before Maxime caught a taxi to the airport, Gunther reported back. Word has been sent out to the Search and Rescue people in Italy. He was given the assurance that they would broadcast it on the local and national news every day. The Italian coastal border posts would pass the details on to their Greek counterparts.

———

Sandro encountered setbacks from the start. Extreme nausea set in on the third day and remained his close companion for the entire course of the chemo. He lost two to three pounds a day— due to fluids and electrolytes loss, along with significant muscle and subcutaneous tissue wastage. Nurse Friesen enforced strict barrier protocol—more rigid than before.

Sandro entered his second solitary confinement.

Maxime landed in Vancouver by the end of Sandro's second day. The toughest part was not being allowed to visit his son. Not even Michelle was allowed.

What if, Maxime kept asking himself. *What if I never see my eldest again?*

Maxime took it on himself to keep Michelle, little Donald and himself sane. There was no Gunther this time to take charge of team-building and recreation. They would have a picnic every day, he decided. They would work their way down the coastline—with Maxime at the wheel of Sandro's silver van. Donald was impressed with his *Oupa* from Saskatchewan who insisted on going to the beach every single day. It was almost as good as Christmas.

Gunther promised to come as soon as they had located Simon and his girlfriend. This time Mary MacDonald would accompany him. She was forced to take a break from running, having injured a hamstring muscle.

On day five of Sandro's treatment, Gunther phoned. They had located the hikers.

"We were *lucky*, Maximus. I've got a lot of respect for those Italians. They tracked them down in a small village just inside the Greek border. The two are flying back to London as we speak. Simon promised to phone you as soon as he sets foot in the UK."

"What was the bloody boy thinking?"

"Don't be too harsh on him, Max. We had *all* assumed Sandro's cure was permanent. We forgot about the sleeping dragon in his bone marrow. You've forgotten about when you fell in love with Donna; you were *unreachable*. You *also* refused to listen to any reason."

"I did?"

"As if you don't remember, you Philistine. I'll email you our flight number and arrival time. Mary finally gets to see the land of frozen tundra. At least, we'll fly across it. On the Pacific coast, we'll probably only need an umbrella. *Auf Wiedersehen, mein Bruder.*"

41

Nurse Fanny Ferguson Refuses That Maxime See His Son

On the tenth day of round two, Sandro developed a nose-bleed that persisted through the morning.

Maxime had set up camp the previous day in the hematology waiting room but was completely unaware of what was transpiring in the isolation room. The staff, following hospital policy, did not inform him of anything. Instead, he sat waiting for Simon, who was expected early that morning. No other matching donor had been found. Despite Maxime and Michelle's pleading, Simon refused to rush to his brother's aid. He had timed it perfectly, he claimed—he would be there in time.

By early afternoon, Sandro had lost so much blood that he passed out. By three, his nose had been packed four times, but it continued to ooze blood. Aggressive intravenous fluid therapy slowly stabilized his blood pressure, but only a late-afternoon platelet transfusion brought the bleeding under control. By six, Sandro became confused, and a CT scan was urgently performed: they had to rule out a brain bleeding.

Dr. Pauls contacted Michelle to inform her about the scan and her husband's worsening condition. She immediately phoned Maxime, who at that point, was lounging in the waiting room.

Maxime stormed to the front desk, demanding to speak to the charge nurse or, better still, one of the physicians. He stood at the counter, light-headed, breathing fast. His heart pounded. The terrible pressure in his chest had returned.

Anybody who knew anything about AML and bleeding and brain scans knew that none of this was to be taken lightly. To have been kept in the dark for close to eighteen hours about your son's rapid deterioration was unforgivable. It was a bloody disgrace—and it happened right under his nose. They had told him nothing.

"Hello, Mr. Baumann ... Maxime."

Maxime spun around. She was as gorgeous as ever. He swallowed his angry words. "Nurse Ferguson ... what's happening to my son? Where's Sandro?"

"He's still in the X-ray department."

"Why didn't anybody tell me? I've been sitting in the waiting room around the corner, since yesterday."

"Mr. Baumann, this was not my decision. Doctors' orders. Hospital policy. Dr. Pauls did contact his next of kin when they rushed him to the scanner."

"Am I not his next of kin?" Maxime cried out. "*Mein Gott,* he's *my son.*"

He turned away, then spun back and stepped forward, stopping inches from the equally upset nurse. His eyes brimmed. "Have you *ever* had a child, Fanny?"

Her eyes said no.

He was now whispering. "Have you ever *lost* a child?"

She shook her head.

"Can I speak to Dr. Pauls?" he begged. "*Please* ..."

"Mr. Baumann, I'm afraid doctor will only talk to Mrs. Michelle Baumann, once she gets here."

Maxime pulled himself up to his full six-foot-and-a-half-inch height. "Nurse Ferguson, stuff the hospital policies. I've had *enough* of this bullshit. We're talking about my son, who's *dying*. I've been here eight days, and you people have prevented me from seeing my son."

"Mr. Baumann, *wait!*"

Maxime stormed toward the elevators, hollering over his shoulder, "Too late. I'll find Dr. Pauls *myself*. Thank you for the *empathy*."

She may be as beautiful as ever, but she's still a bitch. Where's their compassion? Do these people have no hearts?

Maxime went down four floors, located the imaging department and insisted at their front desk on speaking to Dr. Pauls. The clerk started explaining how the hospital policies work, when Maxime, who found it impossible to continue speaking with an "inside voice," glimpsed Dr. Pauls as he stepped from a 'staff only' area.

Maxime hollered after him. "Dr. Pauls, *excuse me!*"

"Hello, Mr. Baumann. What a surprise."

Maxime grasped the physician's hand and shook it. "*Tell* me about my son," he insisted, locking eyes with the man, refusing to let go of the doctor's hand.

"The scan was *negative*. There's no intracranial bleeding, but he's not doing well. He's in crisis at the moment. The next twenty-four to forty-eight hours will determine whether this is going to be the end. If he improves, I still want to do the stem cell transplant. Without that, he *will* die." He freed his hand, putting his hand on Maxime's shoulder. "I'm sorry, Mr. Baumann."

———

Sandro was returned to the ward but remained restless. Throughout the night his lucid intervals continued.

"Simon," he muttered. "Where's Dad? I'm thirsty. Someone, please call my wife. *Michelle*. Where is Michelle? Donald, come here, son. Come. Give Dad a hug. Daddy's dying … my bloody nose won't stop bleeding."

"Mr. Bowman, calm down. Everything's okay." It was Nurse Collins.

"My nose … everything is *not* okay. Can someone please take this packing out of my nose? I can't breathe. *Nurse!*"

"Mr. Bowman, I'm right here."

"Please hold my hand … I'm cold. Why am I so cold, Nurse Collins?"

Sandro whimpered and shivered, curling into a fetal position. He couldn't stop the shaking.

"My nose—please take the packing out of my nose." He bolted upright, thrashed about, then fell back. "For *fuck's sake,* take this packing out! I'm choking!"

"*Mr. Bowman. Please.* Do *not* pull that plug out. Do you want to bleed to death?" Nurse Collins was by now crying herself, clinging to his arms. She had managed to press the call button. "I'm sorry, Mr. Bowman, but you leave us no option than to restrain you."

Sandro fell back onto his pillows, perspiring and hyperventilating. His eyes were closed—set deep in its sockets.

He allowed the nurses to attach the wrist restraints. The moment the second nurse left, he glanced at Nurse Collins. "I'm sorry, Nurse Collins. Did I swear? I'm so terribly sorry ..."

"It's all right, Mr. Bowman. It's all right. You're terribly ill."

Sandro rattled the bedframe as he shook his arms. "*Nurse!* Where is Nurse Ferguson? I want Nurse Ferguson." Sandro fought with his restraints, glaring wild at Nurse Collins.

"She's gone off duty; I'm helping you now."

"I want that foxy nurse, nurse Ferguson. Nurse Collins, are you *sexy?*" Sandro gave a manic laugh, shaking the bed once more.

"Mr. Bowman!"

"I'm sorry ... for being such an ass. Please hold me. I'm cold."

A violent shiver shook him, and he lay back. "Nurse Collins, be honest. How many times can one die?"

The fight had left him. He rested, now limp, against the pillows.

"Mr. Bowman?"

Sandro had fallen asleep—his breathing came fast and shallow.

42

Simon And Charlotte Run Into A Winter Storm In London

Maxime was worried.

Where he sat in the darkness, he noticed the chairs of the waiting room as they became visible, one after the other, like the rows in a graveyard at sunrise, as the fluorescents sputtered to life; he squinted his eyes against their eventual brightness. Night was falling on the tenth day of Sandro's treatment.

There had been no word from Simon.

Maxime phoned Michelle and asked for his brother. "Gunther, why don't you pack a picnic bag and bring Mary along, plus your laptop and a blanket? You can set up camp with me while we wait. I can't leave Sandro, and I'm worried about Simon. A winter storm has struck Central Canada, but I've no idea what's going on in the UK."

Maxime wandered down to the cafeteria to wait for his brother when his phone rang. It was Simon.

"Dad, it's *snowing*."

Maxime gazed out the foyer's windows. It was raining. He rolled his eyes. "Where are you, Simon? In Calgary?"

"I'm still in London, England. We had to dig ourselves out from a foot of snow. A blizzard had struck the entire city. We're on our way to Heathrow *now*."

Maxime's legs failed him, and he plopped down on the nearest couch. His heart pounded as he gulped for air.

In London. Good Lord.

He licked his parched lips. It required all his self-control not to yell, "*How* were you hoping to be on time for the cell donation? It's taking place in *Vancouver*, not in Southampton." Maxime said nothing.

"Dad, it's two in the morning. My flight leaves at six. It's a direct flight. I'll be on time. Remember, we're eight hours *ahead* of you guys. Don't panic."

Maxime hung up and stomped to the cafeteria. He needed an extra strong, extra black coffee. *Don't panic.* The bloody cheek of the boy. Anybody who knew anything about weather conditions and freak winter storms knew that it could be impossible to get out of a snowed-in city.

Your older brother is lying upstairs, dying, and you built a snowman outside your apartment. Asshole. You are not emotionally related to me or your mother, Simon Baumann.

Maxime found a table and cradled his steaming paper cup—he took small sips of the scalding dark fluid. It was impossible not to glance at his wrist—Gunther should be here soon. He texted his brother to meet him in the cafeteria. He was sipping his second black coffee when Gunther and Mary walked in with a cooler and a small shoulder bag. In his distress, Maxime gave Gunther and Mary each a prolonged hug until they wiggled free from his tight embraces.

"Maximus?"

"It's Simon." Maxime sagged back down on his chair. "He's still in *bloody* London."

"How was he planning on—"

Maxime jumped to his feet when his phone rang. The sudden movement was too much for the lopsided table, and his coffee cup toppled over. "Oh, damn it! *Sorry, Gunther.*" Maxime stepped away from the spill. "*Simon.* What's happening?" He gestured with one hand at Gunther to get themselves something to drink—he would clean up in a moment.

"My flight's been canceled, Dad. But we're still heading for Heathrow. There's a flight at six-thirty and another at seven."

"And if *those* get axed?"

"Dad, don't you have a *little* faith? That's what you always taught us, remember? The rulebook? Not *every* flight will be canceled."

Maxime hung up and turned around. Mary was busy cleaning up his mess. Muttering under his breath, Maxime took over and made her sit down. He updated his brother and soon to be, sister-in-law.

Then he gulped down what little had remained of his coffee.

Maxime resembled Mr. J. Johnson who was born in 1936 as he leaned across the table. "What will happen if it keeps snowing in London?"

Gunther chuckled, his glance shifting between Mary and Maxime. "He's a handful, your youngest. First, the two disappear off the map; now he's dragging his feet to get here." He shrugged. "They might close the entire airport."

Gunther flipped his laptop open. He caught Maxime's eyes. "What's happening in the rest of Western Europe, weather-wise?"

"The Mainland?"

"Yes. What about the Channel Tunnel? If the weather's not too shitty in France, he might be able to take the Chunnel train to Paris and catch a plane from there, even a direct flight."

Mary and Maxime peered over Gunther's shoulder as he scanned the weather reports. Maxime mumbled that his son's head was so messed up by a certain two-legged vegan in a skirt that he could no longer think straight. Why didn't Simon and Charlotte think of the tunnel themselves? Bloody puppy love.

Paris had recorded only one centimeter of snow, and no flights had been canceled. Maxime dropped back on his chair and dialed Simon. His fingers trembled.

"*Simon*! Change of plan. Forget Heathrow and go straight to the St. Pancras train station. If the tunnel's still open, you can get out *that* way."

"St. Pancras?" Simon grumbled.

"*Yes*. Take the Eurostar to Paris. Their airport is open. They didn't get much snow. It's a two-hour, fifteen-minute journey. They have direct flights to Vancouver."

"What about my ticket from Heathrow?"

Maxime felt a surge of anger. Remaining pissed off at your dead mother was one thing. Being an asshole was another. But to be unwilling to listen to logic? "*Lieber Gott,* Simon. What *more* do we need to do? Please let me speak to Charlotte."

There was a pause, then a tentative "Hello?"

"Charlotte! *Hello.* Do you know how to get to St. Pancras Station?"

"Mr. Baumann? Yes, *of course.*"

———

At three a.m. Simon turned the car around and headed for St. Pancras, London. He considered the possibility that driving in such weather could be seen as a suicide mission.

"According to the GPS," Charlotte said, "St. Pancras is only thirty-five minutes away."

"Charlotte, the bloody GPS doesn't know it's snowing."

"No need to use that language with me, Simon Baumann."

Simon rolled his eyes as Charlotte fiddled with the device. A husky female voice filled the cabin.

"*In 500 meters, turn right. Turn right onto M4 highway.*"

"Charlotte, do we *need* the voice prompt?"

The wipers fought a desperate battle to retain visibility through a windshield battered by sleet and ice.

"I love her voice," Charlotte said. "It's reassuring when *some-one* at least knows where we are and remains calm. And now you don't need to take your eyes off the road to look at a silly map."

They took the ramp onto the M4, and Charlotte turned to Simon. "You never told me whether there were risks involved with the stem cell donation. Are there?"

Simon shrugged. He explained to her how they would hook him up to an apheresis machine through a large vein in his arm, and that it would take about four hours to complete the donation. He might feel nauseous for a few days and lose his appetite.

"And that's all?"

"I might also have difficulty sleeping, and experience some bone pain."

"And?"

"In rare instances, I could have a stroke or a blood clot or a severe allergic reaction."

"Simon *Baumann*. A *stroke*. And you didn't *tell* me?"

She gave a sob and turned her face away.

Simon glanced at her in alarm. He'd never expected this kind of reaction from her. He had to see her eyes.

"Simon! *Watch out!*" The panic in her voice brought his eyes back to the road. It was only partially visible through the now fogged-up windshield. Brake lights ahead of them were approaching fast. *Too* fast.

"Hold on!" He geared down and touched the brakes, which immediately swung the car's tail out as the tires searched for grip on the iced-over highway. The snow in the air scattered the multitude of brake lights ahead into dancing specks, red blurs that raced toward them.

Simon counter steered, geared down again and again and waited for the impact as the car skidded.

"Brace yourself, Charlotte!"

Simon followed his own advice; eyes shut tight. He waited. The skidding slowed down. Then nothing. The only sound was that of the wipers scraping over an irregular iced surface. His eyes flew open. Their car stood sideways across the highway, six inches from the vehicle in front of them, which also stood sideways. The windows fogged up as he tried to bring his gasping breath under control. The occupants of the other vehicle waved at them through a little peeping hole in the condensation. Simon returned the wave.

"Simon!" Charlotte called out. "The officer in the fluorescent vest is waving a torch at you."

Simon managed to get the window three inches open before it got stuck. "Bloody *snow*."

"Sir," the man said, shining his flashlight into the car, "we are redirecting traffic. You must take the off-ramp to your *right*."

"But I have to take the turn-off to the *left*, officer. We have to get to St. Pancras."

"That's not my problem. You *will* take the turn-off to the *right*." He directed the beam into Simon's eyes.

Simon drew his breath and bit his tongue to stop him from cussing as he followed the new directions. Charlotte squeezed his thigh hard until the officer was left far behind.

The husky GPS voice immediately joined in: "*Recalibrating … Drive four hundred meters, then turn left. Turn left.*"

Simon slapped the steering wheel. "Oh, *thank you*, Miss Know-it-all."

43

Sandro Undergoes A Stem Cell Transplant

Simon and Charlotte touched down in Vancouver, in time for morning tea.

By the time Simon was connected to the apheresis machine, Sandro's confusion had cleared.

Maxime, Gunther, Mary, Simon, Charlotte, Michelle and little Donald showed up the evening after the transplant had been completed, optimistic of being granted visiting rights.

At the unit desk, Fanny Ferguson was in charge. Maxime waved in passing as he herded the group down the hallway.

"*Excuse me*! Mr. Baumann, please wait."

Maxime nudged Gunther ahead as he turned back to give his attention to Nurse Ferguson with a broad smile. Gunther brought the rest of the group to a halt just down the hallway.

"I'm sorry, but Mr. Sandro Baumann cannot receive any visitors."

Maxime's smile disappeared. He had been looking forward to seeing his son. "Why do you have an issue with us, Nurse Ferguson? We're not visitors; we're *family*."

"I don't have an issue with anyone, Mr. Baumann. Your son has developed a fever. He's not out of danger yet. My instructions were clear: *no* visitors."

"I haven't seen my son in *eleven* days."

"I appreciate that. But I can't allow a busload of people to come in contact with an immune-compromised patient."

Maxime felt dizzy. His heart pounded. Was the world suddenly populated entirely by assholes? This beautiful woman will be responsible for his premature demise. He hissed through clenched teeth, "It's not a *busload* of people. It's my *family*."

Crimson crept up Fanny's neck. She reached out a hand toward Maxime. "Sorry, Maxime. I'm not trying to be vindictive. But Sandro is deadly ill."

Maxime dropped his hands to his sides. His shoulders slumped like Mr. J. Johnson who had turned eighty-two. "At least allow Michelle—his wife—to slip in and say hello." Maxime swallowed the venom in his mouth. "*Please,* Fanny."

He had to focus on his breathing not to lurch forward, take her face in his hands and kiss her miserable attitude away. *That's what this woman needs, damn it. She needs a damn good kiss; perhaps two.*

Maxime touched her outreached hand. A burst of static made them both jerk their hands away. Fanny's hue intensified. She pursed her lips. "But *only* her."

Maxime grabbed her hand and gave it a quick squeeze. "I'll tell them. *Thank you.*"

He spun around and raced to where his group had gathered down the hallway. He held up an index finger. "Only *one* can go in. I've negotiated a peace treaty with the United Nations. Michelle, they'll let *you* go in."

Maxime took his grandson's hand. "Come, Donald. Mommy will go with the nurse to say hello to Daddy." Then he faced his family, "It's the waiting room for the rest of us."

They had not yet reached the waiting room when Gunther exploded. "What's that woman's problem, Maximus? Does she appreciate how far we've come to visit your son? From the bloody *other side of the planet.* Max, what did you *do* to her?" His thundering laugh echoed through the room. "You must have pissed her off."

With everyone's eyes on him, demanding an explanation, Maxime filled them in on what had happened between him and Fanny eighteen months earlier. He omitted the part where she had straddled him in her bedroom and made him fondle her breasts. About the part where he had bailed. He could feel his face glowing.

"Dad," Simon said, "what are you *not* telling us?"

Maxime sunk into a chair. "Nothing." His face was hot. *Damn that bitchy nurse.*

"I saw how you touched her hand," Simon said. "You both jerked away, and then you touched her *again*." Simon peered at his father. "I observed latent chemistry, Dad."

Maxime snickered. "Balderdash." He reached down and lifted Donald onto his lap, challenging Simon with his eyes.

Michelle swirled in from the hallway, bent forward and scooped Donald away from Maxime. "Donald is also going to say hi to his Daddy," she whispered. Michelle's eyes drilled into Maxime. "She's quite a sweetheart, this Nurse Ferguson. *I* don't have a problem with her. Come, Donald. Daddy's waiting."

Gunther leaned forward and slapped Maxime on the back. "Out with it, Maximus. We should have let *Michelle* do the negotiations with the UN—then we could *all* have been able to say hello to Sandro."

Maxime had had enough. He held up his hands in surrender and went to sit across the room, next to Mary, who raised her brows at him. "Why didn't you *kiss* her?" she whispered.

"*What* do you mean?"

"Maxime, I'm not blind."

"It would have been inappropriate—there in the hallway. Fanny would have slapped me."

Mary laughed and put her hand on his arm. "You're wrong. Didn't you see how she *looked* at you?"

"Yes, she wanted to *kill* me."

"I don't think so. She was only following hospital regulations."

Michelle stood in the door opening with Donald on her hip. "Sandro sends his regards."

Donald added, "Daddy give Donny a hug, *Oupa*."

"That's wonderful, Donny!" Gunther hollered. He pulled Maxime by the sleeve. "Come. I need refreshments. Coffee, or something stronger—to soothe the disappointment. Let's go."

As they passed the front desk on the way to the elevator, Maxime caught Fanny's eyes. He gestured for the others to continue without him, then waited to the side of the nurses' station until Nurse Ferguson finally walked around.

Maxime grinned embarrassedly. "Thank you for allowing the two of them in, Fanny."

She smiled at him. "I'm not *really* a bitch, Maxime."

"I never said that."

"I read minds."

"I need proof of that. Will you join me for a coffee tomorrow afternoon? New place, different time."

She hesitated.

"I missed you," Maxime blurted out.

She laughed her soft little bells. "Is this a date?"

"Yes," Maxime said. "For *coffee.*"

44

Maxime Discovers A New Coffee Shop, Among Other Things

Maxime had done his homework.

He had researched the coffee shop, first online, then in person. Fanny Ferguson would love the place. He would prove to her that he was a changed man—it was possible to escape a rut.

She declined his offer to pick her up—she would meet him there.

Maxime waited for the lunch-hour rush to pass before he entered the coffee shop, settled down at a table next to the floor-to-ceiling windows and texted Fanny the address. There was no haste. Except for Maxime, the place was deserted. He opened the book he had purchased from the store next door, one with a blue and white sticker: Staff's Choice.

Maxime inhaled the aroma as he read—the crisp paper smell of a never-before-opened book, and in the background, freshly ground coffee. Heaven. For a moment, he was back in his little drinking hole in Saskatoon, where he had escaped to after work and after gym—when Donna would wait on him in the kitchen, along with an overbearing Columbus.

Maxime was into the fifth chapter and his third espresso when he became aware of her.

"Maxime."

"*Fanny.*" He stood and pulled out a second chair. "Have you been *watching* me?"

"The book took you to a faraway place."

Maxime shrugged. "It's not bad. Let's get you something. I still have coffee left."

Maxime sat across from Fanny, sipping his now lukewarm drink. He said nothing as he observed her, suddenly uncomfortable. *What is she thinking?* He willed her to meet his eyes.

"You think I was unreasonable not to let you see your son."

"You were."

"I was only doing my job."

Maxime drained his paper cup and stuffed the napkin inside with force. "I thought your occupation wasn't a job, but *a calling.* Called to take care of the ill, to alleviate pain and suffering, to assist the dying and their relatives—*with* compassion."

"I'm not a saint, Maxime. It *used* to be a calling—when I was young. It's only a job now."

"You could have let me in."

"I had my orders."

"*Bullshit.*"

"Believe what you will." Her lips pulled into a thin line.

Maxime leaned forward. "*Why* did you agree to come today?"

She tossed her head to the side. "I'm in need of uplifting company. But I'm also a sucker for pain."

"My son is *dying*. I might not see him alive again. Why can't you understand that?"

"I *do* understand."

"That's not true. You've *changed*."

Fanny clutched Maxime's hand, shook her head and blinked several times. Her eyes were moist. They had *all* changed, she claimed. And, for the record, she was not a cold-hearted bitch. She'd had trouble sleeping after her refusal to let them see Sandro. She had rolled around the entire night, feeling horrible about her unyielding stance. But her patient was deadly sick. She feared for his life. They dared not take the chance.

Maxime scoffed, then covered her hand with both of his. "Have you seen anybody since ... since I ...?"

She nodded, a rosy hue inching up her neck as she freed her hand. "It only lasted a couple of months. Nice and all, but he had commitment issues."

"Did you sleep with him?"

"Maxime, please ..."

"I *need* to know."

Fanny rose and glared at him. "You have *no* right to ask me. *You* were the one who walked out on *me*." She stomped from the café.

Maxime bolted after her. "I wasn't ready. You rushed me. I'm not an appliance, with an on–off switch."

Out on the sidewalk, Fanny turned to face him. The tears were gone. She smiled, bemused. "I thought that was a woman's prerogative—her inborn right—to be slow to be aroused."

"I guess I'm different."

Fanny snorted. "That won't be a lie."

Maxime shook his head—a second time at loss for words. It's not what he'd had in mind when he'd asked her out for coffee. They couldn't go their separate ways like *this*—totally at odds with one another. They were further apart than they had ever been. "I've missed you, Fanny. I was hoping we could get closer—"

"Have we *ever* been close?"

"Fanny, please. I can't leave like this." He walked down the block with her to her car.

She opened the door and hesitated. "It was a mistake to have come. Sorry that I wasted your time, Mr. Baumann."

Maxime held the door open as she tried to close it. "Can I visit my son tomorrow morning?"

"Come after ten; then we can reassess the situation."

"Thank you, Nurse Ferguson."

"That was not a promise. Goodbye, Mr. Baumann."

45

Isolation

Maxime was worried.

He had on the gray suit with thin pinstripes, a white shirt, and a yellow polka-dot tie. His socks matched his tie. He had been sitting alone in the hospital foyer since nine. He had finished four black coffees. It was time to take the elevator up to Sandro's floor. His heart thumped against his breastbone. It had required much effort to prevent Gunther and Simon from accompanying him this morning. He had come early to give himself time to think.

He thought about his life. About Donna. About Mr. J. Johnson. About Simon. About Michelle and Donald. About Sandro, and about Fanny.

Nurse Collins was at the desk when Maxime arrived on the hematology wing at exactly ten a.m. "You can go through, Mr. Bowman. Nurse Ferguson had informed us of your visit. Come, let me walk with you. He's not doing too great."

Maxime accompanied the nurse down the endless hallway. As they slipped the overclothes on, she said, "He has developed jaundice. On top of everything. But, come."

"Dad." It was a hoarse whisper.

"*Sandro.*"

Maxime was careful as he hugged his firstborn. Sandro seemed sculpted from the finest bone china, which could shatter from a sneeze. Only half of the once muscular man had remained, reminding Maxime of pictures he'd seen of concentration camp survivors. It wasn't hard to imagine the striped pyjamas and barbed wire.

Maxime collapsed onto the chair and faced the nurse. "*Thank you*, Nurse Collins."

"Mr. Bowman?"

Maxime pierced her with his eyes, waiting, willing her to get the message. Only after she had left, did he turn to face Sandro.

"How was it, son?" he asked. "This *second* time around?"

Sandro grasped his father's gloved hand with his now bony fingers. He described being let down into a dark, narrow well on a frayed rope. The farther he was lowered, the damper it became, and now and then his head bumped against the ragged sides. Dirt rained down on him, blinding and choking him. If he ever allowed himself to reach the bottom of the pit, he believed, he would indeed die. Therefore, since day one, he had been climbing back up as fast as his arms and legs could manage.

"I was more scared this time," he confided.

"You probably had fever dreams."

"I heard the voices of angels. I'm certain of it. How many times can we die, Dad?"

"Sandro? Only once …"

"No, Dad. I've already died once, with the first chemo treatment. This was my second time. I'm commencing with life number three."

Maxime laughed softly. "We're not cats."

Sandro's voice rose and he talked faster and faster. His skin became warm to touch. Did his father forget, he implored, how many people were alive but had already died? One didn't have to be a corpse with rigor mortis to be dead. Didn't one die the day one started believing that life was expendable, worth nothing? That another's life was there for the taking? Does part of one not die the day one stops caring and loses compassion for one's fellow humans?

He grasped Maxime's hand, with surprising strength. "Do we not die when honesty becomes a foreign word to us, Dad? When making money becomes our sole mission in life? How much of us is still alive when we find it impossible to forgive, and we hold on to bitterness, even rightful resentment?"

"Rest now, Sandro …"

"No, Dad. Are we not practically dead when we have forsaken hope? But there's a worse fate: having hope *stolen* from us, taken by force. The powerless get robbed of their hope by the powerful. Are the influential and powerful not inherently dead when they accrue their positions, and ability to rule, through virulence, cunning, and foul play?"

Maxime glanced at his son as if for the first time. *And I thought I knew you. When did you gather this wisdom?*

He laid his free hand on his son's forehead only to yank it away. "Sandro, I'm calling the nurses. You're *burning*."

He reached for the call button—pressed it long and hard. Sandro had slumped back into the pillows: pale, yellow, and covered with purple blotches. His skin oozed perspiration. The clumps of remaining hair were matted to his scalp.

Movement at the door made Maxime turn. It was Nurse Ferguson. Maxime met her gaze but kept his distance.

"Thanks for coming, Fanny. Won't you please take his temperature? He's on fire."

Fanny Ferguson busied herself and took her patient's vitals. "Forty-one Celsius. Pulse hundred and fourteen, blood pressure hundred over forty-two."

"That's not good?"

Fanny glanced at him. "That's why I didn't want to allow visitors the other day. He's *sick,* Maxime. I'll alert the hematologist on call, and get a few things to make him feel better."

Sandro had fallen asleep.

Maxime went out into the hall and stripped the disposable clothes off. He would wait until Nurse Ferguson had administered the medications. Anybody who knew anything about this second trial of chemo to knock the AML off its feet would know that it was serious. *Deadly* serious. That much was bloody obvious. There was nothing he could do for his son now but pray.

Maxime waited in the hallway until Fanny had stepped from Sandro's room and had removed her over-clothes.

"Thank you for allowing me to see him."

"Did you get a chance to talk?" Her eyes were gentle.

"Sandro spoke non-stop. He claims he's now in his second or *third* life—like that of a cat. He insisted on knowing how many times one could die."

"He talked about it the other day. I agree—we *can* die more than once."

"*Come on.*"

"Maxime, we're talking about *emotional* death, *spiritual* death. It's still *dead*."

Maxime shrugged. "Okay, technically. I'm sorry about yesterday. I was a bit of an asshole."

"I prefer the bit that's not part of a donkey." She laughed her little bells as she held his gaze.

46

Sandro

Sandro's fever subsided the next day, but he remained in isolation for a further three weeks. Dr. Pauls wanted to ensure that the donated cells "took," rather than chance a rejection.

Sandro had become a regular on the ward, a semi-permanent resident, akin to family. It didn't take him long to grasp the dynamics of the day-to-day operations of the unit—especially the invisible power nuances.

Being a long-time regular, he assumed, allowed him special privileges, with certain liberties. His favorite instrument, since he wasn't permitted to leave his room, was the call button. He loved pressing it.

A head appeared at the door. "You called, Mr. Bowman?"

"Nurse Collins. I'm *so* glad to see you. I hope you can help me."

"What seems to be the problem?"

"I have a fever."

Cathy Collins donned the barrier clothes and stepped into the room, frowning. "I took your vitals only fifteen minutes ago. They were all satisfactory."

"I *definitely* have a fever."

She quickly redid his vital signs and sighed. "As I suspected: temperature normal. Mr. Bowman!"

Sandro looked at her with a wide grin. "Sorry— I should have been more clear. I have *cabin fever*."

"Cabin fever? I don't have time for silly games. We're *busy* on the ward." And she spun around to leave.

Sandro immediately changed his tone. "Please, Nurse Collins, this is serious. You must be familiar with the term 'solitary confinement.' Well, this room has become my prison cell, and for all I know, it could become my death chamber."

Nurse Collins turned back at the door. This man was well known for his smooth ways with the staff. "Mr. Bowman, with all due respect, you were critically ill not long ago. We feared for your life. However, the moment your condition improves, you exploit the situation. Cabin fever—*please*. I don't have time for this."

Sandro sucked in his breath. "Nurse Collins. You may think I am being facetious, but my condition is potentially fatal. I suffer from reactive depression. You guys are working round the clock, and I appreciate that immensely. I know I'm a high-maintenance customer. But my fear of death is real. Isolation is messing with my head. I'm not making this up." He patted the thick textbook on his bed stand: *Blood Diseases,* 9th edition. Dr. Pauls had lent it to him.

"It says so in this book," Sandro said. "You can ask Dr. Pauls."

Cathy Collins knew she was in a corner. Nearly everything the poor man said was true. But still... she didn't trust him. Mr. Bowman was known for his appreciation of everyone wearing a skirt, especially the younger ones.

"*What*," she asked, "Does the big book says is the treatment for cabin fever?" She immediately regretted taking the bait.

Sandro was ready. He opened the book to a marked page. "It says here, and I quote, 'Patients with suppressed immune systems, subjected to prolonged periods of isolation, are likely to develop symptoms of depression. An effective way of addressing this potentially lethal condition, seen in the light of their frail physical status, is sufficient human interaction, in spite of isolation measures in place.'"

He glanced at her and smiled. "It then continues with, 'Interaction with females have been shown to be far more effective in alleviating the depressive symptoms in patients.'"

Nurse Collins snorted. "*Shame* on you, Mr. Bowman. You made that up."

Sandro strained. "Please hear me out. I'm not making sexual advances toward you. Lord knows I wish I could—you're gorgeous. But look at me." He blushed. "I look like death. I'm only a shadow of my former self. I was merely *paraphrasing* what the book says. I need someone to talk to, someone who can listen, someone with whom to interact. I need meaningful conversations. *Please*."

He fell back against the pillows, catching his breath.

The nurse smiled. Perhaps there *was* something she could do. "I'll speak to Nurse Ferguson as well as Nurse Friesen. I think it's time to reconnect you with your family. You need your *wife* in your room. Good day, Mr. Bowman."

———

Nurse Collins kept her word. Sandro received visitors that same afternoon. He celebrated time with his wife and son and extended family. But the excitement exerted him.

By the next morning, he had developed a new fever. He now had sores in his mouth. An irritating cough tore through his wasted frame. Dr. Pauls diagnosed pneumonia and placed him on a double course of antibiotics.

Simon, meanwhile, complained little. He remained inconspicuous and on the sidelines, quietly recovering from the side effects of the apheresis donation. It was nothing in comparison with Sandro's ordeal. His biggest problem was a nagging bone pain, which improved with gentle massage and exercise. Another issue, however, was how to break the news to his family that it was time to return to London.

In order not to stress the hematology staff, and to retain visiting rights, the Baumanns started visiting Sandro in smaller groups, or one at a time. Maxime would often come with only Simon and Charlotte.

Charlotte rolled her eyes at the two men each time they got into Sandro's van as they argued about who should drive. Simon usually won, although Charlotte was convinced that Maxime conceded only to pacify his obnoxious younger son.

They were tying up their gowns outside Sandro's room when Simon said, "Dad, Charlotte and I are planning on returning to London the day after tomorrow. I have to get back to work."

Maxime looked up sharply. "But your brother's condition has worsened. I don't think it's a good idea."

"I'm not retired, Dad. I *have* to get back. I have clients with needs... projects to complete."

"Clients? Projects? Where are your *priorities?* Your brother is *dying.*"

Charlotte stepped between the two men and steered Simon into the room. Then she turned to Maxime. "It's okay, Mr. Baumann. We'll see how things are faring with Sandro before we make a final decision. Come."

Sandro was fast asleep. They didn't have the heart to wake him. Instead, they stood at the foot of his bed—like three hangmen, taking measurements of their client. There they remained: unmoving, unflinching, each toiling with their dark thoughts. No one said a word. It was impossible to ignore the obvious: Sandro had become a shadow of a man—he was nothing but bone, yellow skin, and sparse bits of flesh.

After half an hour, as of one mind, the trio stepped out into the hallway.

"Dad," Simon said in a quiet voice, "it's *over.* I'll come tomorrow and say my goodbyes."

"Simon! *Nothing* is over."

"*Wake up*, Dad. It's how life goes."

Maxime stepped closer to his son. Their faces were inches apart. "Do you have *no* compassion? You're repeating the same spiel you did when your mother passed."

"Don't *mock* me, Father. Leave Mother out of this. She made her choices. She whored around—"

Maxime had never before struck his son with a fist. He had given him a few spankings as a child when he misbehaved—and rarely so—but never with a fist.

Simon swore and stumbled back, holding his lip, eyes wide. Charlotte shrieked and lurched forward. Footsteps clattered down the hallway toward them.

"Retract that, Simon Baumann," Maxime hissed. "She was *not* a slut."

Simon gave a sob as Charlotte clung to his side, dragging him away. "You chose to remain *blind*," he yelled at Maxime. "You lived your perfect life with your perfect firm. You left Mom alone at home—day after day after year after year. She was *lonely*. I should hate you for doing that to her, to us. But I can't help it—I hate *her*. I tried to protect you from the stories going round—"

"*Stories?*"

"You lived in a perfect fantasy world governed by your ridiculous rules." Simon licked blood off of his fast swelling lower lip.

Fanny Ferguson reached the end of the hallway and planted her feet in front of Maxime. "Mr. Baumann!" Her glance shifted between the two men. "Gentlemen, *what's* going on?" Two male orderlies who had accompanied her stepped forward with purpose. "We could hear the two of you from the front desk." Fanny continued. "I cannot allow this. It's *not* a schoolyard." She lowered her voice, piercing Maxime with her gaze. "Did you just *hit* your son?"

Maxime was unrepentant. "He called my deceased wife—his mother—a *whore*."

Maxime suddenly bent forward and rested his hands on his knees. The world swirled around him, his heart pounding in his ears. He took several deep breaths.

There's that suffocating pressure again. Like a bloody boulder on my chest. Mein Gott, I'm going to die.

He straightened up and shuffled down the hallway without a word—the same shuffle, he thought, as Mr. J. Johnson, senior partner of Johnson, Johnson, and McBride.

47

With The Help Of Caffeine

Maxime wept.

He sat in the hospital foyer, in a far corner, away from the main entrance and its never-resting revolving doors. He had no desire to watch people come and go.

Lieber Gott, what has become of us?

Minutes earlier, by the time the elevator had reached the main floor, Maxime had recovered sufficiently to free himself from Mr. J. Johnson's gait. He had ordered four of the strongest double espressos and came to hide here.

Maxime hunched forward on the couch, swaying gently, his shoulders shaking. The four paper cups were stuffed in the cardboard tray, in perfect symmetry—all empty.

He tried to remember. It was the fourth time in his life he had cried, perhaps the fifth. Anybody who knew anything about the effects of drinking four double espressos, within ten minutes after hitting one's son in front of his girlfriend, inside a hospital, would know it was all madness. Utter, blooming insanity. He leaned back, surrendering to his racing heart and the whooshing in his head. Tears ran down his cheeks.

Donna, dearest Donna … What have I done?

After half an hour of weeping, his eyes had run dry. His soul was empty. But his heart was in no hurry to slow down.

Congratulations, Maxime Baumann. You have distinguished yourself by breaking almost all of the thirty rules in a single interaction with your son. Brilliant. You didn't stick to one of the rules. You took what didn't belong to you. You didn't consider all your options. You showed contempt, not respect. Your nose was where it didn't belong.

You have lost your faith. You spoke out of turn. You listened not to your heart, but to your ass. You stirred things up. You didn't accept what you couldn't change, and you forgot the worthwhile stuff. You did not help Simon. You hurt everybody's feelings. You're such a smart aleck; it's painful. You did not use the head the Good Lord gave you.

You're not a bad person, Maxime. You're only an asshole.

Purposeful footsteps approached and came to a halt in front of him—two shining ladies' shoes, planted next to each other entered his field of vision. Maxime followed the sculpted legs upwards until he reached the shoes' owner: Nurse Fanny Ferguson.

"Maxime?"

"*What* do you want?"

"May I?" She didn't wait for permission but perched on the edge of the seat next to him, knees together, hands clasped in her lap, head tilted. "I don't *want* anything," she said. "I'm trying to *understand*."

Maxime sighed. "It's complicated. I can't seem to make peace with Simon. It freaks me out when he talks like that about his mother. Perhaps it's me who's the idiot in the story. I'm a dumb asshole."

Fanny shifted closer and took his hand. "Don't chastise yourself like that. I've spoken to Simon and Charlotte. That's why I only came here now, not earlier."

Maxime wiped with his free hand over his eyes. "What did Simon tell you?"

"Who is Donat Drabik?"

Maxime jerked his hand away. "Simon told you about that man?"

Fanny nodded. She reached for Maxime's hand again.

Maxime looked at his hand in hers. Then he told her about the thirty rules. He told her about his marriage to Donna. Next about Mr. J. Johnson, Mr. C. Johnson, and Mr. McBride. About the RV trip with Gunther and about Donna's aneurysm. How they all waited during the attempted embolization and the final surgery, and how Simon refused to attend the funeral. He told her about the chiropractor's visit to his house, two days after the funeral. About the fancy Italian leather boots. And the six kitchen knives.

"You *head-smacked* him?" Fanny said, eyes wide.

"I'm not exactly proud of it."

"I never thought of you as a man of violence, who would use excessive force—"

"Those were *all* exceptional circumstances. I'm usually meek and mild—ask Mr. J. Johnson."

Fanny grinned and brought his hand to her lips. "I'm pulling your leg, Mr. Baumann. Come … I came to fetch you. I'm worried about Sandro. I've asked Dr. Pauls to examine him again."

Maxime grabbed the paper cup tray and rose, using his other hand to pull Fanny to her feet.

"Simon and I didn't get to speak to Sandro," he told her. "He was sleeping, and we dared not wake him. We stood around his bed for half an hour before we piled into the hallway. That's when Simon and I had our altercation."

As they waited for the elevator, Maxime asked, "What's the matter *now* with Sandro?"

Fanny faced him and shrugged. "I don't know. It's a *feeling*. I went in to take his vitals after I spoke with Simon, and I all of a sudden felt this heaviness—he looked different, and not in a satisfying way."

They strode down the long hallways—in total silence. They passed the empty waiting room and reached the hallway in front of Sandro's room. Of Simon and Charlotte, there was no sign.

"Did you let Sandro's wife know?" Maxime asked.

"They're all on their way."

"And Simon?"

"I sent him and his girlfriend for a walk. Told him to go clear his head, then come back in an hour and make peace with his father."

48

Making Peace Is Not Simple

When Maxime and Nurse Ferguson entered the room, Sandro's eyes flew open. He smiled and raised his hand, but it plopped right back down.

"*Sandro.*" Maxime bent forward and hugged his son's fragile frame with caution. The taut skin glared lusterless—the neon light was unforgiving to the blotches.

Maxime sat down and pulled the chair close.

"I feel terrible for doing this," Sandro said.

"What? There's no reason for you to feel sorry."

"For leaving you all behind."

Maxime forced a laugh. "Where are you going? Nurse Ferguson told me you're still in isolation. They won't give you a weekend pass, not for a while."

Sandro coughed and sighed. "I can feel it coming. Look at me. There's nothing left." His breathing came fast. His voice dropped to a whisper. "Remember what I told you about the well?

I'm further down now—I've almost reached the bottom. It's pitch dark down here ... and yet, far above me is this speck of brilliant light." He sighed as he glanced at the ceiling. "At least it's driving out much of the darkness."

Fanny squeezed Maxime's shoulder and whispered, "I'll come back" and left the room.

Maxime's gaze never left Sandro. "Then we'll *pull* you out of there. Just hold on."

"No, Dad. It's no good. I'm waiting for Michelle and Donald. I had other plans for my boy, for us. I never got to finish that tree house. We got the floor in ... when this thing relapsed."

Maxime shook his head. Behind his mask, he silently mouthed, "Damn it. I'll pull you out *myself.*"

His cheeks were wet. He kissed his son's forehead with his masked lips. Sandro had fallen asleep.

Maxime slipped out into the hallway. The next group had arrived; he hugged Michelle, Mary, Gunther, and little Donald.

"Oupa, I made Daddy a picture. *Look.*" Donald pulled a crumpled piece of paper from his pocket and handed it to Maxime. "Will Daddy like it, Oupa?"

"Oh, yes. He *will*. Go in now with Mommy." Then Maxime stood and watched them walk into the room—Michelle with Donald, then Mary and Gunther.

Gunther stopped in the doorway and turned back. "Maximus?"

Maxime hugged his brother a second time and shuddered. "He's *leaving* us," he whispered. "My sweet son ... We must say our final goodbyes. Go in. I'll be here."

Maxime turned around and plodded back to the front desk. There he waited until Nurse Ferguson noticed him. When his eyes met hers, she rose and steered him toward the waiting room, which was empty.

"*Sandro?*"

"You were right, Fanny. He *knows* he's lost the battle."

"*Maxime.*" She glanced around, gave him a quick hug and stepped back.

"Where did you send Simon?" Maxime asked. "Do you think he'll return? Perhaps he took the ferry to Victoria. He's not *anywhere.*"

"He'll come. He *promised.* I told him to be back in an hour."

She steered him down the endless hallway toward Sandro's room.

"Go *in*," she prompted.

"Come with me," Maxime pleaded.

"It's not my place. Go. Your son needs you. I'll be at the front desk."

"Fanny ..."

She stood on tiptoes, took his face in both hands and kissed him full on the lips. Then she turned his head and whispered in his ear, "I love you, Maxime Baumann. Yes, you are high maintenance. We'll have to work on those two pages with rules. But you're *not* an asshole. Never say that again. Now *go* in."

Maxime stood at the back of the room, watching his daughter-in-law and grandson. They sat on the bed, one on each side of Sandro, his arms draped around them.

Gunther and Mary stood next to the bed, holding hands, looking on.

Maxime took a step closer. Was Sandro still breathing?

Michelle leaned forward and took his hand. "Come, Daddy, hold his hand. Sandro..." She nudged Sandro gently in the ribs, whispering in his ear. "Your dad is here. Come, say goodbye to him."

Sandro's eyes fluttered open, and he smiled at Maxime. "Dad," he mouthed. He smiled at Gunther and Mary, then looked to each side, at his wife and son, and pulled them closer. "Michelle ..." he whispered. "Donald ... I ... love you ... Tell Simon ..."

Sandro Baumann's breathing slowed down.

Maxime could not remember later how long they had remained like that. It must have been a long time. He must even have dozed off in the chair by the bed. Voices outside the room startled him, startled them all.

Sandro's eyes were closed. He had stopped breathing.

Maxime kissed his daughter-in-law and grandson before taking Gunther and Mary by the hand and leading them outside.

Simon and Charlotte were slipping into the disposable gowns. His younger son's lower lip was purple and swollen. He smirked. "Dad, we *have* to talk."

Maxime shrugged. He would like that. "Yes, perhaps we should. You don't have to bother with that barrier clothing anymore."

Simon paused and looked at him. "*Dad*?"

"Go say goodbye to your brother. I'll be here. I'll wait for you."

He would like to talk to his son. He would also like to add two new rules. # 31: *Make provision for a time-out when none of these rules apply.* # 32: *Constant worry can no longer be a bloody option.*

LEBENSREGELN—LIFE RULES
(MAXIME BASTIEN BAUMANN, 1971)

Page 1

1. Stick to the rules.
2. Be true to yourself.
3. Don't ever tell a lie.
4. Work hard.
5. Don't take what doesn't belong to you.
6. Consider all your options before acting. Always.
7. Show respect for other people.
8. Never eat charred meat.
9. Your nose does not belong in other people's business.
10. Never be jealous of assholes.
11. Greet everyone you meet with a genuine smile.
12. Never be found without faith.
13. Be clear in your vision. What do you wish to achieve?
14. Don't speak out of turn.
15. Listen to your heart.

Page 2

1. Accept what you cannot change.
2. Don't stir things up.
3. Set deadlines if you hope to achieve anything.
4. Remember the worthwhile stuff. Write them down.
5. Be grateful—every day.

6. Don't be late. Never.
7. If it's in your power to help others, do so. (Don't close your heart to others.)
8. If you give, don't expect reciprocity.
9. Go through life with open eyes—behold the world's beauty.
10. If possible, don't hurt other people's feelings.
11. Don't ever think of yourself as a smart aleck.
12. Don't waste: not time, not money, nothing.
13. The good Lord gave you a head—so use it.
14. Life is short—make it count.
15. Stick to the rules.

Page 3
The two new rules:

1. Make provision for a time-out when none of these rules apply.
2. Constant worry can no longer be a bloody option.

THANK YOU FOR READING!
Please consider leaving an online review for this novel.
Reviews matter. By leaving a review more readers will gain
access to the novel—hence enable the author to write more.

ALSO BY DANIE BOTHA
Be Silent
Be Good

Visit me at http://www.daniebotha.com